The Hidden Queen

of

Hy-Breasail

The Hidden Queen

of

Hy-Breasail

Donna Marie George

DEDICATION

Many thanks to all of family and friends for their love
and support during my writing journey.

To my husband, Rick, thank you for always believing in
me,
And having the patience of a saint.

To my children, Kelsey, Connor & Bridget,
thank you for cheering me on.

To my O'Flaherty cousins,
thank you for welcoming me into the family.

Mom & Dad, thank you for encouraging me to write,
and not squelching my very vivid childhood imagination.

ACKNOWLEDGMENTS

To the *Lettermullen & Garumna Heritage Center &
John Bhaba Jack O'Chonghaola*
For helping me bring life to my history.

To my cousin, *Caroline Reaney*, thank you for being my
Irish translator and inspiration.

To my friend, *Chasie Zeitler* @Chase Photography, thank
you for your friendship and your expertise in capturing the
real me.

To my illustrator, *Ingvard the Terrible*, thank you for
bringing Maeve O'Flaherty to life.

To my editor, *James Oliveri*, thank you for your
constructive criticism and sound advice.

1 The Queen of Hy-Breasail

For over one hundred years, every year, on the first of November, the citizens of Rowan would gather in its center in waiting. It was a tradition that none missed. Young and old gathered to enjoy the celebration. The center of town decorated in holly, twinkling lights, and a huge tree topped with an angel. The ancient Irish Gaelic language spoken by most of the elders in the community floated like musical notes through the air. Games played by all. Food carts were aplenty selling everything from boxty lunches to ice cream and cotton candy. In every business and residential window, a candle glowed brightly awaiting the good news.

The reigning Mayor of Rowan traditionally read from a book. The book was tattered and worn from generations of reading. It contained the tale of a mystical, magical place. The place so far away its existence was inconceivable to the listener. Children and adults brought blankets to the village center to hear the legend believed to be based on Rowan's fairytale history. The Mayor cradled the precious book in his hands, opened it, closed his eyes as if praying, and began reading Rowan's most beloved tale. The tale of "The Queen of Hy-Breasail."

~~~~~~~~~~~~~~~~~~~~~~~

Many, many years ago, a mystical, magical place called Hy-Breasail existed. Royalty, Warriors, Protectors, Oracles, and Guardians all had lived together harmoniously for thousands of years without any unrest. The Queen, born without royal blood, chosen by the Guardian of the Realm of Blessings, was beloved by all as she ruled with purity, honesty, and strength. She faced no conflict or adversity for many years during her reign.

On her twenty-first birthday, the Queen would learn of an arranged marriage, her own. Shocked by the news, the Queen requested the presence of the Guardian of the Realm of Blessings. The Guardian, who made few appearances, would not fulfill the Queen's request of a meeting. Instead, a messenger of the Guardian delivered a brusque and concise message addressed to the Queen. The message stated that the Queen and her betrothed's heart had been bound before birth, therefore, there would be no other. The Queen, saddened by this news, became full of worry and despairing questions. Thoughts pervaded her mind conjuring images of her marriage to a vile King.

Rumors spread among the people of Hy-Breasail as to the identity of the future king. One rumor in particular spread within the castle walls. This rumor identified the Queen's betrothed to be the youngest born to the mightiest warrior family in Hy-Breasail. The Queen's attendant brought news of this rumor. With the deepest of hope, she believed she knew who her mysterious King would be. In that, the Queen found solace.

The whole kingdom attended the Royal Wedding. The Queen nervously stood before God and her people, her betrothed walked toward her, his identity shrouded by the cloak of concealment. He stood, taking her hand in his, their touch dissipating the cloak, revealing the future King's identity. The Queen gasped, flinging herself into his arms. Her King had been her secret love, friend from birth, her heart's secret for years. Torrents of love emanated between them, leaving everyone in their presence overcome with emotion. Joy and peace filled the Realm for many years as the people of Hy-Breasail revered the Queen and King.

Several years after the Royal Wedding, the Queen delivered a beautiful set of twins – a boy and a girl. Three years later, another child blessed their family, a son. The Queen and her little family flourished in Hy-Breasail. As the first-born children of the Queen, on the prince's and princess' tenth birthday, the Guardian of the Realm of Blessings would make an announcement. She would name the Queen's successor. Inhabitants from all over Hy-Breasail believed the throne should be passed to one of the Queen's children as love for the present Royal family was boundless. Yet, never in the history of Hy-Breasail had the throne passed to a descendant of a reigning Queen. All felt the Guardian would feel as they did. As a result, excitement rippled throughout the kingdom awaiting news of the future Queen's identity.

The Guardian's announcement caused shockwaves to radiate the castle and throughout the realm. To the peoples' dismay the Guardian made clear that never would the lineage of the crown change. Therefore, the one to succeed the Queen would not be one of her children. It would be a babe not yet born. And the identity of the future Queen would remain concealed. Disheartened by the news, discourse among the people of Hy-Breasail was rampant.

Most were riled by the anonymity of their future Queen. Others were angered as their wishes had been ignored.

The Queen reminded them of the King's hidden identity before their marriage, and that his anonymity had not quelled any waves of dissension in Hy-Breasail. The Queen demanded deference for the Guardian's decision as it had been for centuries, insisting that no unjust worry or discourse ensue. The people in reverence to the Queen waited respectfully for changes in the Guardian's decision. None would come.

Many months later, as if her words had fallen on deafened ears, the Queen's pleas were long forgotten. Many demands made to uncover the future Queen's identity with the insistence that the rules of succession change. Factions formed, some against the Guardian of the Realm of Blessings, others against the Queen intensified. Threats of harm against the Royal family were received by the Queen. For the first time, there was unrest in Hy-Breasail. People were worried as broken trusts and danger lurked throughout the Realm. The decision of the Guardian had left the Royal family vulnerable.

One night, while the Royal family slept, the castle was overtaken by one of the newly formed factions. One faction's carefully formed plan ensured attacking the Queen and King in their most defenseless state. The King awoke, picked up his sword, and fiercely fought against the intruders. The King received fatal wounds protecting his family. Within minutes of his death, the Queen succumbed to her broken heart as she cradled her beloved in her arms.

Hy-Breasail never recovered from the loss of its beloved royal family. The factions that had attacked the Queen and her family were banished from the land and imprisoned in a Realm between Hy-Breasail and the Realm of Blessings. None would escape. The world they now lived ensured an unending tortuous existence – a life without love.

Mourning for the Queen and King continued for centuries. It is believed that that the Queen's Hierarchy, consisting of her most well-regarded Warriors, Protectors, Oracles, and Guardians, saved the royal children; yet, their whereabouts remained unknown. Many believed they lived in an unknown realm, a realm far away from Hy-Breasail.

Centuries later, Hy-Breasail waits patiently for news of the princess and princes' whereabouts and for the birth of their new Queen.

~~~~~~~~~~~~~~~~~~~

Mayor Keane looked up from the book, hundreds of eyes lay upon him. He knew he must answer the silent query permeating the atmosphere around him. Slowly, yet without hesitation, he answered the question that had not faltered for the last one hundred and fifty years. "When will she return?" Today, he would have news. "I do not have a definitive timeframe, but she will be coming soon, very soon." Exhalations and sighs of relief flooded the crowd. Smiles adorned the faces of Rowan's townspeople. The festivities renewed.

2 Maeve

Maeve is beautiful, intelligent, and charming, the trifecta. She is dating the captain of the football team, her best friend is class president, and all the girls at Hawthorn High want to be her. Everyone thinks Maeve has the perfect life, except Maeve. She is very shy, with a magnetic charm drawing people of all ages to her. Her voice's soft melodious cadence touches a person's inner being. Yet, Maeve has a secret. She sees what others cannot – people who were living, dead, and imaginary. She can read people's minds – friends, family, and strangers. She is a visionary of the beautiful and chilling. Too many secrets to think of as gifts. Gifts, she thought were not secreting, kept from everyone, especially those she dearly loved.

At the start of puberty, Maeve began to have unsettling experiences that she, at first, was unable to decipher as fact or fiction. She thought she might be having a psychological breakdown. It felt as if she was having out of body experiences. She labeled them "transcendence". These transcendence episodes were short snippets of time when she would transport to other places and times - the past, future, present, and other realms. These encounters increased exponentially around her sixteenth birthday. They were insightful, sometimes scary, yet clues to the reason she bore her gifts. Maeve did not know its true meaning but like everything else strange and unusual in her life, she had become used to blinking and being somewhere else entirely.

Today was extraordinarily ordinary, unbelievably uneventful. Nothing, nothing was amiss but a small nagging in the pit of Maeve's stomach. Something was awry. Her morning had gone smoothly. So, there was no reason that Maeve could think of to cause this feeling. Normalcy could be the culprit. Her normal did not consist of peace and tranquility. This morning, her alarm rang promptly with the added benefit of her sisters being extremely quiet. She giggled at the thought: 'now that is unusual'. The girls were as quiet as mice, there had been no screaming, fighting, or banging on the bathroom door. Plus, there were no last-minute texts or phone calls from Shae or Liam about the presentation. Maeve placed her hands on her belly, then took a huge, deep breath and exhaled her nervousness.

Maeve studied her reflection in the mirror. Red waves of hair streamed down her back to perfection. She braided a small strand pinning it back leaving soft, baby curls surrounding her heart-shaped face. Her only makeup was a soft gloss on her full, strawberry-colored lips. Her complexion beautiful, radiant, and natural with glowing rosy cheeks sprinkled with freckles. Her cerulean-blue, doe-shaped eyes highlighted by dark auburn eyelashes. Her outfit was perfect. She wore fitted black jeggings and a sweater that perfectly accented her gorgeous eyes paired with her signature black Converse™ sneakers. Maeve completed her look by wearing an antique key pendant, a gift from Liam on their first month anniversary. The pendant hung daintily around her neck on a silver woven necklace Maeve sighed at her reflection and smiled.

Maeve turned away from the mirror to scan her room. She was a neat freak. Her clothes picked up and her bed made. Everything was in its place. Her choices in décor were simple, yet elegant. Her bedding was a lush, soft baby blue. Her walls were gray with tiny sparkles infused in the paint. Her lamps, picture frames, and accessories were a shimmery white crackle. The room glittered like sparkly new-fallen snowflakes. The room's ambience was serene and peaceful. In her bedroom, she felt enrobed by a cloak of protection encompassing her body with an ethereal feeling. Suddenly, Maeve felt a soft feathery shiver down her spine causing a tingle of love rush through her body making her smile even wider.

The timer on her phone chimed, alerting her to go downstairs for breakfast. Quickly, in preparation for her science presentation, Maeve massaged lavender essential oil into her temples. Shae said it would emit a calming effect. It was worth a try since presentations and Maeve were not the best of friends. They always made her a bit nervous. Her shyness would overwhelm her. One on one Maeve had no problem. She could have a deep intellectual conversation with a stranger, but a room filled with people would turn her into a bundle of nerves. As always, Shae knew the oils would help. Maeve took one last twirl in front of her mirror and nodded to her reflection in satisfaction. Off she went to start her day.

3 Mam

Mam finished putting away the dishes from last night's dinner of bacon and cabbage – an O'Flaherty specialty. Mam's kitchen was renovated in a farmhouse style replicating her childhood kitchen on the farm. Mam sighed. Niall surprised her with the renovation for her last birthday. The carpenter repurposed the flooring and cabinetry from her Da's barn. The cabinetry was white with a barely visible crackle infused with tiny silver blue hues blending the histories of the O'Flaherty's and the O'Connor's in her family home filled her with a loving nostalgia.

Mam could hear Maeve moving around in her room. Her heart ached for her oldest baby knowing the secrets she had to keep. The memory of telling Maeve to never divulge her gifts seared deeply in her heart. It was a tricky situation due to Maeve's young age. Mam did not want to teach her that lying was acceptable behavior when suspicions and questions arose, but she had no choice. The secret must be kept for the safety and protection of Maeve, the family, and the people of Rowan. The difficulty Maeve faced every day concealing it from her best friends devastated Mam. It was time to talk to Niall and call a meeting for directives. It was not fair for Maeve to keep up this façade any longer. Mam listened as Maeve's feet hit the stairs on her way down to breakfast.

"Morning, sweetheart. Did you sleep well?" Mam asked as Maeve entered the kitchen.

"Yes, Mam," Maeve added, "but I did wake up with a bit of a nervous stomach. Probably because of the presentation."

"Sweets don't worry. Your Dad and I loved it. So, did your sisters and they are tough to please. I am sure Miss Almath will love it, too. You all did a fantastic job, honestly. You have nothing to worry about," Mam replied.

"Thanks, Mam," Maeve answered modestly, "I know, it's just that I hate standing up in front of everyone. But Shae is presenting, so I should be okay," said Maeve with a tremendous sigh of relief.

Since silence was a rarity in the O'Flaherty house, with Maeve's three sisters bickering about something twenty-four hours a day, Mam and Maeve agreed to enjoy at least thirty minutes each morning in peace. On nice days, Mam opened the kitchen window to enjoy the chorus of songs the birds would sing each morning. Listening to the choir helped Maeve focus on eating her breakfast, her least favorite meal of the day. Mam tried not to lecture her, but truthfully, Maeve had heard the "nutritional speech" more times than she could count. Mam started to say something when Maeve cut her off and said:

"I know, Mam, I'm working on it."

Since her fifth birthday, Maeve was able to finish her sentences. It still amazed Mam.

"Maeve, how in the world?"

Mam continued to mumble under her breath shaking her head back and forth. Luckily, Maeve could hear only bits and pieces of Mam's mumbling. Most of it garbled. Until she became loud and clear with: "You'd better hurry before..." This time Maeve finished Mam's sentence with a hint of sarcasm.

"Shae gets here."

"Maeve!" exclaimed Mam.

Maeve panicked. She did not mean to sound disrespectful, but when she replayed it in her mind, she did. Maeve held her breath. No matter how close she was with Mam, answering back was unacceptable behavior. She could lose privileges for the rest of the day or worse grounded. Part of her punishment during grounding would be no contact with Liam or Shae, a fate worse than death. She felt her heart catch waiting for Mam's response.

"Maeve hurry up. Shae will be here any minute. She is doing me a huge favor picking you up. Get moving, sweetheart."

Maeve looked relieved. Mam had given her a "pass" on her sarcasm.

"Yes, Mam. I'm almost done."

Maeve ate as fast as humanly possible. Her sisters had begun their bickering. Bridget, Caitlín, and Breana were awake less than five minutes and loud enough for Maeve and Mam to hear every word. So loud it was if they were all in the kitchen.

"I'm the oldest! I need more prep time," Bridget screamed.

Breana chimed in, "That's for sure. You look like a beast."

Sweet Caitlín played intermediary. "That's not true. We all look alike, so if one of us looks like a beast, we all do."

It was an endless cycle of complaining and fighting. Their voices escalating as they talked over one another.

"Too bad for you. I'm the oldest and it takes me longer to get ready!" yelled Bridget.

"I can take a shower, get dressed, eat breakfast and you'll still be staring at yourself in the mirror. I'm not waiting for you to primp and pamper yourself, PRINCESS!" screamed Breana.

In a small, sweet voice, Maeve could hear Caitlín. Calmly, she tried to quiet her sisters.

"There's no need to fight. I'll figure something out. Please, please just be kind."

Maeve and Mam both looked up at the ceiling at the same time and sighed. After realizing that their reaction was identical, they giggled, rolled their eyes, and shrugged their shoulders. This was a normal morning.

4 Shae

Shae pulled up to the sidewalk in front of Maeve's house and gave her horn half a beep. She had inherited her Ma's vintage car when she got her driver's license in May. Her Pa had saved it for her and kept it in perfect condition. He knew Shae's Ma, Branagh, would have loved for Shae to have it.

Maeve quickly picked up her backpack and coat, and kissed Mam on the cheek. "Bye, Mam", looked up toward the ceiling, giggled, and said, "have fun."

Mam chuckled and said, "Have a lovely day, Maeve...and good luck!"

Her sisters' voices echoed from the house to the street where Shae's car was idling.

Maeve thought of her poor neighbors. Listening to her sisters first thing in the morning while having your first cup of coffee must be annoying. Maeve was sure that the "Irish triplets" argued all the way down Laoch Street. She was surprised if Irish triplets was not their only nickname. She could think of a few names she would like to call them if it would not get her in trouble.

Maeve practically ran to Shae's car. She had helped the Chief surprise Shae on her birthday. It was a day to remember. The thought brought tears to Maeve's eyes. She fastened her seatbelt and let out a huge sigh. Shae turned to look at Maeve.

"Okay. What's up?"

"Nothing, why?"

Shae knew she was lying. "Maeve, I know you best. Are you nervous about the presentation? Don't be. It's great, plus I'm doing all the talking. Your part is done."

"I don't think that's it. I just have this strange feeling for no reason Like something bad is going to happen and I can't explain why."

Maeve's stomach felt like an erupting volcano. Suddenly, she felt faint. Shae gave her a side glance. Maeve was white as a ghost.

"Maeve, do you need me to stop the car? We are close to home. We could go back."

"No, I'm okay, really. I just need a diversion. Some humor will make me feel better." Maeve laughed half-heartedly. "I'm going to say something ridiculous and the first one to laugh loses. Okay?"

Shae nodded. So, Maeve continued in an exaggerated tone.

"I think Liam…is cheating on me. It's obvious really. The other girls drool over him. How could he not be? With my flaming red hair and freckles, you know I'm right!"

Dead silence. Shae tried so hard to keep a straight face. Maeve played this game so well. Maeve's face did not show the laughter boiling deep in her belly. Shae could not hold it in any longer, she exploded in laughter, tears started streaming down her face.

"You're insane, you know that don't you?"

"And you lost, didn't you? You didn't even last thirty seconds."

Hilarity at its finest. But Maeve was still a wreck inside. The closer they got to school the worse she felt.

Shae was laughing hysterically. She tried her hardest to stop, but it was almost impossible. Every time she caught her breath, she had another laughing fit. When she was finally able to compose herself, if you could call it that, she responded to Maeve.

"What did you eat this morning? And your game, joke or not, there's no way that Liam likes anyone else."

Shae could hardly talk. She had to take deep breaths in between each little fragment of sentence, she was laughing so hard.

"Oh, if I don't stop laughing, I'm going to wee in my pants. Maeve, you're crazy."

"Hey, stop laughing at me. I'm trying my best not to vomit in your car." Maeve could not stop laughing either.

"Okay. So, let me just add that the boy is madly in love with you. AND, I'm extremely jealous of that fact." Shae turned to look at Maeve and with all seriousness said, "Oh, no, Mae, you're looking a bit feverish. I think you need to go to the health center as soon as we get to school."

They both burst out laughing after Maeve squeaked out a reply.

"Seriously, not funny."

At the stoplight, Shae reapplied her eye makeup. She wanted to make sure she had applied her mascara and eyeliner perfectly.

Shae had a model-like, natural beauty. Her features were symmetrical, no makeup required. She had long, straight hair that was raven black, so black, it appeared to have blue highlights. Her eyes were the loveliest shade of blue, the color of the cobalt blue Irish pottery in Rowan's history museum, rimmed with the longest, blackest eyelashes. Her eyes looked even bluer against her porcelain white skin.

Shae's style was different than Maeve's. She had the tiniest bit of hippie in her clothing choices. Maeve thought it was from all her New Age reading about crystals, essential oils, yoga, meditation, and philosophies. Maeve was always in awe of her best friend. Her beauty radiated from within. She was a kind, genuine soul.

Just as Shae finished reapplying her lip gloss, the light turned green. Shae turned to Maeve to reassure her again about Liam. Sometimes Shae's beauty took Maeve's breath away.

"Maeve, seriously, he's been in love with you since kindergarten You're his one and only."

Maeve could not hold it in anymore. "Shae, it was a joke. I promise. I just needed a laugh. I know he loves me! Geesh!"

Shae gasped for air and replied, "I'm sorry. I know. You just worried me for a second. Your relationship with Liam is no joke. Our friendship is sacred."

Maeve started to laugh, then stopped herself. Shae was being so serious.

"Honestly, Maeve, I'm not kidding! You're my forever friend, my only sister. And him, oh, never mind."

Maeve transcended into the past.

5 The Playground

Maeve wondered the significance of this memory as she watched it unfold. She remembered the day very clearly; it had been terrifying for a third grader. She took a breath as it played out.

All the students began lining up on the blacktop after recess when Maeve realized she had forgotten her water bottle. She left it at the bottom of the slide by the jungle gym. She turned to Liam and Shae and said, 'Ooh, I will be right back. I forgot my water bottle. Save my place, please.' Both Liam and Shae nodded.

Maeve ran like a stallion, her ponytail a red mane swaying back and forth, the sun shining down on her in the cloudless sky. As Maeve grabbed her bottle, the sky directly above her blackened. The clouds began to swirl creating marble-sized hail. The hail began pinging down on her. Maeve became immobile, her feet felt as if encased in cement shoes. The hail was hurting her skin with needle-like piercings. There was nowhere to hide. She did not want to cry, but the pain was intense.

Everyone was staring at her, but not one person tried to help. She could see Liam, Shae, Declan, Raegan, and Finn in the distance. Declan and Raegan, Maeve's cousins, were special, too. All three were able to hear each other's thoughts without speaking. She telepathically cried for their help. It had only been a few seconds, but she already had red marks on her face, shoulders, and arms. Simultaneously, Declan gave Liam a little nudge on the shoulder as Raegan whispered for him to help. Shae stood in shock. Finn remained expressionless. Liam knew it was up to him.

Liam, instantly, turned into a mini superhero. He ran at warp speed - a blur of light reaching Maeve's side in seconds. Seemingly his size increased enabling him to scoop her up in his arms using his body as an umbrella to shield her. The storm intensified; it was angry. From the distance Liam looked toward his friends, Declan and Raegan were visibly worried for them both. Shae was on the brink of hysteria. Finn stood on the fringe with his arms folded across his chest and a grimace on his face. Liam thought his behavior strange but quickly diverted his attention back to Maeve.

The hail stopped as Liam stood up and carried Maeve confidently. Shae could not contain herself; she ran up to Liam and Maeve embracing them with the greatest of ferocity. Her action unknowingly caused a silver bonded strand to wrap itself around the trio. The strand, illuminated with light and tiny silver speckles, weaved a triquetra encompassing the small group. Liam pulled the girls closer as if tightening the bond of protection tighter. Those teachers with sight gasped; the ungifted remained impervious to the silent message delivered in this incident.

Miss Flannery, the principal, came running toward them. The entire incident had been visible from her office window.

"Liam, Shae, Maeve, are you okay? Come, come with me."

Maeve thought she heard Miss Flannery call her "our poor, sweet princess". Maeve tilted her head in a questioning manner. Declan and Raegan nodded in the affirmative; they, too, had heard Miss Flannery's reference. Finn's reaction puzzled Maeve, he was angry, huffing like a petulant child. He was her friend and Shae his best friend. His behavior was bizarre, yet she dismissed it quickly, shrugging her shoulders. The little group followed Miss Flannery as she chattered and flittered back into the school.

6 Miss Flannery

Miss Fae Flannery was the youngest principal to ever run the Rowan Primary School. She was a tiny waif-like lady with a sweet, cherubim face. The same year that Maeve, Liam, and Shae entered kindergarten, Miss Flannery became principal. Her students responded well to her because she had the sweetest, melodious voice accompanied by an adorable, joyful demeanor. Everyone who met her at once became happier, her personality was infectious, a perfect fit for leader of a primary school.

Miss Flannery sat down with Maeve, Liam, and Shae to explain her role as principal. She would have to call each of their parents informing them of today's events. They would be scared to hear of the incident any other way. The three responded with a nod of indifference, it had been no big deal. Miss Flannery went into her office to make her calls then returned soon afterward. She told the "triquetra" that Officer Kerrigan, Shae's father, would take them home.

Mrs. Bohann, the school nurse, overheard Miss Flannery's conversation and interrupted her. She could not release the students without a medical evaluation.

"Miss Flannery. Excuse me. School policy prescribes that I examine all injured children before releasing them to their parents. Plus, there are the reports that I need to complete," Mrs. Bohann said with a raised eyebrow.

Liam, Maeve, and Shae sat with Mrs. Bohann. She asked them many questions about the playground incident. Liam noticed her taking a lot of notes. Their answers were noticeably short, condensed eight-year-old versions of what had happened. Being extremely perceptive, Liam thought it strange for the school nurse to ask so many questions when there had been no injuries. Mrs. Bohann looked very worried as Liam scooched himself closer to the girls. Her questioning continued.

Liam began challenging Mrs. Bohann's questions. Thankfully, Miss Flannery interrupted the interrogation. Liam felt relief course through his body. Mrs. Bohann had no choice but to release the children. Officer Kerrigan had arrived. Mrs. Bohann greeted him and filled him in on the events that occurred on the playground. He just kept nodding his head. Liam knew that something was wrong, today's incident meant something. He just did not know what.

Miss Flannery crouched in front of the three children, touched each of them under the chin and told them how brave they were. As she stood up, Officer Kerrigan pulled her aside. Liam could hear some of the conversation.

"It is important that you interview all of the witnesses from the playground. You must include all students, teachers, and aides, sighted and unsighted. Leave no one out. I need an incident report no later than tomorrow morning. I will arrange a meeting with the "proper authorities" upon its receipt. It is of the utmost importance."

Miss Flannery shook her head in agreement. She placed her hand on his arm as she responded: "I will be calling *all* of you with my report." She squeezed his arm and released it.

On the way home, Officer Kerrigan was emotional. He was not one for sentiment. His behavior puzzled Maeve, Shae, and Liam. He stressed the importance of their friendship. He told them multiple times that they were brave. He told them he loved them. The three just stared at him in disbelief. Maeve grabbed Liam and Shae's hands. His emotions were making all of them nervous, especially Shae.

Officer Kerrigan continuously talked the rest of the way home. The three were incredibly quiet in the backseat of his police car. Maeve glanced down at the hands she was holding. Out of nowhere sparkles began radiating from their grasps, so, she held their hands tighter. Warmth spread through her heart growing in intensity the tighter the grasp became. The triquetra had united them eternally. She wanted to show Liam and Shae the sparkles, but she remembered her secret:

"Maeve, never talk about any of your gifts."

Later that night, Officer Kerrigan received Miss Flannery's report. It said that many witnessed Liam running toward Maeve like a gazelle, with ease and grace. Many felt confused by Liam's strength, he had lifted Maeve up as if "she was as light as a feather". The rapid change in weather bewildered the witnesses. Beautiful blue skies rapidly changed into a swirling gray mist creating an eerie atmospheric tornado with red wisps that swirled as if self-directed toward Maeve. After reading the report, Officer Kerrigan made a call to an unidentified person.

Maeve watched as each moment flashed before her. One memory was unsettling. She shook her head in disbelief. Finn's behavior was shocking. His lack of empathy frightening. He was a few years older, and just stood there, not helping. Now, it was obvious to her that she and Liam were a threat to his friendship with Shae. Poor Shae. Maeve knew she had to keep a closer eye on him. It was obvious he was not trustworthy.

7 The Parking Lot

One minute, Maeve and Shae were laughing like hyenas; the next each was deep in her own thought. It still amazed Maeve that she could transcend in front of people so discreetly. She wished she could share her experience with Shae. What she had seen was disturbing. There had to be a safe way she could. The only person she trusted to give her good advice was sitting right beside her. She just needed one person she could confide in, just one. Maeve gasped when she realized she had said "just one" aloud.

Maeve waited for Shae to ask, "one what?" Surprisingly, Shae did not say a word. She knew she had to cover up her flub. She could not lie. Telling a fabricated story of a half-truth was different than an outright lie. Plus, Shae knew her too well, she would never be able to pull it off. So, Maeve just pulled a tiny little story out of nowhere. Maeve felt a little sense of relief knowing her response would mostly be truthful.

"Did I think that aloud? Ha, ha, ha! I was thinking about the mornings with Bridget, Caitlín, and Breana and how nice it would be to have just one quiet, peaceful morning. They seem to know how to destroy it."

Out of nowhere, Finn's face flashed before her leaving her uneasy. Her transcendence uncovered another side of him that Maeve had never seen before. A side of him Maeve found unfavorable. A side, that unfortunately, Shae had experienced. She knew Finn would prove to be an adversarial acquaintance more than she originally thought. A sudden rush of relief flooded over her. She knew that viewing the triquetra banding her, Liam and Shae together gave her the aptitude to tackle any adversity that challenged her. She had the ability to diminish the volcanic turmoil inside of her to ash. Maeve smiled to herself contentedly.

Shae pulled into the Hawthorn parking lot. Maeve saw Liam waiting for them as was his usual morning routine. His assigned space was near Shae's. It was a benefit of being captain of the Hawthorn Huathe football team. Maeve felt butterflies flittering in her belly, a welcome feeling after this morning's doom and gloom. No matter how many times she saw him; she felt the same. In kindergarten, Maeve told Mam that little fireflies lit up her belly when she saw Liam. Mam had nodded her head and said, "That's nice".

At six feet, four inches, Liam was pure muscle and the quarterback for the Hawthorn Huathe. He had mahogany brown, wavy hair, with magnificent marine blue eyes. Gazing into his eyes was like floating on an endless, oceanic horizon – their depth eternal. Mam's friends said that Liam had eyes like a movie star from the 1950s. When he leaned against his car, Maeve's friends said he looked like James Dean on steroids. Liam acknowledged their arrival by nodding his head in their direction. Maeve smiled happily to herself.

Liam was extremely protective of Maeve and Shae. But, cool about it. His norm was to wait by his car, but not today, his walk was brisk, hurried, as he walked toward Shae's car. Maeve knew he felt what she had all morning. She knew it without a doubt. When she turned to look at Shae, Shae was worried, too.

"Maeve, somethings up with Liam. The presentation?"

"Nah, it wouldn't be that. Presentations don't bother him. It must be something else. I'm sure he'll tell us."

"True."

Shae continued to look concerned.

"Shae, relax. I'm serious. There's nothing to worry about. You know Liam, he WILL tell us." Maeve hoped so. "Here's some advice. YOURS. Breathe! Or we'll both have a panic attack. One of us has to be the calm one."

Shae's face relaxed as she slowly transformed into yogi Shae.

"We're going to do this together. Ready? Close your eyes. We are going to breathe slowly. Inhale. Exhale. Inhale. Exhale."

Maeve felt rejuvenated. A million thoughts were running through her head, the empowered Maeve inside her head screamed confirmation, "Stop worrying over things you can't control! This has nothing to do with Liam and you. It doesn't have to do with Shae either. It's something else." Maeve and Shae opened their eyes simultaneously and burst out laughing. At the same time, they both called each other, "Idiot!"

The girls, wrapped up in their excitement, forgot Liam. Both girls screamed when Maeve's car door opened. Once again, they were in hysterics. Liam had been standing outside of the car watching them, shaking his head. His favorite two people in the entire world were certifiably nuts. Liam was beaming as he softly took Maeve's hand into his, gently pulling her up into his arms and hugging her close.

"Mo shíorghra," Liam whispered into Maeve's ear – my eternal love in Irish.

Maeve looked up at him searching for a sign.

"Liam are you okay?" asked Maeve.

Squeezing her hand, Liam replied, "Yeah, there's a bunch of stuff going on, but nothing that can't wait until after school. No worries, I promise I will tell you and Shae later."

In her peripheral, Maeve saw something in the distance. Shimmering figures stood just beyond the trees surrounding the perimeter of the school. The figures were breathtakingly familiar, very much like Kían, her secret friend. The brightest one, whom she thought to be the leader, had the ability to speak directly into her heart. His words were causing an overwhelming warmth to pulsate through her body. His message clear and concise.

"Maeve, you are destined for greatness and the revelation of your fate will soon be revealed." He bowed his head upon the conclusion of his message, and all disappeared into a wisp of sparkles.

Thankfully, Liam and Shae, so immersed in conversation about last night's basketball game, did not notice a thing. As they walked together, the triquetra illuminated, forming a protective boundary of strength around them. Overcome with a sense of joy and familiarity, Maeve suddenly found herself transcending to her first meeting with Kían.

8 Kían

Kían was Maeve's mystical friend. Most of the family and Maeve's friends knew about him. Most thought it was cute that Maeve had an imaginary friend, others indifferent. Maeve would become annoyed if someone called him "imaginary". Kían had his own place setting at the O'Flaherty dinner table, a seat at church, and a spot in the backseat of the family's van. He was her most trusted companion.

Kían was no taller than five feet, two inches. He looked more like a fairy but without wings, his features slightly pointed yet chiseled like a movie-star. His hair was a deep silvery blue that he wore combed and manicured in a business-like manner. His slight Irish brogue along with his charming personality and handsomeness would make one think he was six feet tall. Genuineness and goodness spewed out of him like sparkling fairy dust. In his lapel he wore a single sprig of furze – a deep yellow flower with a pungent coconut smell. After leaving a sprig for anyone in need of hope, faith, courage, and determination, one would magically reappear in his lapel.

Maeve would often be in Bridget's nursery telling her the most fantastical stories. Bridget would coo in her crib as

Maeve sat on the floor right beside her. The stories and tales she wove with her imagination were incredible. Her favorite story was that of a princess who mysteriously disappeared. Blonde-haired, Bridget with eyes as big as saucers was giggling away as she listened to her sister's story.

Halfway through the story, Kían appeared. He stood in the doorway of the nursery listening to the story of the hidden princess. The moment he met Maeve he knew he would protect her with every ounce of his being.

He watched the two sisters for a few moments before he said, "Hello, sweet Princess Maeve and darling Bridget."

Maeve stopped the story mid-sentence. Tilting her head to the side, she studied him intently. Excitedly, she began to giggle, causing her bouncy red curls to bob up and down. Her blue eyes sparkled in amazement.

"Hi! I'm a princess? Then so is my sissy, she is Princess Bridget."

Maeve giggled again as she continued telling Bridget her story in her tiny, little animated voice. Occasionally, she would look over at Kían and smile.

"What's your name? Mammy says not to talk to strangers."

"Maeve, your Mammy and Pa know I am here. I am your friend, Kían."

"Oh, okay."

The day Maeve started kindergarten Kían told her their friendship must be a secret. He explained that people would think her odd for still having an "imaginary" friend. Maeve understood because Mam already told her about secrets. Maeve and Kían communicated telepathically, the same way she could talk to Declan and Raegan. Maeve preferred to use her audible voice, but it would sometimes cause an inexplicable, uncomfortable gnawing in her stomach that was distracting and unnerving.

Occasionally, Maeve would forget that her friendship with Kían was private. Once, at fourteen, she and her sisters were home with the flu. Running up the stairs to her bedroom, she tripped. She yelled for Kían's help. Some profanities followed. Her sisters heard her. The three appeared around the corner to stare at her. Maeve freaked. The girls would think she was crazy. Bridget being Bridget was the first to speak up.

"Maeve, who were you just talking to?"

"No one. Why?"

"Yes, you were. We heard you!"

"No, you didn't! I yelled for Kían." Bridget looked at her like she was crazy. "Geesh B, I just didn't want to use God's name in vain. You know the rules. If Mam heard me, I'd be punished so I blamed it on Kían instead." Now, the three of them were staring at her shaking their heads in disbelief.

"Stop looking at me like that! Did you know that I just read a study and it said that people who talk to themselves have genius IQs? So there, what do you have to say about that? Nothing, I bet."

Caitlín glanced at her with a look of concern, Breana laughed at her, and Bridget just shook her head sympathetically. Out of the corner of her eye, Maeve caught a glimpse of Kían at the top of the stairs. Maeve pouted at him, stomped up the stairs, and slammed her bedroom door. Kían was waiting for her in her room. As soon as he saw her, he burst out hysterically laughing. She started yelling at him when suddenly she felt her belly fill with giggles. She could not help herself and joined in the laughter. Both stood with tears streaming down their faces.

9 Hawthorn High

Maeve began to put all the pieces together. Every important person in her life was significant. Liam, Shae, Declan, Raegan, Kían, the figure in the woods, and even Finn had their purpose, whether love, friendship, peace, danger, or uncertainty. Her gifts began to take on meaning; they, too, given to her for a reason. Tonight, she would review today's events and figure out how and why they were important in her life. Her answer would be the key to the change looming in her near future.

Maeve was relieved that Shae and Liam were still talking about last night's game. It seemed to be taking her a bit longer to reacclimate from her latest transcendence experience. Two times in one day was a first. It had left her in an intense contemplative state. Maeve felt as if trapped in the center of a snow globe, snowflakes swirling around her, her body unstable like someone had shaken the globe. Beyond the glass, she could see Liam and Shae, but she could not find her way through the snow to break the glass and be with them.

After a minute or two, she felt more like herself, grounded in Liam's arms with Shae by her side. She was in her happy place with her two-favorite people. Shae tapped her on the shoulder.

"Maeve, did you hear me? Shae asked.

"Huh?" Maeve replied. "I must have been daydreaming. Sorry."

Both Liam and Shae stared at her. Maeve shrugged her shoulders.

"I was daydreaming and truly wasn't paying attention to your conversation. Sorry, what did you just ask me?"

At the same time, both Liam and Shae said: "Nothing. No worries. We were just asking you a question about the game."

Liam squeezed Maeve a little bit tighter and brought her even closer to him. Maeve looked at him as if to say, "What's up?"

He just stared into her eyes. His eyes told her, "Everything's okay. Trust me."

Maeve tilted her head as if to say: "I do trust you."

For the first time ever, she heard him call her "my princess". Princess? She needed to find out why people kept saying that. She was so not a princess, not in any way, shape, or form. She would add that to her list to review tonight. Her instincts had never been wrong. The uneasiness she had felt earlier stemmed from her intuitively knowing that Liam had a secret. Maeve remembered the presentation.

"Hey, we'd better pick up the pace. We still need to set the projector up. It's a big day for Miss Almath. We don't want to be late."

10 The Question

Miss Róisín Almath was everyone's favorite teacher. Her cousin, Miss Fae Flannery, was Maeve's principal at the primary school. The cousins had become an integral part of the community after moving to Rowan from another province. Everyone thought they were twins, both had short, curly auburn hair and petite statures. The only difference between the two were their eye color. Miss Almath had big, emerald green eyes and Miss Flannery's eyes were robin egg blue. Maeve always said they reminded her of fairies. They both had the sweetest dispositions and smiled even on the worst of days.

About a month ago, Miss Almath faced an unsavory dilemma. She was fraught with worry about her upcoming lesson on lab safety. Last year had been a colossal disaster, she knew she would need to call upon her favorite students for a huge favor. So, Miss Almath kept Maeve, Liam, and Shae after class. Their classmates gave them looks of sympathy; some even wished them luck. Maeve, Liam, and Shae nervously moved to the front of the classroom in wait. The three of them heard Miss Almath take a deep inhale before she asked, "Would you please take a seat? I would like to speak with all three of you."

Barely audible, Maeve thought she heard her mumble 'dear me'. Miss Almath propped herself against her desk and said, "Oh my gosh, you guys look terrified. Do you think you're in trouble? Mercy! No, no, no. I just need your help."

They looked at each other and all exhaled a sigh of relief. She needed help with presenting the next chapter in their textbook. It was a simple, self-explanatory lesson. "Would you be interested in helping me. Lab Safety is the easiest lesson." She hesitated for a second and said "...until last year that is. Last year was a disaster."

Maeve heard the story from Mam. Miss Almath taught the Lab Safety lesson earlier in the week. A few days later, Maeve's neighbor, Baeth disregarded all safety precautions during lab. His blatant disregard caused injury to another student. The injured student suffered severe burns. She was in hospital for over a month. The experience scarred Miss Almath. She had nightmares for months.

Miss Almath took a deep breath and said, "Maeve, Liam, and Shae would you please make this presentation for me? The students in this class have profound respect for each of you. Honestly, I trust no one else."

Without hesitation, Maeve agreed. Shae and Liam seemed blasé. Yet, Maeve committed.

"Miss Almath, we would be more than happy to help."

"Thank you so much! I forgot to tell you that you each will receive five extra-credit points at the end of the semester."

"We would do it even if you didn't offer any extra points.

Shae gave her an evil look that spoke volumes. Chemistry was Shae's worst class. She needed those points to get a B+. Maeve ignored Shae's indignation and continued.

"But, if you don't mind, I'd like to make one suggestion. Would you object to us making a video?" As soon as Shae heard "video", there was a huge look of relief on her face. Liam's too.

"Oh, my goodness," Miss Almath replied, "that is an outstanding idea! If your video is a success with this class, with your permission, I would be able to use it in the future. Would that be okay?"

Of course, they agreed. Liam asked one last question. "Miss Almath would you be opposed if we added humor to the presentation. I think it may keep students interested."

Miss Almath looked elated. She resembled Bridget, Caitlín, and Breana when Mam says they can have ice cream for dessert.

"Liam that's a great idea! I am so happy you thought of it. Maybe everyone will finally listen and understand how important safety is in the lab."

Shae was a natural in front of the camera. Her charisma and magnetic personality won her the school election for class president. So it was unanimous, Shae would host and narrate the presentation. Maeve with her regal persona and creative abilities would be writer, director, producer, and camera person. Liam, the most handsome boy in school, would be the lead actor as well as play multiple parts.

Maeve, Liam, and Shae had two goals. First, they wanted Miss Almath to gain the respect she deserved. Second, they wanted everyone who watched it to really listen and learn about lab safety.

The film covered all the typical safety rules:
- Read Chemistry Safety Instructions as posted in class.
- Dress appropriately.
- Identify/know the location of all safety equipment (fire blanket, extinguisher, eyewash station, shower).
- Don't taste or sniff chemicals.
- Don't eat or drink in the lab.
- No horseplay.
- Always be prepared before lab.

11 The Visitors

Maeve, Liam, and Shae entered the class and found that Miss Almath had everything ready for the presentation. The only thing left to do was for Liam to insert the flash drive into her laptop. Maeve could hear hushed discussions throughout the class. Everyone was wondering what the presentation would be about. Maeve smiled. She knew the presentation would be a success. Her toughest critics already loved it.

Miss Almath stood in front of the class. She was so excited she could hardly contain herself. She announced that instead of a lecture, today's class would be a video presentation about Lab Safety.

"Everyone, please sit down and quiet yourselves. We have a surprise for you. Today, there will be no lecture. Maeve, Liam, and Shae have made a video presentation for you. I hope you all enjoy it. Come up here, you three."

She noticed some exasperated eye-rolling which did not surprise her at all. Yet, most of her students looked relieved and happy not to hear her lecture for one day. Shae made a quick introduction.

"Hey everyone, good morning. Maeve, Liam, and I made a video about Lab Safety. We hope you all enjoy. Thanks!"

Liam moved to the back of the class. Miss Almath joined him so she could watch the whole class to ensure no disruptions arose. Maeve and Shae stayed up front so they could answer questions at the end of the video, if necessary.

The video was an obvious success as the whole class was entertained laughing throughout the whole presentation. Miss Almath was beaming like a little girl with her first puppy. At the end, everyone started clapping. A couple of the boys whistled. Maeve, Liam, and Shae were ecstatic. Success! Five extra points for them and a momentous day for Miss Almath.

Maeve and Shae squeezed each other's hands tightly. They both were deep in conversation when they realized the classroom became eerily quiet. They looked around the room and found everyone with looks of terror across their faces. Maeve and Shae were so confused by the change in the room. Maeve turned around in her seat to find Liam. Miss Almath was frantic. Her eyes met Liam's. He motioned for her to look toward the windows.

Maeve elbowed Shae nudging her to look where Liam had directed. A creepy chill-like presence enveloped her. Shae grabbed her hand. Maeve whispered to Shae, "We'll be okay, I promise." The girls held each other tightly.

Four ghostly shapes, moving at tremendous speed, had entered the classroom through closed windows. Because of the intensity of their movement, it was impossible to see their bodily forms. They had long streaming hair of silver and black with grey cloaks over green flowing dresses. The dresses cinched with shimmering silver belts placed high under the bodice. The shapes' eyes were pea green in color, with pale skin and darkened circles around their eyes. No sound came from their open mouths. Their keening and shrieking muted.

Liam's brain was racing. He could not believe his eyes. He thought the banshee was a legend. He had read many folk tales describing them, never expecting them to be real. In Irish mythology, the banshee was a messenger. Banshees warned family members of impending death. Normally, one visited, today there were four. Liam's stomach lurched. He remembered the significance of the visitation of four. Four banshees beheld news of death: death to one of royalty or holy blood.

The banshees reached the front of the classroom forming a protective shield over Maeve's head. They conjoined into one, enlarging their diameter around her. Unexpectedly, another foreboding entity entered the room, its presence felt, yet, hardly visible. It began to form a large cloud becoming darker and darker. As the entity's spinning intensified it formed a cyclonic force. Tinges of green mist ran through its blackness. The entity emitted a strange aroma. The smell of blackthorn began to permeate the room. Not the sweet smell of the newly flowering bush but the smell of its rotting cut flower.

Maeve turned to Liam in desperation. At that moment, he knew she knew. Maeve was the intended target. Liam flew out of his seat; but he was seconds too late as the entity was stronger than the banshees. The banshees' protective strength did not compare to the threat against Maeve. The black entities exploded over the girls' heads. Both girls catapulted out of their seats like military projectiles. They flew across the room stopping only from their collision with the whiteboard landing on the floor crumpled like old rag dolls. Resultant of the explosion, the banshees magically disappeared, leaving a path of glittering filaments in the air.

12 The Aftermath

Liam's actions were seconds too late. His reaction time too slow. He knelt next to Shae. Shae's injuries were minimal enabling her to cradle Maeve in her arms like a baby. But Maeve remained lifeless. Liam kept calling out her name until she began to regain consciousness. Groggily she opened her eyes. In the distance she could see Miss Almath and her classmates gathered round. There was chatter in the background praising Liam's heroics. Liam kissed Maeve's hand then stood up. He was upset and uncomfortable. Not a good combination, but he composed himself as he talked to his classmates calmly.

"Hey, everyone, listen up! I'm just like you. I can't believe what just happened. It was like watching a movie. It was the weirdest thing I've ever experienced, so we have to stick together. We need to be there for each to help understand how lucky we all were, even Maeve. We all could have been seriously hurt. The police are coming. They'll want to know what happened so they can investigate and find out who ordered the attack. We all must remain calm. Remember we are all okay."

There was a collective mumble of yeses and head nods from the crowd. Maeve could see Liam's shoulders relax.

Everyone was being receptive. Maeve thought: 'thank God' if they did not, she was afraid that emotions could escalate. Liam kept talking to the group in a calm voice, "We're safe. Shae's dad will be here soon. Remember he's the Chief of Police. He'll take care of all of us. Listen up, if you're injured, see Miss Almath. She needs to know so she can let the EMTs know when they get here."

Maeve scanned the crowd for Raegan and Declan. She would not be able to relax until she knew they were okay. She looked for small gatherings. She knew they would be in the center. Her twin cousins were special; both had magnetic personalities. Raegan had a sweet, beautiful aura, and Declan complimented her with his calm, peaceful demeanor. Liam would need relief soon and they were the perfect duo for the task.

Finally, she saw her beautiful cousins across the room. Their father was Mam's brother, Uncle Donall. Both had red hair like Maeve, although, Raegan's hair was long and straight. Raegan was stunning. She was extremely tall with emerald green eyes, strawberry red lips, and a flawless complexion. Her natural beauty and height had caught the eye of many model agencies. Declan was extremely handsome, with wavy, thick, shoulder length hair. He was tall, about six feet, six inches, with the same emerald green eyes as Raegan, and the same freckles as Maeve.

Maeve caught Raegan's eyes and gave her a quick nod. She needed Raegan and Declan to be a calming force to the crowd forming around her and Shae. Raegan was talking to a group of girls. She knew Raegan would bring comfort to the room. Maeve was sure Liam had had about enough.

"It's okay, I know it was very scary, but it's over now. Relax, okay. You know Shae's Dad? I know you do, you met him at her birthday party. Well, he's the Chief and he's going to be here soon."

Raegan was amazing. Just beyond Liam, Maeve caught a hazy glimpse of Declan. He was talking the guys down. A few of them were planning to go hunting to find the "bombers"

"Oh, my gosh!" Maeve thought. "Bombers!"

Maeve felt a tightness in her chest. The panicked energy in the room was overwhelming. Declan brought his hands together in a prayer-like position and the whole room miraculously calmed down; so, did Maeve. She smiled to herself.

Maeve could hear someone in the hallway. The voice was booming and very authoritative.

"Excuse me! What classroom are they in?"

When she heard someone say, "Why are you here? Parents haven't been notified." She knew exactly who it was.

13 The Chief

Everyone in Rowan knew Shae's Dad, Chief Ólan Kerrigan. He was a man with many names: Chief, Mr. K, Ollie, and Pa. He had a soft spot for Maeve, so he allowed her to call him "Papa K". He loved her like a daughter.

Maeve hoped whoever was being disrespectful to the Chief was a seasoned teacher responding off nerves. The Chief did not tolerate disrespect. There was an edge in his voice when she heard him reply:

"Do you know who I am? I do not need your permission to be here. Everyone out of the halls. I need this pathway cleared. Patrol and ambulances should be here any second. All of you need to move! Questions?"

A pause permeated the hallway. It was an uncomfortable silence. The Chief asked impatiently. "I didn't think so. Room?"

This time there was not a hint of hesitation in the reply.

"End of hall on the right."

Maeve could just imagine the look on his face.

"Thanks! Send the other officers and the EMTs to Miss Almath's class ASAP. Understood?"

The Chief's voice became louder. The girls glanced at each other.

"Excuse me! PLEASE! Move!"

The Chief was a tall, intimidating man with jet black hair, and gorgeous blue eyes like Shae. No one messed with him. He was able to part a crowd like Moses had parted the Red Sea. Both girls felt a rush of relief flood through their body. He nodded at Shae and Maeve, his face filling with emotion.

The Chief pulled Liam aside. His voice barely audible, he spoke, "Liam, what happened. I need details. The Hierarchy will need to know how to proceed." Maeve's ears were ringing, a result of the blast. She only heard random words. "Maeve". "Target". "Banshee". "Hierarchy" "Cloud-like figure". Other than random words there was just a bunch of hand, arm, and body movements. Then the Chief hugged Liam and whispered something into his ear. Liam nodded.

It was obvious the Chief had an agenda. Miss Almath was next on his list. Maeve heard him ask her, "Are you okay?" She just nodded her head. She was so emotional. Maeve was not sure her account would be decipherable. The Chief kept nodding at Miss Almath's attempts. He gave her a quick hug of comfort before walking over to Shae and Maeve.

In the short distance from Miss Almath to his girls, he reviewed Miss Almath's story in his mind. She concluded that the formation of the cloud, the lightning, and heat appeared threatening, but the explosion caused the most damage and injury. Unlike Liam, Miss Almath did not mention the banshees' warnings and their attempt to protect Maeve. An emergency meeting of the Hierarchy needed scheduling expeditiously to discuss today's attack. Things were happening much sooner than expected. There would be great concern over this development.

The Chief smiled widely as he walked over to the girls. It was obvious he was masking his emotions; there was a slight quiver in his lower lip. He wanted to be strong for his girls. He kneeled in between them, pulling them gently into his arms. When he pulled away, there were tears brimming in his eyes. The Chief inhaled deeply before he started his questioning.

"Miss Almath told me you were both incredibly lucky that your injuries were minimal. We will talk about the incident later. For now, the three of you need to stay together. Liam will sit with you shortly."

The Chief needed to keep his composure. Today's event had been personal. He would alert Rowan's mayor and school officials. Another attack was imminent. For now, it was imperative to organize students into groups. His officers would need to start getting statements from all witnesses. Interviews would begin as soon as guardians arrived.

Maeve was concerned for her classmates. She instinctively knew without a doubt today's attack would have traumatizing effects on her friends. Shae's concern was different. Maeve's safety was at risk. Shae took Maeve's hand in hers. Maeve looked at Shae for an answer.

"Shae, I know you too well. You're scared. What is it? Please tell me."

Shae squeezed Maeve's hand. She tried to offer Maeve comfort but was finding it difficult to find the right words.

"Maeve, keep calm, okay? There's no easy way to say this. So, here goes."

Maeve felt bile rising from her stomach. Shae continued.

"I don't want you to freak out but I'm 99% sure that you were the target."

Maeve had just had the same thought. She knew Shae was waiting for a reaction. What could she say? Nothing, really, except: "Shae, I was just thinking the same thing. I overheard Liam saying "target", and "Maeve" when he was talking to Papa K. So, I'm not surprised."

"Maeve, it's going to be okay," Shae said as she pulled Maeve closer to her. She whispered, "I truly mean that."

The girls huddled together. Anger was beginning to stir in Maeve's belly. Strange, but this anger gave Maeve a bit of relief. She looked up to see Liam walking over to her dissipating the anger boiling in her. Liam had the ability to absorb any unsettling feelings she had. Maeve sighed with relief.

Liam sat against the wall and drew Maeve and Shae closer to him. He had one girl on each side of him with his arms protectively shielding them. He knew how much Maeve loved the *Sleepsong* lullaby from "A Secret Garden". Quietly, Liam sang to the girls. His voice was hypnotic. Maeve felt her thoughts drifting away. Both sank deeper into his arms as he sang.

Loo-li, loo-li, loo-li, lai-lay
Loo-li, loo-li, loo-li lai-la
Lay down your head and I'll sing you a lullaby
Back to the years of loo-li lai-lay
And I'll sing you to sleep and I'll sing you tomorrow
Bless you with love for the road that you go
May you sail far to the far fields of fortune

With diamonds and pearls at your head and your feet
And may you need never to banish misfortune
May you find kindness in all that you meet
May there always be angels to watch over you
To guide you each step of the way
To guard you and keep you safe from all harm
Loo-li, loo-li, lai-lay
May you bring love, and may you bring happiness
Be loved in return to the end of your days
Now fall off to sleep, I'm not meaning to keep you
I'll just sit for a while and sing loo-li, lai-lay
May there always be angels to watch over you
To guide you each step of the way
To guard you and keep you safe from all harm
Loo-li, loo-li, lai-lay, loo-li, loo-li, lai-lay
Loo-li, loo-li, loo-li, lai-lay
Loo-li, loo-li, loo-li lai-lay
Loo-li, loo-li, loo-li lai-lay
Loo-li, loo-li, loo-li lai-lay
Loo-li, lai-lay

Liam's strength and love flowed through the verses of the song. Maeve could feel herself drifting in and out of consciousness. She needed to fight to keep awake. Maeve felt so tired, but through the fogginess, she knew she needed to stay cognitive to the situation unfolding. "Liam, I must stay awake." He pulled her closer. She could hear his heart beating, syncopated with hers.

Maeve knew that there was something or someone after her. Whatever it was, the banshees were trying to warn her? Of what, she did not know. Everyone was concerned. She was certain of that. Maeve was starting to think that Shae, Liam, Papa K, and her parents knew more than they were sharing with her. She knew she would have to tread carefully in her approach with any of them. She would get the information she sought after. She had no doubt.

Maeve's head hurt slightly, but she felt comforted by Liam's voice. Maeve kept thinking about Liam. There was something she could not remember. As he was coming to the last verse of *Sleepsong,* Liam sang, "to guard you and keep you safe from all harm". Maeve remembered what it was. Earlier there had been sparkles all around Liam's aura. The same as the figures in the woods. The same that emanated from their hands forming the triquetra on the playground so many years ago. All three incidences interconnected. She just did not know how. Maeve kept her eyes closed for a few moments ruminating over her thoughts.

Liam's voice was hypnotizing. It had a calming effect on most of his classmates. Others were just gawking. Some were crying. Those who were most effected gravitated toward him forming a semi-circle of protection around the three of them. Declan and Raegan were in front keeping everyone at a distance from the three huddled on the floor. It seemed like forever since Miss Almath had called emergency response. Maeve was starting to get impatient. Liam tightened his hold on her. He knew her better than anyone. He knew she would try to get up.

The Chief was getting progressively agitated. The Emergency Response Team was taking an extraordinarily long time to arrive. Shae jokingly told Maeve and Liam, "My

Pa's head looks about to explode. Look at his cheeks. They are fire engine red."

Finally, they heard a few of the staff mutter: "They're finally here."

Maeve and Shae simultaneously sighed with relief. Relief was short-lived as the Emergency Response Team entered the classroom. The team members consisted of Finn and Cillín Darroch. Shae looked at Maeve with concern and angst. Just when Maeve thought the day could not get worse, she transcended.

14 Kerrigans & Darrochs

Branagh Kerrigan and Catriona Darroch had been friends since childhood. They met the first day of preschool. Quickly, they became closer than sisters. When they married, their families blended making them one big family. The Darroch boys called Branagh, Auntie B. All the Kerrigan kids called Catriona, Auntie Cat. Auntie Cat became a surrogate mom to Shae after Branagh died. Sadly, the relationship between the Kerrigans and Darrochs frayed in the summer of 7th grade.

Maeve was sleeping over Shae's house one summer night. It was a few weeks before the start of school. After dinner, the Kerrigans and Darrochs played competition dodgeball. Dodgeball was not Maeve's forte. She begged not to play. The kids would not take "no" for an answer. Why? Either they all played, or no one played. Those were the rules enforced by Papa K and Auntie Cat. It was a ruthless competition. Knowing that, Maeve offered to be scorekeeper.

Maeve's team was losing, and it was her fault. She kept making error after error. Maeve could hear the boys cursing under their breath. Shae was the only one who did not add to the commentary, but Maeve knew what she was thinking. She was just being a good friend. Out of nowhere Finn called a timeout to talk to the team. He huddled them all together, "Guys give her a break. She doesn't play all the time like we do."

One of Shae's three brothers, Aedan, rolled his eyes at Finn and told Maeve, "Maeve, you stink. I told them you shouldn't play. We're losing because of you."

Maeve was so embarrassed. She warned them all, but did they listen? Nope. Suddenly, Shae nonchalantly walked up to Aedan and punched him in the face. Maeve just stood there speechless. It was no secret that Shae would always defend Maeve over her brothers. Shae was so infuriated, anger spewed as she yelled at Aedan.

"Leave her alone, JERK! Do you want me to get Auntie?" Aedan backed down. He did not want to upset Auntie Cat.

Maeve noticed that when Shae made eye contact with Finn, she had a gleam in her eye. A gleam in her eye that Finn may misconstrue as something more. Knowing Shae as she did, Maeve knew it meant nothing. Maeve was right. Finn was beaming. There was no doubting the fact that Finn had a crush on Shae, and now he thought Shae liked him back.

Aedan replied as he rubbed his eye where Shae's fist had landed: "Seriously, Shae. Did ya have to hit me? Geez! Sorry, Maeve. I just like to win."

Finn stepped up again and put his arm around Aedan.

"Good man, Aedan. Nice recovery."

The rest of the game went smoothly. Maeve regretted not warning Shae about Finn's feelings. Honestly, she was afraid Shae would not believe her because of how much Maeve disliked him. Out of all the Darroch boys, Maeve liked him least and only tolerated him for Shae's sake. There was something about him that left her disconcerted. He worried her and she did not know why. He was not as nice as Shae thought.

Maeve had forgotten about Finn's infatuation with Shae until a few weeks later. It was after dinner when Mam answered a frantic call from Shae. Mam had her come over straight away. By the time Shae arrived at Maeve's backdoor, she could hardly breathe. She was frantic. Her eyes were bulging, her arms and hands were flailing as she tried to explain what had happened.

"Finn." Panting. "Me." Deep breaths. "No!" Maeve never saw Shae so panicked.

"Shae, calm down, I can hardly understand a word you're saying. Take a deep breath." Shae nodded.

"Remember when we learned Anjaya breathing during our yoga unit in gym. That's it. Inhale left nostril, exhale right nostril. Inhale right, exhale left. Slow down. One more time. That's better. Keep breathing."

Shae continued her yoga breathing for the next few minutes. Once Shae was calm, Maeve started asking her questions.

"Okay, now slowly tell me what happened. Can you do that?" Shae nodded as Maeve continued questioning her. "What about Finn? Did he hurt you? Shae, you're making me nervous."

Shae took a deep breath. She was desperate to talk about it. So, she began by saying that she always thought that Finn was cute. But she never thought of him in the boyfriend kind of way.

"Gosh, Maeve, boyfriend? Never! I explained that he, Fagen and Cillín were my brothers. I told him he was handsome, and sweet, but I wasn't the girl for him. Any girl would be lucky to date him. Plus, I told him I could not date until I was sixteen. He knows my Pa's rules. I thought he would understand."

Maeve nodded in agreement then added. "Same rule applies for me."

"I know. Everyone knows."

"For sure. They've made it known since we were born."

Shae paused for a second, then took a huge gulp of air.

"He lost it, Maeve. It was terrifying."

Maeve stared at Shae. She was talking nonstop without a pause between sentences. Her tone was flat and vacant. Then she suddenly stopped and became quiet again to recollect her thoughts. At one point, Shae put her head in her hands, simultaneously, Maeve became overcome with fear. It was true, she was right about Finn. The fear was Shae's and felt like an injection into her heart. It was disturbing.

Shae continued, "He wasn't our Finn. Maeve, he was so intense, filled with hatred and rage. The more I explained why we couldn't date, the redder and redder his face got. He started sweating and screaming. His arms were thrashing around. He was having a freakin' tantrum. Then he started threatening me. He told me I'd be sorry."

Maeve placed her hand on Shae's trembling shoulder. For the first time, Maeve could vividly see the confrontation between Shae and Finn with her mind's eye. The experience was so realistic it was mind-blowing. The emotion was overwhelming. Maeve's gifts were evolving. This was more difficult than transcendence. The ability to peer into her best friend's mind was beyond anything she ever imagined. Maeve tried hard to keep her composure. She did not want to upset Shae any further.

"Shae, you need to tell Papa K. And your brothers. What if he comes after all of you?"

Shae sighed again. "I can't tell Pa. He'd go crazy. Once I'm calm, I'll tell the boys. They need to know Finn's nuts."

"Well, that's a start."

"I don't know what happened. I didn't defend myself. I just sat there whimpering like a blubbering idiot. Nothing I said was coherent. He took me by surprise, and I couldn't react."

"Shae, you need to tell someone. How 'bout Mam? She's right down the hall. She can help. And she can keep a secret."

Shae started ranting to herself, not really listening to Maeve's advice. This situation was dire. Maeve quietly watched Shae. Shae looked comical. Her face masked countless facial expressions. After another deep breath, Shae started to reply.

"Maeve, you're right. He's coming after me." Shae's voice started to quiver. "Plus…"

"Plus, what? Shae, what is it?"

"I can't tell you. Not right now anyway."

"Can't tell me what?"

"I'm not sure. I honestly don't remember."

"Try to remember."

"I can't. It's gone. I'm too upset. If I remember, I will tell you."

"It's okay, Shae. It's okay."

Maeve grabbed Shae and gave her the biggest bear hug. Maeve knew deep within her soul that Finn meant every word he said. Shae was in extreme danger.

Maeve and Shae decided telling Mam about Finn was the best decision. Mam met with Papa K and explained everything to him. Papa K's fury was indescribable. He severed all ties with the Darroch family for Shae's safety. With one exception, for continuity, Auntie Cat and Shae meet Saturdays to keep their relationship strong. Papa K knew it was what his wife, Branagh, would have wanted.

15 The Confrontation

Finn's true self had never been clearer. Maeve's recollections were clicking together like puzzle pieces. She now saw him with great clarity. His foreboding presence was at every supernatural incident since kindergarten. Memories flooded her mind. Each one pictured Finn sitting on the sidelines vehemently watching. Maeve was so angry at herself at how blind she had been, especially for giving him the benefit of the doubt for Shae's sake. Shae needed her protection from Finn. If only she was privy to his agenda.

Finn's arrival was panicking Shae. Her struggle to keep her composure was clear to those who loved her. The Chief's eyes spoke volumes. Today's events had been terrifying. Adding Finn to the mix was unfair. Finn's presence even unnerved the Chief. In hindsight, he should have called the Chief of First Responders and reassigned Finn to another unit, not the Hawthorn team. The Chief needed to pull in a favor. Better late than never. His daughter needed limited contact with Finn. He would make sure that happened.

Maeve could feel Shae's fear. Her hands and body were trembling. She was trying so hard to keep her emotions in check. Luckily, her hands were the only give-away. Maeve thought there was only one plus in the situation unfolding.

Finn had to be on his best behavior. He would never reveal his true feelings for Shae. Hate was something that he must hide, especially from the Chief.

Shae leaned into Maeve, cupped her hand, lifted it up to her ear and whispered:

"Maeve, I haven't talked to Finn in two years. Why? Of all the First Responders in Rowan. Why HIM? Ugh!"

Maeve replied: "I thought the same thing. Remember, he's nothing. And everyone here loves you. He'd never try anything. There are too many witnesses."

Shae rolled her eyes: "Gee, thanks. That makes me feel better now."

"Seriously, you'll be safe. I promise."

"You can't promise me that."

She had to keep Shae calm. "You can do this. I know you can. Finn won't act up in front of everyone. I don't think he's that stupid."

"Ha don't be so sure. But I truly hope you're right."

Maeve closed her eyes and with every cell in her body wished calmness to flood over Shae. As she slowly opened her eyes, she realized that Shae's hands were no longer shaking. It had worked. She did not know how, but she also did not care.

Finn was walking toward them. Goosebumps began to tingle down Maeve's neck. With every step the tingling on her neck intensified. Maeve could see the real Finn. He looked directly into her eyes. She could see pure evil flowing from his cavernous inner core. Maeve took a deep breath embracing her newfound internal strength. For a second,

Finn retracted, then smirked quickly regaining his composure.

Maeve squeezed Shae's hand tightly as Finn knelt beside Shae. Gritting his teeth into a forced smile, he spoke to Shae with a voice void of emotion. Maeve was straining to hear him.

"How are you feeling, Shae? Nervous?" he snickered. "It's just you and me. Not Maeve, Liam, or your precious Daddy will be able to help you. You are going to the hospital with ME. Doesn't that just make your heart flutter. Mine is. I've waited a long, long time for this."

He placed his hand on her shoulder and squeezed it.

Before he could get up, Maeve grabbed his arm and pulled him down to her level on the floor. Under her breath, she said, "FINN, you don't know what I'm capable of. YOU really don't want ME to come after YOU! Don't mess with me or my friends. Do YOU understand me!? Finn Darroch, my warning is no joke!

Finn looked at her with contempt.

Shae was so upset she could not respond. She looked worse than right after the explosion. Her whole body was trembling. This angered Maeve. She had finally calmed her down. She would have to try her new technique again. Unfortunately, it would have to wait.

Cillín was on his way over. Glaring at Finn, he loudly announced for the whole room to hear, "Girls, I will take great care of both of you. Okay?"

Cillín emphasized "I". Both girls nodded "yes". Although Shae was one step away from hyperventilating, Maeve squeezed her hand and said, "Focus on Cillín. Forget Finn. He can't hurt you. I'm stronger than him. Believe me."

Shae could not speak but her eyes spoke volumes. The thought of being alone with Finn was terrifying her. Maeve could not blame her. Maeve watched him from across the room. He was talking with the Chief and Miss Almath. Finn's aura was flowing like water from a fountain. The aura illuminated red fire beams of light.

The Chief was visibly agitated. Not only by the delay in medical evaluations, but by Finn's presence. Suddenly, he turned away from the group and started walking toward them. He could not stay away from Shae. Cillín tried to stop him, but Finn shoved him out of the way. He was trying to induce fear. Once again, he crouched down and began taunting them. The comments audible only to Maeve and Shae.

Just above a whisper he said: "Hey, girls, you know what's ironic?

"Ah, no!" replied Shae and Maeve simultaneously.

Finn continued, "Did you know this high school has a barrier of protection around it? It's true. That's why the cornerstone says 'Cosanta 1850'. Cosanta means 'protected' in Irish. I guess the protection didn't apply to either of you. Obviously, someone doesn't like you. I wonder who that could be? Hmm?"

Finn's presence infuriated Maeve. With her teeth gritted together she said: "Finn, did you not hear me? My threat is no joke!"

She could see Liam out of the corner of her eye. He looked like a lion readying to pounce. Thankfully, Cillín intervened. He looked as irritated as the Chief and Liam with Finn.

"Thanks, Finn. Breandán is on his way. NOW leave."

Finn's lips tightened into a thin line so taut she imagined cutting them with a scissor. He was struggling. Maeve knew that he had to be. She had humiliated and angered him as did Cillín. She felt a deep-seated satisfaction in that knowledge. The Chief had thwarted his plan to terrorize Shae.

"You know, Finn, that's enough. None of us have time for this." He turned to Shae and Maeve, and said "Sorry, girls." He continued to reprimand Finn. "So, make yourself useful and get the equipment so I can get the girls ready for transport."

Finn angrily replied: "YOU? You mean US!"

"No, I just told you Breandán is on his way. You're no longer transporting the girls. You've been reassigned to triage. Go, see Miss Almath, NOW!"

"BUT I'm…"

"You're not listening. Rían and Seamus will drive the ambos. Breandán will be aiding me in the girls' care and transport."

As Finn walked away, he replied smugly: "This doesn't change anything, bro. No one can stop what's coming."

"Whatever, Finn, just do as your told for once."

Maeve mouthed "thank you" to Cillín.

16 A Message

Maeve observed Cillín as he assessed her. Not unlike Liam, he had a thin brilliance of illumination surrounding his whole body. He looked up at her and stared into her eyes. As if she was peering into the sea of his inner being, she found a calm and goodness flooding throughout his soul. Cillín held his eyes on hers for a second longer. Suddenly, Maeve saw a shift in the calm. There was now a whirling pool of darkness at its epicenter. Cillín had been involuntarily tainted. Maeve felt her face flush and a small sweat break out on her forehead. She broke eye contact with Cillín.

Maeve inconspicuously redirected her gaze toward Finn. She was thankful that students, faculty, and emergency personnel filled the room. He moved through the swarm of people with an air of confidence that wreaked from insolence. Even at a distance, his repugnant energy was overwhelming. It was vibrating like electrical currents making her body hairs stand on end. Maeve wondered if he knew she was watching him because his energy force was intensifying.

Finn closed his eyes entering a meditative trance-like state. Suddenly, a cloud of darkness enveloped him. The darkness soaked into every pore of his body. It soon dissipated transforming Finn right before her eyes. His body language and facial expressions changed drastically. It was as if he had put on the costume of Finn – the Finn of pure heart. Maeve was thunderstruck. Who was he? What had he become?

As Cillín started to talk to Shae about her symptoms, in her head Maeve heard Kían's voice. His message was cautionary.

"Quickly, I must warn you. Today was the first of many attacks against you and the people of Rowan. This faction against our people has experienced exponential growth in the last month. Its' membership tripling in size. Finn is part of this faction. It teaches hate; a hate for you that is unimaginable. Please be wary of Cillín as he is contemplating joining this faction. Cillín is still of pure heart but we know not for how long. Finn wears a protective shield against you. You are stronger than him which infuriates him. Do not be afraid. He is unable to hurt you when the triquetra is together. I will explain more soon. Be strong, Princess, I must go now."

Kían's message made her shudder. It was a bit cryptic but confirmed her feelings about Cillín. Maeve evaluated what Kían had just told her. His message just formulated more questions in her mind that needed prompt attention.

So entrenched in her own thoughts, Maeve did not notice Breandán trying to get her attention. She jumped when he touched her hand. "I'm sorry, Maeve, I didn't mean to startle you. You were so deep in thought; you didn't hear me."

Maeve mumbled: "I'm sorry, Breandán."

"No worries, Maeve. It's okay."

Cillín looked over to him and nodded for him to start.

"We have to get you ready for transport."

When it registered in her mind that Breandán was evaluating her, Maeve let her guard down worsening her symptoms. Her head began spinning, she became pale, and felt extremely nauseous.

"Maeve, are you okay? You look like you're going to faint." Maeve grabbed his forearm. "Okay, let's stabilize your neck. Then I'll take your vitals. Temperature. Blood pressure. Pulse rate. Then, I'm sorry, once we're in the ambulance I must insert an IV needle. It won't hurt. I promise, everything will be fine." Maeve just nodded her head.

Between all the events of this morning, and the message from Kían, she was beginning to feel ungrounded. Maeve rested her forehead in her hands and rubbed her temples.

"My head really hurts and I'm very nauseous. I think I've just crashed."

Maeve reached across to Shae and grabbed her hand. They held hands stretcher to stretcher.

The Chief was guiding students into small groups. The crowd responded to his directions swiftly. Maeve kept noticing him glancing over at them. As Officer Rooney walked into the classroom, Maeve saw the Chief's shoulders drop in relief. The Chief filled Officer Rooney in on the details of the attack. He gave orders on how to continue with interviews and forensics.

It took only seconds for this whole transaction to take place. Officer Rooney then patted him on his back. Maeve could hear him tell the Chief, "Go, Chief. I've got this. The girls need you."

The Chief replied, "Thanks, Rooney. Much appreciated."

The Chief walked toward Cillín and Breandán.

"Let's go. We need to get the patients to the hospital."

17 The Ambulance

Officer Rooney remained at the school to complete witness interviews. Finn stayed to triage the students with minor injuries. He would not be riding with them to the hospital. Both Maeve and Shae were relieved. The Chief had pulled in a few favors. His nephews, Rían and Seamus Kerrigan, would drive the ambulances, and his wife's nephew, Breandán Flaherty, would ride with Shae. These changes ensured everyone would get to the hospital safely.

As soon as Maeve settled in the back of the ambulance, Cillín took her hand gently in his. He spoke with such sincerity and concern, overwhelming Maeve. She knew the truth about him. She saw his protective nature shining bright, yet she could sense his internal conflict. Darkness tainted his heart. Kían's warning was correct. She needed to keep her distance from Cillín. He would not trick her by using kind words. She was relieved that the distance to the hospital was short.

He kept apologizing for Finn's behavior.

"Maeve, I'm so sorry about Finn. My Mom is devastated. None of us know what to do about him. Aífe won't even come over anymore. We know he's gotten involved with bad people. We just don't know who. It's ruining my family. All I can do is apologize to you for his behavior today."

Maeve did not know what to say. She knew Aífe. She was Liam's oldest sister. Long before the confrontation between Finn and Shae, Aífe told us that she avoided all contact with Finn. She stopped going to the Darroch's house and made Cillín come to her house. Maeve tried to make her reply sound as natural as possible.

"No worries, Cillín. It's not your fault." Maeve giggled, then continued. "Honestly, I thought my sisters were horrible and there's three of them. I'll admit Finn's worse than all of them put together. I'm so sorry. Things must be difficult for your family, especially your Mum."

Her head was starting to pound harder. She felt sorry for Cillín, but his tainted energy was beginning to affect her negatively. She had hoped Kían was wrong about him. Now she was not so sure.

She knew if Kían's predictions were right, Liam would be devastated. Liam loved him like a brother. Why else would he let him date his sister? Cillín and Aífe were an adorable couple. Everyone talked about them in town. The rumor mill spewed an impending marriage within the next two or three years. Maeve was not surprised. It was common for couples to marry young in Rowan. She had to admit it was the furthest thing from her own mind.

"Cillín, I really don't feel well but I want you to know that I'm so sorry for you and your family. It's a lot to deal with. It must be stressful. Thanks for the explanation, though. That was really sweet."

"Thanks, Maeve. You're amazing. After all this, you can still have compassion for me and my family. You truly are special."

They both smiled. The rest of the ride was quiet. Maeve needed to close her eyes. The pounding in her head was getting worse. Plus, she was exhausted. Maeve just drifted off to sleep when Seamus pulled into the emergency room ambulance bank. She felt Cillín remove his hand from hers. Through a haze of sleepiness and pain, Maeve noticed the sparkle emitting from Cillín's hand as she drifted off. The next thing she knew she was in an examining room with Shae.

Maeve kept getting a tingling, hair-raising feeling on the back of her neck. She was not able to decipher if her imagination was playing tricks on her or it was resultant from the excruciating pain coursing through her head. She had to fight to keep her eyes open. She knew someone was in their room. If she could only speak. She was desperate to find out if Shae felt it too. The feeling had become so intense. As she drifted off again, she felt a coldness overwhelm her. Someone was watching her. The someone had incredible powers. Maeve struggled. Was it Conaire?

When she was a little girl, Kían told Maeve there were Guardian Protectors from another realm living among them. Hers was Conaire, the Strong and Mighty. Maeve knew he must have protected her during the attack. Maeve was sure of it. She should have died today. The blast was so close to her head, there was no way there had not been someone interceding on her behalf. Plus, Kían's message insinuated that she had protection. It had to mean that Conaire was close by.

18 Conaire

Conaire, Guardian of Protection, a descendant of Archangel Michael, was a protector of the O'Flaherty's for centuries. He was the son of Conor, King of the Guardians. His back adorned huge wings. His chest emblazoned with a gold plate. In his hand, he bore a staff of gold and silver. His age progression emulated Maeve's to ensure her trust. They met when Maeve was nine years old. She nicknamed him ConCon. He acquiesced only because she was his Princess. Otherwise, other Protectors would have ridiculed him.

The first time Maeve and Conaire met was at a recess swing set contest. The winner must swing the highest without being scared. Maeve and Shae were competing against each other. They were swinging in-sync when the swing set footings became loose. The structure was becoming unstable. Maeve glanced over at Shae. The fear on Shae's face paralleled her own. The swing set flipping over was inevitable.

Magically, Maeve saw this beautiful boy fly toward both her and Shae. His wings covered her and Shae in a sparkly white light. She could not believe that a boy her age could wield the power against a danger so great. Maeve became overcome with emotion. She realized that this boy was an angel. She had many questions. Where was he from? Why was he protecting her? She could not wait to talk to Shae about him. She was sure that Shae and the other kids could see him, too.

"Hi! My name is Maeve. This is my friend, Shae. Thank you for saving us. You are so brave."

"You're welcome. I'm Conaire. I came to protect you from danger. I'm always nearby. I did not know you could see me."

"Yes, I can. How do you know me?"

"My family has been protecting your family for a long, long time. You are royalty to us."

Maeve stunned by his use of the word "royalty" continued questioning Conaire.

"I don't understand your use of the word "royalty". I am just a girl. My family is not royal. We live just down the street from here. We don't live in a castle."

Conaire realized that he divulged too much information to Maeve. Luckily, their conversation ended abruptly when Shae interrupted them.

"Umm, Maeve, are you okay?"

Maeve turned to look at Shae. Shae and their friends were staring at her. The realization that she alone saw Conaire shocked Maeve. Everyone thought she was talking to herself. She knew this could become a big problem. She would make them think she was pranking them. So, Maeve quickly began laughing.

"Fooled you. Y'all thought I was talking to myself. Ha! Just seeing how you all would react."

There was an awkward pause and then they all started laughing. Maeve knew she had come close to revealing one of her secrets. She had to be careful. She heard Mam's warning clear as a bell. If anyone found out about her, she could be in great danger.

Conaire appeared a countless number of times over the years. He saved her from little things like falling off her bike; from a near car accident while chasing her dog; and even, tripping over her own feet. No matter the situation, he never made her feel stupid. He said it was an honor for him to protect her. Maeve knew that there was more to her gifts than anyone had told her. It was the beginning of her questioning who she really was.

19 Rowan General Hospital

The Chief leaned in the doorway of Maeve and Shae's exam room blocking its' entrance. He stood with his arms crossed and his foot tapping, waiting for the doctor. As Finn and Cillín passed the girls doorway, Finn stopped and waved mouthing 'feel better'. It was clear he would not gain entry. Both girls gave him a dismissive wave, rolling their eyes at each other when he was out of sight. Maeve thought 'good riddance!' as the Chief grabbed his arm and escorted him out of the hospital. He, too, felt the need to remove all Darrochs from the premises.

The first thing out of Shae's mouth when he was out of hearing range was "What a jerk!!! I can't stand Finn. Have you ever met anyone so obnoxious? I can't believe I let him get to me like that."

"Shae, geez, under the circumstances I think you handled it well. Not your best, but okay." Maeve chuckled weakly.

"You're just being nice. I acted like an idiot. Thank God I never went out with him! He's not the Finn I grew up with who was so NICE." Shae could not help but emphasize the word 'nice' with a tiny bit of cynicism. She continued. "Plus, he was like my brother. It's just unbelievable. Other than you, Liam, and my brothers, he's the one I could turn to no matter what. I really loved him. Now, it's just sad."

Maeve had to ask, "Shae, I'm so sorry. Don't get mad, but do you think he still likes you?"

Shae sounded melancholy when she replied: "No. I don't think so. Why would he? He has hardly uttered a word to me since I told him I wouldn't go out with him."

"But it doesn't mean he doesn't like you. He may not want you to know. This sounds really mean, but I never liked him and now, I would call him evil."

"Yikes! That's great. I'm loved by the evil Darroch brother. Aren't I the lucky one?"

"Mmmm, well, uh." Maeve was unsure how to answer.

"I'm sure you're right about the evil part. He was so mean to me. Not the best way to show you like someone."

"Agreed."

"Your sixth sense is always right so I'll have to believe you. But it does make me terribly sad." Shae paused for a second. "Maeve, I miss my mom. None of this with the Darrochs would have happened if she were still alive. My Ma and Auntie Cat were like sisters. The Finn situation would have ended long ago. My Ma would have made sure of it."

"I know, Shae. Your Ma would have kicked his butt." Maeve had a glimmer in her eye. She was reenacting Ma kicking Finn's butt then said: "She was great. I miss her too." A little tear formed in Maeve's eye.

"Thanks, Maeve. You know what? Even if there had been a one-percent chance of me changing my mind about him, he blew it today."

Maeve nodded in agreement and then hesitated before she asked her next question. "Shae?"

"Sure!" Shae replied automatically.

"Can I ask you a weird question." Maeve hesitated. "Did you get goosebumps when we first arrived?"

"Umm, no? Did you?"

"A little bit. Probably just my imagination." Maeve half-laughed. "Back to Finn. I got the feeling it made him happy to see us hurt. It's the reason I said he's a little evil."

Shae hesitated a second. She looked as if she was watching a scene from a movie replay in her head. She looked up at Maeve.

"Geez, it did cross my mind, but I thought it was my imagination. He must be crazy to be happy but then…he is a bit off. It wouldn't make sense at all if he was the old Finn. This new one? It's a possibility."

Maeve was having a challenging time formulating the right sentence. She did not want it to come out wrong. Plus, Kían had warned her not to talk too much about Finn. Hurting Shae by making an unkind statement would be insensitive. Maeve had to know if Shae saw what happened to Finn.

"Okay, this is going to sound crazy."

"Geez, Mae, come on, just say it. I can't imagine anything you'd say would be a surprise to me after today."

"Ha, you're right. Well…I saw Finn transform. He instantly changed from a sarcastic, obnoxious idiot to a professional, caring EMT. He had two distinct personalities."

It was obvious that Shae was still trying to reenact today's events in her head to see if she saw what Maeve did.

"Maeve, I'm not sure. You saw me. I was in full panic mode. I was so wrapped up in Finn's presence I didn't notice much else."

"Well, I'll tell you what I saw. He was hell bent on having an altercation with you. You had to notice that. Am I right?"

"Yep, couldn't ignore that," Shae replied.

"Then out of nowhere, POOF, magically a new Finn appeared. Polite and caring. So weird. I've been trying to figure it out ever since. It doesn't make sense."

Both just sat there pondering the timeline of events concerning Finn.

Alone in their silence, the girls startled when the doctor and the Chief came barreling into the room.

20 Dr. Lynch

Maeve and Shae were both irritated. The Chief and doctor had barreled into the room then completely ignored them. Both were oblivious to the girls. Maeve wanted to shout "HELLO". Instead, she strained to hear the conversation, but it was useless. The Chief and doctor were whispering in a language familiar to the elders of Rowan. Maeve and Shae looked at each other in frustration until Shae spoke up: "Ahem, hello. We're over here. You know the patients that you're talking about."

The Chief and doctor became so engrossed in their conversation they totally ignored Shae. Maeve and Shae looked at each other in disbelief. Were they invisible? They were beginning to feel that way. The conversation was intense. Not heated, though. Both kept turning to look at the girls. This angered Shae. Her face was beet red. This time she yelled, "Hellooooooo!"

Both the doctor and Chief replied at the same time.

"Sorry, girls." It was obvious they had a silent agreement to continue their conversation later. Both walked over to Maeve and Shae's beds.

The doctor reached his hand out to shake their hands as he introduced himself as Dr. Peadar Lynch. He was a young intern and very handsome with dark curly hair and piercing eyes. Shae raised her eyebrow at Maeve. Maeve looked back at her. Her eyes said, "I know, wink, wink, cuuuute". The Chief cleared his throat. He hated when they talked boys in his presence. The girls reverted their attention back to Dr. Lynch. They knew if they did not, the Chief would embarrass them.

"Girls, I'm Dr. Lynch. I'm going to be taking care of you while you're in the ER."

Both girls replied "Hi" simultaneously. A slight blush crossed both their cheeks. The Chief let out an exasperated sigh.

"Girls, the Chief filled me in on what happened at school and the EMTs also reported their findings to the nurses. And, Maeve, I just spoke to your Mam. She has given the Chief permission to act on her behalf. Okay, now that is the business part, let us get to your health. Just to make sure you are both okay, I'm going give each of you a routine exam."

Dr. Lynch turned to the Chief and asked: "Chief, would you mind leaving the room. I am not sure the girls will be comfortable with you in here while I am examining them.

The Chief replied, "Girls, it's okay if you want me to leave. I do not mind. I can get one of the nurses to come in here."

Both replied at the same time.

"Nope, we're fine. You can stay." Each letting out a small chuckle. Saying the same things at the same time was a common occurrence for best friends.

Maeve did not care. She saw Papa K more than her own father, so she was comfortable with him. Plus, whatever happened in this exam room was nothing compared to his experience as Chief of Police.

"All right let's proceed then." Dr. Lynch took all their vitals: blood pressure, pulse, etc. "Vitals are all within normal range. I am amazed. EMTs told me the explosion threw both of you against a wall. I expected greater visual injuries." Both girls nodded. "We must make sure you don't have any internal injuries. Please lay down. Now I am going to press on different parts of your belly. Let me know if anything hurts."

Both giggled and replied simultaneously, "Okay". No internal pain. Dr. Lynch and the Chief both looked relieved. Next Dr. Lynch did a concussion screening. Shae passed. Maeve failed.

"No headache, pain. Nothing? Are you sure?" Maeve nodded.

"The EMT report states that you had nausea and an excruciating headache. This is especially important, Maeve."

Maeve paused. "I did earlier. I was tired, nauseous, and I had a horrible headache. But I honestly thought it was just stress related. Sorry."

Dr. Lynch diagnosed Maeve with a moderate concussion and ordered a CT scan of her brain. The CT results cleared her of further brain injury. So, Dr. Lynch ordered both girls bedrest at home until all symptoms, if any, subsided.

The Chief excused himself to call Mam to update her on Maeve's condition. "She's doing fine, Treasa. I promise. The doc said they will go home in the next couple of hours. I will call you if anything changes. I do not expect it will. See you soon! Yes. You're welcome!

Three hours later, the girls went home.

21 Home

The drive home was noticeably quiet. No one was talking not even the Chief. Maeve and Shae were starting to feel extremely uncomfortable. Maeve was increasingly more nauseous, and her anxiety level was escalating to levels she had never experienced before. Shae grabbed her hand and held it for the rest of the car ride.

Maeve's thoughts clashed. While she could not wait to go home, she did not want to leave Shae. She knew Mam was going to be hovering over her all night. Maeve could not believe how quick a drive it had been. Before she knew it they had pulled into her circular drive. The Chief parked in front of the porch steps. Before he could get to the passenger side of the car, Mam flew out onto the porch. She must have been peering out the window predicting their arrival. He opened Maeve's door, took her arm, and guided her to Mam.

Mam pulled Maeve into her arms and squeezed her voraciously. After a few seconds, she drew her back and kissed her multiple times on both cheeks like she was baby. Treasa thanked the Chief profusely. Maeve looked back at Shae thinking 'please help me' and smiled. She knew it was going to be an exceptionally long night.

"Ollie, thanks so much for everything! Thank you, thank you, thank you." Mam hugged him so tight Maeve thought he might pass out.

He gently pried her arms from him, looked her straight in the eye and said, "Treasa, no worries. You and Niall have always been there for me especially since Branagh passed. This is the least I could do. You're family."

Treasa hugged him again. Nodding her head as he spoke, she tried to ward off tears and asked him, "Ollie, why don't you and Shae come in. I have already made dinner and there is plenty. You can call the boys to come over, too."

Maeve thought: YES, there's hope. If they stay and eat, then Shae and I can talk. We can go over everything that happened today.

The Chief replied, "Treasa, I think it's best that the girls rest tonight. You, too. You have been worried sick about Maeve plus you have three sick little girls. If you need anything, let me know. I will be home for the rest of the night."

"Thanks, Ollie. If you change your mind, just let me know."

"I will, thank you Treasa." He started to walk toward his car and remembered something. "Oh, Treasa, I talked to Niall. He is on his way home. He will get a message to me if he will be late. If you need anything, call me. Do not hesitate. Everyone is on stand-by and ready. Okay?"

Mam looked relieved. "Thanks Ollie. I'm sure we'll be fine." She smiled as she waved and closed the door.

The disappointment Maeve felt was overwhelming. She had hoped Papa K would accept Mam's invitation. Even with her concussion, Maeve questioned his comment about everyone being on stand-by and ready. What did that mean?"

They were in the house less than five minutes and Mam had asked Maeve four times if she was okay.

"Mam, I'm fine, I promise. But I do need a nap. I'm exhausted."

Mam was wiping tears from her eyes as she said. "Scoot, Maeve. Go and rest. I am just so relieved that you are okay. The girls are upstairs sleeping. They shouldn't be a bother." Mam gave Maeve one last huge squeeze and pushed her gently toward the stairs.

When Maeve entered her room, a heaviness in her chest overcame her. It was unexpected in her place of refuge. The heaviness plus the feeling of a disturbing presence frightened Maeve. When her sisters were little, they would pounce on her chest and not let her up. All four of them would end up laughing hysterically. The pressure in her chest felt the same, but without the jollity. Maeve was starting to panic.

Maeve felt more scared now than after the explosion. She was lucky to have an army of protection close. Kían, Conaire, and her special angels just a call away. She screamed for them in her mind.

"Please I need you. I'm really scared."
Maeve was not scared; she was terrified.

22 Maeve's Angels

Maeve was in the nursery with her sisters when she saw angels circling Caitlín's crib. The angels looked like cherubim. Each were small, toddler-like angels except for one. The one who stood out among the rest. While most were chubby, sweet faced, and curly haired, one was older with more authoritative, leader-like qualities. He did not look much older than the rest – a few years at best. His innocence and grace wafted through the room as he made his way over to Maeve after her asking who they were and why they were near her sisters.

He told her that her family was royalty and special. Special in ways this world would not understand. She would see, hear, and know things that no one else could. She would not experience undue fear because she had an army of protection around her.

"My princesses! You are the most royal of your family, Princess Maeve. You and your family are special to all of us. Special beyond the understanding of this world. Your gifts will allow you to see, hear, and know things no one else can. We will all protect you so never be afraid." Maeve shrugged her shoulders and giggled.

Maeve never needed to call upon her army of angels. Threats, danger, or fear would make them automatically appear. They would gather and enfold her in their wings protecting her from any typical childhood fear – scary stories, nightmares, monsters, and thunderstorms. Her reactions perplexed most of her friends, especially when the boys tried to scare the girls on the playground. Maeve would just shrug them off.

Raegan was having a sleepover party for her tenth birthday. Her sister, Moira, entertained the girls at the party. They had so much fun. They could not wait to tell everyone that Raegan's sister, a high school sophomore, chaperoned the party. At bedtime, Moira sat all the girls down in a circle to tell the story of a spirit lady. The spirit lady who went on a rampage of revenge. In death, she would appear to any girl who called her name three times in front of a mirror. If she visited you, she wanted to be your friend. If you saw her reflection peering back at you, she would kill you in your sleep.

Maeve was terrified. Her gift told her the spirit lady was real. She told Moira to stop. Moira just laughed at her. All her friends at the party told her to grow up, it was just a story. She pleaded with them to believe her. Raegan tried to convince everyone to listen to Maeve, but everyone wanted to hear more of the story. For the rest of the night, she avoided every mirror in Raegan's house. Even when she went to the bathroom, she crouched down so she could not see her reflection. Maeve called to her angels to watch over her cousins and friends.

The angels came quickly warning her never, ever to call upon the spirit world. Danger lurked in that world. She was too young and inexperienced to conjure up evil spirits. Maeve heard the word evil and that was all she needed to know. She would never play that game again. The girls from the party teased her at school mocking her for refusing to play the spirit lady game. She blamed it on her Mam. Mam said she would call Father Roan if she played it again. After that, no one teased her again about it. No one wanted to mess with their neighborhood priest.

23 Sacred Space

Over and over, Maeve called to her angels. Why did she even have to call on them? Couldn't they feel her terror? What was happening? Conaire was nowhere and now her angels were missing, too. What was she going to do? Something was terribly wrong. Without their help, how was she going to handle whatever this was? She dropped to her knees overcome with helplessness.

Maeve held her head in her hands, elbows on her knees, and shins to the floor, just rocking back and forth like a little kid's rocking horse. She continued to sway until she could not move anymore. She grabbed the pillow and blanket from her bed and lay right where she was. Overcome with exhaustion, she fell asleep on the floor. Maeve woke up curled in the fetal position.

"My whole body feels like its covered with a weighted blanket. My eyes are so heavy as if sewn shut. This is crazy. I won't panic. I'll be fine.

Maeve slowly pushed herself up with her hands. When she finally sat up and crossed her legs in a pretzel, she began to open her eyes.

"Yikes, that was hard." She chuckled and thought, "I'll never make fun of Mam again when she walks stiff and craggy." Her and her sisters would imitate Mam all the time, mocking her by saying "Hey, old lady when's your ninety-fifth birthday again."

Finally, her eyes were open wide, and her drowsiness was wearing off. Maeve knew she was not alone. Whoever was in her hospital room today, was here now. She started to repeat her mantra: "My room is my sanctuary. I'm always safe here."

Today's message from Kían flooded her mind. She was strong. Stronger than she knew. If that was true, why did she feel incredibly vulnerable. She started talking to herself.

"Okay, Kían, sure it's easy to feel strong when your support system is nearby. I have no one right now. You are nowhere. Conaire is God knows where, and the angels, pfff? I wish Liam and Shae were here."

Maeve rubbed her eyes as if it would stop the glowering presence, she felt laden with. She slowly and dreadfully turned toward her window. She thought, "It can't be. There's someone in my room."

Maeve's heart was beating wildly in her chest. Clenching her teeth, she let out a stifled cry. It was not her imagination. The someone or something watching her earlier was here now. When Maeve totally focused on the figure, she gasped. The figure was dark and foreboding wearing a dark hood covering its face with one exception. It had glaring red eyes. She could not scream for help. She tried and tried but all that came out was, "mmmmmmmmmhhhhheeeeemph.

Its powers were keeping her from screaming. She felt an invisible mask covering her mouth. Its contemptuous demeanor was terrifying. It mocked her defenselessness. She tried to uncover its identity. It was difficult as the figure did not have a definitive shape. Man or woman was unclear. Maeve realized it truly did not matter. Its powers were overwhelming. It jeered at her knowing it was controlling her and she was defenseless.

Maeve's breathing became labored. She was panicking. Dark figures never entered her room. She saw them in her house, at school, and in public places. Never were they as terrifying as this. Dark figures and shadows began to form in Maeve's mind in swirling snippets of memories. So real, her head was pounding. Maeve placed her palms against her temples and massaged them hoping to alleviate the pressure. She felt the blood running through her veins like a fast-flowing river.

Before her, memories of the first encounters with shadows came alive. The encounters long forgotten. The memories she had buried deep. One right after another she saw them in front of her. She felt as if she was watching a film on fast-forward. These were not the shadows you see when the sun shines from behind a tree and falls onto the sidewalk. They were not peaceful or pretty like that. These shadows were scary. They were the shadows you hid from under your bedcovers wishing them away.

Kían, Conaire, and her angels' intervention had taken those memories and hidden them away. Why and how did this thing have access to them? More importantly, where were Kían, Conaire, and the angels? They told her there was protection around her and so she was safe. Was she? Had they lied to her? Maeve lost control of her own body and senses. Flashes of scenes from the past flooding the invisible screen in her mind until she passed out.

24 Shadows

There were times when Maeve would see shadows out of the corner of her eye. Thinking someone was there, she would turn, and they were gone. She was eight when Mam questioned her during a picnic lunch with her sisters. Maeve saw a shadow in her peripheral vision, not her direct line of sight. She would turn quickly to talk to it, and it would disappear. After a few times, Mam asked her what she was doing.

"Maeve, what are you looking at?"

Maeve replied, "Umm, I keep seeing someone. When I turn, they're gone."

Mam looked disturbed by Maeve's reply. It was obvious even to a little girl that Mam did not know how to respond.

"Umm, sweetie, sometimes when the sun is strong and shining brightly it may cast shadows. It makes us believe that there is someone or something nearby. Our eyes can play tricks on us as well. If we are tired, or have not had enough to drink, things are not always what they seem to be."

Maeve just looked at her Mam. She was aware that Mam was having a challenging time formulating an answer that sounded believable. Mam was worried. "Why" was a question that Maeve was not able to answer.

Maeve's next encounter was in third-grade recess. She was playing tag with her friends. Suddenly, her body would not move. Her feet felt weighed down with heavy blocks of cement. The entity encompassing her body kept her from moving. If she fought against it, it became stronger filling her with a sensation that felt like she was pulled or dragged down beneath the earth's surface. Everyone yelled at her to run. Not only was she unable to move her feet, but her body had also become immobilized. Her heart was pounding in her chest. Tears were readying to flow. Maeve was terrified.

Shae saw terror on Maeve's face and ran to her. She grabbed her by the shoulders. "Maeve! Are you okay? Look at me!!!"

Shae tugged at Maeve's shirt. "Come on, run, you can do it."

Maeve could hardly speak. She started sputtering words. "I. Ca. Ca…n. T. Help me!"

Out of the corner of her eye, Maeve could see dark shadows in the woods near the playground. Too many to count. Everyone started yelling "RUN". Maeve thought everyone could see them. It took a second for Maeve to realize why they were yelling. Recess was over. She did not hear the lunch aide blow her whistle. Shae tugged on Maeve again. When she did, Maeve stumbled falling into Shae. Both girls started running. Maeve ran filled with a feeling of pure terror.

25 Imagination

After a few years, the shadows began to take form. Human form void of faces or gender. Some resembled a black silhouette in old-fashioned pictures. Other dark shadow in the fairytales Mam read at bedtime, but creepier. Some jeered at her. Others disappeared as if shy. Today, they were strong, bold, and violating her sanctuary. She wondered if today they would overtake her.

Maeve's heart beat harder and faster. Her breathing labored. Her senses heightened. Her hearing amplified. The hollow, spiritless shape across the room was taunting her. Maeve had never felt so abandoned, so terrified, so alone. Fear coursed throughout her body. Maeve felt depleted of fight. Immediately, Maeve knew what was going to happen. It had happened a few times before. It was an inexplicable experience. Maeve, suddenly, found that she had passed into another dimension.

Within this dimension, she experienced a vision. A vision so clear it felt real. Maeve gasped as she saw her alter ego shopping with Mam. Instantly, she knew her name. Her doppelgänger had her name in Irish. Meadhbh after the greatest female warrior of ancient Ireland. Maeve was astonished at how similar they both were in their dress, mannerisms, and expressions.

Maeve could not believe what was enfolding before her eyes. She felt everything that her vision-self did. Yet, Mam did not know she existed, but Meadhbh did.

She watched as a man passed by her other self and brushed her shoulder with his hand. Maeve reached to touch her shoulder. Nothing was there except a tingling of goosebumps that rose from his touch. Both Maeve and Meadhbh became devoid of emotion. Maeve watched as Meadhbh stopped in her tracks and turned to look at the man. Mam asked, "Meadhbh, why are you stopping?"

Meadhbh could not reply. She wanted to answer her Mam, but she was unable to speak. When she tried nothing came out. Not even a stammer. There was silence.

"Meadhbh, answer me. This is ridiculous. What's wrong with you?"

Mam was becoming impatient. Vision. Dream. Vacant. Meadhbh was oblivious to Mam's existence. Mam's words were incomprehensible. Her voice sounded like gibberish, just like the teacher in the Charlie Brown cartoons.

The power of the man's touch was immeasurable. Maeve knew it connected to the dark veil that shrouded Finn. Again, she remembered Kían's message. She was strong. Then why this vision? He told her she was safe, protected; yet she could feel this man's touch pulsate throughout her body. How was he able to infiltrate her bodily form? Maeve kept watching, hoping the vision answered her questions before it ended.

Meadhbh looked into the man's eyes. They were dark, red, and human-less filled with contempt. With a smug smile and sneer on his face, he glared intently into her eyes. He knew the impact he was having on Maeve and Meadhbh. The man's gaze was magnetizing. Meadhbh struggled to disconnect from his gaze. Maeve could feel the fight within herself. She finally regained control. The satisfaction he felt was keenly plain. Yet, shaded with disappointment. He did not expect Meadhbh's strength to equal his own. No doubt he was more powerful than Finn. His goal was to frighten and intimidate both Meadhbh and Maeve. He achieved his goal.

Immediately, Meadhbh began to stutter and tell her Mam about the man.

"Mam, I'm so sorry, but that man frightened me. He had enormous power over me. I don't know how. By grazing my shoulder with his hand, he could control my actions; I became immobile. I heard you asking me questions, but I was unable to speak and understand your words. He was terrifying, Mam. It felt like a bad dream; a nightmare really."

Mam replied: "Sweetie, what man? We are the only ones here. Are you okay?"

Meadhbh shook her head in disbelief. "Um, I must have imagined it. Sorry, Mam, I'm tired."

Both Maeve and Meadhbh realized this Mam was not aware of her gifts. Something felt off about Mam's reaction. She usually was empathetic when something so out of the ordinary happened. Meadhbh felt isolated and alone. Maeve had an overwhelming sense of compassion and sympathy for her doppelgänger. She totally understood what she was going through.

Meadhbh mulled over the event in her head. Maeve could hear her twin's thoughts. "I don't know what to do. Mam doesn't understand. I won't put Liam or Shae in danger. Forget Father Roan. He will get the church involved to put me away. Am I the only one like me? I don't know who I am anymore."

26 Mam?

Maeve and Meadhbh shuddered simultaneously. It was obvious Meadhbh was having difficulty processing her encounter with the mysterious man. Maeve could feel how distraught she was especially after Mam's uncharacteristic reaction.

"Sweetheart, I don't want to discredit your experience, but I believe your imagination is playing tricks on you. I did not see the man you are speaking of. I know you are upset; but I just do not know what you are talking about. I'm sorry."

Mam embraced Meadhbh and whispered in her ear. "Remember this feeling right now. Whether real or imagined, always trust your instincts. Your instincts will never steer you wrong. Meadhbh, do you understand?"

She sounded like Mam. It perplexed both Meadhbh and Maeve since Mam was not acting herself. This was extremely confusing behavior as Mam was always her voice of reason.

Meadhbh nodded her head against Mam's shoulder. Meadhbh had a strange feeling in her Mam's arms. Maeve could feel it, too. This person looked like Mam, but when in her arms, she felt strange and unfamiliar. Whoever this was, she was not Mam.

"I hope that helps." Mam pulled away from Meadhbh lifting her chin so that their gazes met. "Sweetheart, you know I will always be here for you. Even in strange times such as these when your imagination gets the better of you. There was no man. I am so sorry that sometimes I just do not understand you. We may just have to set up that meeting with Fr. Roan. Your father has been insisting. It may be time."

Mam had a smirk on her face shaking her head as she abruptly walked away. She turned toward Meadhbh and said: "Hurry it up, Meadhbh, we're on a schedule remember."

Maeve could hear a woman's sweet, melodic, fairylike voice. She turned to find no one standing there. The voice was familiar but neither doppelgänger could figure out the voice's identity. It was gentle and kind yet unrelenting.

"This entity you've encountered is stronger than your imagination. It is evil. You need to be strong. Keep your head about you. This is the beginning of a raging war against you. Good v. Evil. Yes, you are safe thus far. But this evil, this war is trying to break down the protective forces around you. You must fight. Believe in yourself. You are not alone. But, right now you must, and I emphasize must, get away from this place. Be strong. Fight. Get away before you cannot escape."

Terror raged through Maeve's body. Meadhbh looked directly into her eyes pleadingly. Meadhbh wanted Maeve to take her to Rowan. Maeve knew she could not. She swore she would bring her to safety soon. Meadhbh felt assured her doppelgänger would return as promised. Both felt a deep love flowing from and to each other. A connectedness that was inexplicable. Tears formed in both of their eyes communicating an unspoken good-bye.

Maeve stood with both hands at her side, with her feet planted into the ground. A surge of power entered her soul illuminated with brilliant beams of light. Her body felt emblazoned with an internal fire. She closed her eyes and envisioned herself back home. Within seconds, Maeve was torn away from her dreamlike state.

Maeve was sitting in the corner of her bedroom, hugging her knees to her chest, and rocking back and forth. Her hair was damp with sweat, she felt little droplets dripping down the sides of her face. She must get back to Meadhbh. The voice she had heard was familiar. The warning dire.

Maeve continued rocking back and forth mumbling to herself, "Bad dream. Sensory overload. Crazy day. Visions! Voices. I'm losing it. Kían? Conaire? Angels? Meadhbh? Why the visitation with Meadhbh? What is her importance in my life? Are Liam, Shae, Conaire, Raegan, Declan experiencing this too? You will not defeat me. I am stronger than you."

The dark figure was looming closer to her. "Be strong", the voice said. She was trying but she felt dizzy. Maeve thought: "not again". Maeve transcended to the time when the dark figure touched her for the first time.

27 Games

Maeve and her sisters were playing board games. She was in charge because Mam was making dinner. She had a dim recollection of the scene unfolding before her eyes. Only because it was a rarity for Mam to leave her with the responsibility of the girls. They could be a huge handful. Breana won the first board game played when Mam called from the kitchen. "Maeve, honey, I need another fifteen or twenty minutes. Would you please get another game that will take that long?"

Maeve replied, "Sure, Mam."

Maeve thought, I hate the hall closet. It gives me the creeps. I should have one of the girls get it. Forget it…they'll just fight. I'll get it myself.

Maeve could feel goosebumps creep up the back of her neck. She hated the game closet. She could see the hair on her arms standing straight up. Ugh! She took a deep breath and thought, it's all in your mind.

This was so crazy. Then she thought, "it's pretty ridiculous to be afraid of a closet. What could be scary about a closet?"

She tried talking herself into being brave. "I should just grab the card game "Uno". All three girls love the game.

There wouldn't be any fighting. Plus, I can grab it quickly. Small, easy to grab and run. Okay. I can do this. Just take a deep breath. Move very slowly, then I'll be undetectable. Oh, gosh! You're acting so stupid; it's going to be fine." As Maeve reached into the closet to grab the game, Maeve felt something grasp her wrist pulling her sharply into the closet. Lunging forward, Maeve wacked her forehead on the door frame. She let out a yelp then pulled her wrist away from the unseen entity.

In the back of the closet was an attic door. Maeve noticed it was ajar. Inside the attic she could see the outline of a shadow. The shadow had the silhouette of a man. A man with glowing red eyes. Maeve put her hand over her heart. She could feel each beat through her skin. She thought, "slow down. Slow breaths. Don't hyperventilate. You can't tell anyone what just happened. They're going to think you're nuts. Now stop."

Maeve closed her eyes, tried not to scream so her sisters would not panic, and wished him away. Her heart was still beating crazily. She wiped sweat off her forehead. At that moment Maeve vowed she would never ever go into that closet again. Why should she? That's what she had little sisters for.

Maeve watched herself trying not to have a panic attack. Maeve almost forgot that the little girl she was watching was her. She was so angry, she started yelling at the figure in her vision.

"Who do you think you are? Why would you scare a little girl like that? Why? You coward!!! You should be ashamed of yourself!"

Maeve thought, MMM…oh no! She must have angered him. He was letting her know he could control her. The scene before her dissipated into a foggy haze.

In a flash, her and her sisters were in the family room. Maeve watched herself with her sisters, Bridget, Caitlín, and Breana. She thought, "What now???!!!" She had almost forgotten about that night. They were watching a movie before bed when Caitlín asked Maeve to make some popcorn. Maeve hesitated before agreeing. The movie was one of her favorites. Her and Shae always pretended they were the characters in the movie, twins separated at birth. It always brought back wonderful memories of their elementary school years. Before Caitlín complained to Mam and Pa, Maeve started to get up from the couch.

"Ugh, all right!", Maeve replied.

Maeve stood up and jumped off the couch. When she landed, her right foot felt glued to the floor. Luckily, Maeve was able to regain her balance, so she did not fall on her face. She thought she caught her sock on something. When she looked down, there was a hand grasping her ankle. It was a black silhouette. The same dark figure that had grabbed her in the game closet.

Caitlín, always the concerned sister, asked: "Maeve, why aren't you moving."

"Um, my sock is stuck on the couch."

"Oh, okay." Caitlín replied casually.

Bridget peeked at Maeve's feet, shrugged her shoulders, and continued to watch the movie. Surprisingly, the hand remained wrapped around her ankle and Bridget did not see it. Panic set in. Maeve wanted to scream but she felt like she had a gag over her mouth.

Using her mind, Maeve called her angels for help. Seconds after she called them the dark hand disintegrated and blew away like ash in the wind. Breana started whining, "Mae, hurry up. I'm hungry!"

Here it goes, all three of them would start now. Bridget, Caitlín, and Breana started chanting in unison, "Maeve, Maeve. Popcorn, popcorn, popcorn. Maaaeeeevvvve!"

Maeve rolled her eyes.

"I'm going. If you all don't stop, you can get it yourself!"

In an instant, Maeve was back in her room. She felt so weird. The dark presence was hovering near making her skin crawl. Its message clear. I can control you, your visions, and your transcendence. Do not underestimate my power.

Clearly, she heard, "Listen! Observe!"

Maeve heard the dark figure's voice in her head. "You're all alone. With no one to protect you from me. Just you wait!"

Maeve replied, "I'm never alone!"

"Oh, Maeve, the plans I have for you. This is just the beginning. There's no stopping me now."

It was the same message that Finn had given her this morning. She was momentarily defenseless.

"Why? Unless…"

Maeve suddenly realized why Kían, Conaire and the Angels were not visible. It was a test.

28 Confronting Evil

The transformation in Maeve was inexplicable. She looked like a queen. Her posture changed. She had a renewed look of confidence. Gone was her fear and self-doubt. She confronted this entity with courage and strength. She telepathically annihilated it.

"So far, you've proven nothing. All I've seen are events from my past. Yes, you were there, but what did you do really? All you did was scare a little girl. If you're so brave, GO FOR IT! Let me see what you've got! I'm ready for you now. Come on, I dare you!!!!!"

Maeve was hardly breathing. She was SOOO angry. She received no response from her unwelcome visitor. It continued to stare at her intently with a crooked smile fixed on its face. It was chillingly quiet.

Maeve could hear giggling coming from downstairs. The girls were in the kitchen with Mam. She would protect her family. So, with emphatic strength she said, "Nothing you've done has harmed me. Attempt after attempt, you have failed. Your visions don't belittle or intimidate me. You will never win against me. Now, GET OUT!"

Maeve felt a big gust of wind blow through her bedroom. It was so strong her hair was swirling around her as if caught in a windstorm. Maeve shielded her face and eyes from the wind. She was sure that everything in her room had become airborne. She was wrong. The entity was gone leaving a lightness in the energy around her.

Maeve lifted her gaze. She could not believe her eyes. Her whole room, floor to ceiling, sparkled with twinkling particles that reminded her of fireflies in the summer night. The magnificence before her was glorious. Light streaming through her windows made every sparkle dance. She took in the deepest of cleansing breaths. Her lips started to quiver, and she started to sob uncontrollably. She cried from recognizing her great strength and courage.

Blinking through her tears of disbelief, she realized that it was daytime. She glanced at her bedside table. Only a half hour had passed since she came home. She must have dreamt her encounter with the shadow person. Maeve pinched herself to make sure she was awake. Her pinch hurt like a bee sting. She was not dreaming. This was real. Plus, when she looked around, her room was still a sparkling masterpiece.

Maeve thought, "I don't understand why no one prepped me for this day. I wouldn't have felt so alone. I am proud of who I am, what I am, whatever that is. Princess? All this time, everyone knew who I was except me. I have so many questions that need answering. These need to come from Mam and Pa. Not from Kían. Not from Conaire. Not from the Angels. From my parents!"

Maeve paced from her door to her window. Her experiences of the day flowing through her mind. She stopped in front of her mirror with her hands on her hips.

Looking at her reflection, she saw someone she had never seen before. She saw the real, strong, undefeated, and unstoppable Maeve. She saw Maeve the Warrior Princess. She smiled at herself with a smile of knowing, strength, and courage.

Behind her a smattering of sparkles floated in the air daintily. Maeve took in a deep breath. Maeve felt overcome with a feeling of peace and tranquility. Resting in a state somewhere between cognizance and meditation, Maeve felt a gentle hand cradling her shoulder. It startled her at first. Then she turned her head upward and there stood Grandpa Aaron. He was looking down at her lovingly. Maeve could not believe he was here. She was speechless.

Without words, she heard him say, "Sweetheart, you haven't been alone. I've been here. I cannot explain everything to you right now, but I promise I will. Today, our world was altered."

Maeve did not understand what he was saying. She was going to interrupt him, but he continued speaking.

"This change is going to bring you, your friends, and family uncertainty. It is going to be a very scary time. I've been listening to you for the last few minutes. You now know who you are inside. Today had to happen to open your eyes to the truth. Everything you do not know you will find out soon. You are special to all of us, more than you know. All the power you need for protection has always been inside of you. You alone broke from the evil you faced today. It unleashed your strength and courage. The fight coming is not going to be easy. Your people will depend on you for guidance and strength. Be well, my precious princess."

Before Maeve could ask him what he meant, Grandpa Aaron was gone. She thought, "my people. What????? I know I have gifts. This is so much bigger than I realized. I need to find out more." Things truly were changing but for now she felt safe. She always felt safe when Grandpa Aaron was around.

29 Grandpa Aaron

The first time Maeve met Grandpa Aaron she was sick in bed with a high fever and sore throat. All she wanted to do was go downstairs, lay on the couch, and watch her favorite television shows. But no, Mam quarantined her to her room. She tried so hard to have Mam lift her isolation. "No sweetheart, you need your rest. The more you rest the faster you will recover. And I don't want your sisters to get whatever you have."

Maeve stacked picture books on Maeve's bedside table and a few coloring books. Maeve tried to read between nodding off and napping. To pass the time, Maeve counted the birds that flew past her bedroom window. She missed Liam and Shae. She begged for them to visit.

"Mam, I'm bored. I wish Shae and Liam were here. We could play a game. Tell me what I missed at school. This is the worst day ever."

Mam would not allow any visits, and neither would their parents. If Maeve did not feel so awful, she would have tried harder to convince Mam it was a great idea for them to come.

After her third long nap of the day, Maeve slowly opened her eyes. They felt so heavy, like the cement that Pa poured to make their backyard patio. Maeve could swear someone was standing in the corner near her bedroom window. She knew it was not possible. It must be a breeze blowing the sheers of her open window. Her eyes became as big as saucers when she realized a man, a very tall man, was standing in her room.

Maeve tried not to panic. Pa was on a business trip, but this man looked just like him. She was so confused. Pa could not be in two places at one time. Then she realized, she was hallucinating. Mam told her it was a possibility because of her high fever. Maeve felt goosebumps along her arms and neck. She was not delirious. He was real.

Maeve groggily said, "Hello?"

The man did not respond. He just smiled at her. So, she tried again with all the perkiness she could muster. "Hi, I'm Maeve." He just continued smiling at her and waved. Maeve thought she must still be dreaming or hallucinating. She tried not to panic. He looked familiar like they had met before.

He was very handsome, but not as handsome as Pa. They could have been brothers. Same nose, mouth, and eyes. His eyes were the same color as Maeve. His hair, too. Maeve was confused. She was the only one in her family that had blue eyes with red hair. But this man looks like Pa, but Pa has green eyes. She thought. Pa?

Maeve just shrugged her shoulders. She needed answers. Politely, she asked. "Can I ask a question? He nodded "yes". "Umm. Do I know you?" He nodded "no".

"Oh, you look like someone I know. Do you have a name?" He nodded "yes". "Can I try and guess?" He smiled. "Okay, can I call you Aaron? I like that name."

The man nodded his head excitedly. Maeve said, "It's perfect." He gave her the biggest smile.

Before her eyes, Aaron became illuminated by a glittery, shimmering aura. Sparkles were emanating from his body filling her room with a beautiful radiant light. Maeve took a great big breath. When she did, she saw all the twinkles of light form a line. They began swirling around her body then flew right up her nose and down her throat. Maeve giggled. She thought it was so funny. She could see Mr. Aaron giggle, too. Maeve thought, my belly is tickly. She giggled again. "I'm not sick, Mr. Aaron, I feel all better."

Aaron nodded in agreement. He knew she was better. It was the reason he came. He came to heal her. With his mission complete, Aaron waved at her, blew her a kiss, and disappeared.

30 The Cottage

A few months after meeting Grandpa Aaron, Mam and Pa took Maeve and her sisters on a beach vacation. Auntie Rio owned a small cottage on the shores of Uilleand Mor. Every year she insisted they enjoy the fresh ocean air. Maeve's favorite room in the cottage was Auntie Rio's sitting room. Atop the fireplace mantle sat a picture of a handsome, tall man with red hair and blue eyes. It was Aaron. Maeve gasped. Auntie tilted her head to the side.

"Maeve, darlin', are you okay?"

"Yes, Auntie, I never noticed that picture before. Who is that man? I know him."

"Oh sweetheart, you've never met. He died before you were born. He's your Grandpa Aaron."

Auntie Rio looked incredibly sad talking about her parents. Yet, she continued to tell Maeve about her grandparents.

"Your Grandpa Aaron was a wonderful man. He was kindhearted and generous to everyone. People considered him a type of healer. He had a way about him that would make even the saddest soul happy after speaking with him. Your Grandma Brigid was sweet, shy, and kind. She made everyone feel like they were a part of her family, even strangers. If she met someone passing on the street and felt they needed love, she would invite them in for a meal or to stay for a day or two. She was wonderful and loving. I was so blessed to call them Mammy and Pap."

Maeve saw tears form in Auntie Rio's eyes. Maeve became entrenched in the story of her grandparents. So much so, she did not notice Grandpa Aaron standing beside her. Auntie Rio continued: "Your Dad, Uncle Fergus, and I were devastated by their deaths. We had to move from our home to live with your great aunt and great uncle in Rowan. Your Pa has lived there ever since. Uncle Fergus and I never felt at home in Rowan but would visit quite often. As you know your Dad and I are twins and Uncle Fergus is just a few years younger than us."

"Auntie Rio, why don't we have a picture of Grandpa Aaron in our house. I don't understand.

"Maeve, I can't answer that for your Mam and Pa. I think it is because they miss him and Grandma Brigid so. When he is ready to talk about them to you, he will. I am sure of it. Grandpa Aaron would have loved you dearly, more than life itself. God blessed you with his good looks, that beautiful hair, and gorgeous eyes. You are a blessing, my Maeve. More than you'll ever know."

Maeve walked up to Auntie Rio and wrapped her little arms around her waist and told her, "Thank you, Auntie Rio. I promise I won't ask any questions about Grandpa until Pa wants to talk about him. I'll keep it secret; I promise. I like secrets. Now we have one. Just like me, Shae, and Liam. I even have secrets that I don't share with anyone else. They're just for me."

Auntie Rio pulled her closer and whispered: "Oh, Maeve, I know you do. Go now, have fun!" Auntie Rio kissed the top of Maeve's head, gently pushing her away. Maeve skipped away with a huge grin on her face. Auntie Rio watched after Maeve with a crooked smile. She had her secrets, too.

31 Answers

The attack at school, meeting Meadhbh and Grandpa Aaron, her sinister visitor and the flood of memories prompted Maeve to pick herself up off her bedroom floor. It was time to get some answers. No more stories or fabrications tainted with secrets and lies. The truth was long past due. She was strong, courageous, and no longer vulnerable. Everyone and everything she knew interconnected. She needed to know how and why.

Liam and Grandpa Aaron were without question akin. The shimmering aura that each beheld was a definite clue. She had no doubt in her mind. Her curiosity caused questions to form. What were they? Normal people did not shimmer. Who were Grandpa and Liam really? Maeve laughed to herself. She knew 'who' Liam was. He was her forever, her soulmate. She loved him more than anyone she knew. 'What were they' she could not answer. She would find out tonight.

Quickly, Maeve showered and threw on her favorite outfit. Her oldest pair of holey jeans and a giant sweatshirt that her Mam wore when pregnant with her. She threw her hair up in a ponytail. Her eyes glistening a beautiful sparkly blue, her freckles dancing on the tip of her nose and cheeks, and her lips the color of strawberries. Maeve studied her reflection in the bathroom mirror. She thought she looked surprisingly good after everything she experienced over the last 24 hours.

Maeve noticed that there was still a tiny glimmer of radiance decorating her room. She smiled as she readied herself for her mission. Suddenly, her door burst open startling her for a split second. Like three puppies, her sisters barreled through the door. With her mouth filled with toothpaste and spit, she tried to talk. They were impossible. She sighed loudly. When she finished brushing and rinsing, Maeve gave them a talking to.

"Geez, how many times do I tell you to knock. Five minutes ago, I would have been naked. Knock next time, please."

Before her was a priceless picture; she wished she had her camera ready. Her sisters each depicting their unique personalities. Bridget shrugged off her indifference. Caitlín started blushing. Breana started laughing. Maeve laughed to herself and thought, they certainly are an interesting group.

The three girls just plopped down on her bed not a word spoken between them. A few seconds passed; puzzling Maeve, they were never quiet. All three of them sat staring at her. Maeve just stared back. She thought it a blessing that they had not morphed into three evil sisters. If that happened, it would have been the icing on the cake, the cherry on top, or the last straw for a remarkably arcane day.

Her sisters had blonde hair and blue eyes. Their faces were almost identical – same lips, eyes, nose – except for their freckle placement. Bridget had freckles on her nose.

Caitlín had freckles on her cheeks and nose. Little Breana had the family curse. She had freckles all over her body. Not as many as some of their relatives but enough that they bothered her. Freckles and blue eyes were the only common features between Maeve and her sisters.

Each sister had her own distinct personality. Bridget was the nurse – nurturing, kind, moderately talkative. Anytime anyone in the family did not feel well she was right by their side. Caitlín was quiet but very observant. She always knew what was going on before anyone else whether at home, school, or in the neighborhood. Breana was strong both in personality and physicality. No one messed with her or her sisters.

Maeve was starting to feel extremely uncomfortable. She tried to keep calm and patient, but the quiet was maddening. She tried deep breathing. After two breaths, she lost it.

"Girls, I have stuff to do. I must talk to Mam and Pa. So, either start talking or get out. You are waaay too quiet. One... Two... Three... GET..."

Before she could say OUT, the three of them cracked like a dam swelling and breaking except there was no water. Maeve's room flooded with her sisters' emotions. Bridget started crying. Caitlín started babbling and sounded unintelligible. Breana started ranting about avenging Maeve's attackers. Maeve stood in amazement. She did not know if she should laugh or cry. Her sisters, who were usually intolerable were in her room filled with love and emotion. Today was a first for everything.

Maeve's head was pounding. The noise from all three was beginning to amplify. It was too much. She tried to shush them, but she was sure they could not even hear themselves with Bridget's crying, Caitlín's mumbling and Breana's ranting. The girls' behavior was giving Maeve even more anxiety. She could feel it erupting within her. Suddenly, Maeve screamed, "STOOPPP!" surprising herself. She realized she may have overreacted a wee bit.

The three girls stopped simultaneously. Maeve looked at them. Their eyes were as big as a deer's in the shining light of a car's headlights. Maeve scooped them into her arms and hugged them tightly. She shushed them brushing their hair with her hands. Something Mam would do to sooth them when she was little. She whispered, "Shhh, I'm safe now. No one is going to hurt me. I promise."

Maeve could not believe it. She felt overcome with love for them. She realized love was greater than the darkness hovering nearby. "Girls, I love you more than anything on this planet."

Breana looked up at her and raised her eyebrow.

"Okay, Liam and Shae are up there with you."

Maeve thought, "Wow, she's perceptive."

Maeve continued: "We have an unbreakable bond. You're my blood. There's nothing stronger than blood. No matter what, I will always be your big sister; always looking out for each of you. Yes, even when you drive me crazy. I love you sooooo much!"

Maeve squeezed them tighter. Quietly, and shockingly, she asked if they wanted to have a sleepover. All three looked up at her with love and adoration. Maeve had to blink. She thought she saw sparkles emanating around Bridget.

"Okay, girlies, jump in. I'm going to run downstairs and get a quick bite. You're more important tonight. Don't forget to leave some room for me. Okay?" All three nodded with huge smiles on their faces. She smiled at each of them and thought: "Gosh, they are cute. If only they were this precious every day. Ha!"

Maeve ran downstairs, kissed both parents' goodnight, grabbed a protein bar, and ran back up the stairs to her bedroom. She stood at the foot of her bed for a moment. She realized this was their first sister sleepover ever. They were so cute and cuddly, Maeve had to gingerly squeeze between them. Within minutes, they were all asleep. The wildest dream began.

32 The Dream

Maeve was soaring through swirling clouds. She felt light as a feather – gliding through marshmallow fluff. The earth below becoming more visible as the clouds became gauzier and sheer-like. Her travel speed slowed tremendously. The air around her felt light and revitalizing. She found herself sitting on an invisible ball of cotton hovering buoyantly over incredibly, lovely scenery. She patted the fluff beneath her to make sure it was real. It was. Maeve gasped as she became overwhelmed with emotion. There was something special about this magical place.

Maeve felt a pull, a sweet longing in the depth of her heart. Her eyes scanned across the landscape searching as if in pursuit of something she had lost long ago. Beautiful forests lay below her. Each tree with twisted, curly branches entwined resembling a lover's hug. The number of stories preserved in each rung was limitless. In the distance, Maeve spotted a mighty stone structure. She heard it calling her. Maeve willed herself closer. She gasped upon the beauty of it, an awesomely exquisite castle.

The entryway of the castle was a grand tower. Maeve felt an inexplicable connection to this place. Suddenly, she felt a swelling within her heart. A sense of love and contentment flooded her inner being. She was home. Home in a place she had never been. Home in a place she never knew existed. She needed to be here. Not Rowan.

Maeve willed herself even closer. She saw a veranda close to the top that encircled the whole tower. At the top was a spire of platinum and diamonds spiraled into a weave of Celtic knots. Atop the spire was a symbol of some sort. Maeve was not familiar with its significance. She pinched herself. She thought she must be in a dream.

"I'm home."

Maeve felt a wave of an ocean breeze filled with peace and joy flow through her body. She took a cleansing breath encapsulating the feeling into her inner self. The tower before her was magnificent. It glistened in the sunlight. Its structure made from millions of sparkling rhombus-like jewels. The sparkle was luminous. Maeve was in awe of its beauty and the indescribable feeling deep within her heart.

Captivated by its beauty, a shadow passed by a veranda window alarming Maeve. The shape was familiar. It caused her to feel lightheaded and dizzy. She could not believe her eyes. She was having a challenging time differentiating fact from fiction. It felt real. It looked real. But there was no way it could be real except in this mystical place. No one she knew would be here. Wherever here was.

The shadow cautiously peered out of the tower window. It was a girl. The girl had a familiarity about her. She knew she had seen her before. Maeve chuckled. The girl looked like her sisters. Suddenly, Maeve began to sense this feeling of impending danger. The girl must have known or felt its presence as well; yet she did not look fearful. Maeve saw a thin, dark, cloud-like energy appearing in the distance. Suddenly, Maeve felt a rush of wind blow past her.

"What was that?" Maeve whispered under her breath.

The force was closing in on the castle. The girl was still in the window. Maeve tried to yell to her – to warn her. She had no voice, frustrating Maeve.

Maeve watched the dark energy surround the castle. The girl seemed unaffected by its presence. She stood on the veranda tall and proud. Her stance full of strength and power. The light reflecting from the tower intensified. Its brilliance beaming, equating in heat to the sun's rays on a scorching summer day. The energy's attempts to enter the tower thwarted by the light's powers diminished it to ash.

Maeve could see the tower's occupant more clearly. She was a lady not a young girl. Her auburn hair flowed down over her shoulders. Her dress was a shimmering, white shift that accented her beautifully shaped neck and shoulders. She was ethereal. Maeve had no control over her movement. She moved closer to the tower. This lady represented more to her than she could define.

Movement stopped about fifty feet from the tower. Maeve could see the lady more closely. She gasped bringing her hand to her mouth to stop words from escaping. She was not fearful, but astonished. The lady was Grandma Brigid. The Grandma Brigid who had died more than thirty years ago.

Grandma Brigid gazed out over the vast forest. Maeve caught a glimpse of movement in the distance. It had not been there a few moments ago. It was an entourage of men on horses. Obviously, the castle was their destination. Even though impenetrable, the tower remained surrounded by the dark aura. Maeve questioned the aura's pertinence. It either appeared to overtake the castle, acting as a protective barrier to keep out the unwanted or potentially dangerous.

One man stood out among the rest. He was a man of great stature with an air of majesty. He, too, seemed familiar to Maeve. Yet, he was too far away for identification. He rode a white horse. The horse was a beautiful, majestic steed. Maeve knew his name was Cearul. He carried an air of royalty reminding her of a mystical creature she read in a book at Auntie Rio's beach cottage. The Cearul of her book had the ability to spread wings and fly. Maeve shook her head in disbelief.

The group was getting closer. Maeve hoped to find out the identity of its leader. Goosebumps ran up and down her back and neck. Her eyes grew wide with recognition.

Grandpa Aaron was dressed like royalty. His posture of greatness and strength followed by eight men on horses. Cripes! They are wearing chest plates and carrying swords. On their chest the O'Flaherty crest emblazoned with beautiful jewels. Maeve began to question who her family truly was.

Everything went black.

33 The Morning After

Seconds later, Maeve was back in her bed, her heart pounding in her chest. She gasped then took a deep breath. Without looking she knew; she could feel Grandpa Aaron's presence. She turned finding him leaning in her doorway. She gestured that they needed to keep quiet. Her sisters were still asleep. He smiled, placed his hand over his heart, blew her a kiss and slowly disappeared. Maeve drifted into a deep sleep until her alarm started vibrating at 6:00 a.m.

She laid there thinking about her dream. It had been so vivid and amazing. She still could not believe what she saw. Grandpa Aaron had infiltrated her dreams so he could send her an extremely important message.

"Grandpa wanted me to have that dream. I just know it".

The power radiating from the castle's tower was identical to the sparkling illumination emitted by Liam, Bridget, Cillín, and a few others. As much as she loved Rowan, it was not her true home. None of their true homes. The magical place in her dream was home. Seeing Grandma Brigid was a gift. The blackness surrounding the tower was the blackness in Miss Almath's class. I'm sure of it. The others know about our home. They must. Why the secrets? Today I must get my answers. None of my questions evaded. Of that I am sure.

Maeve turned her head. Breana was still snug up to her side. Bridget and Caitlín cuddled together like little angels. She felt this overwhelming warmth flood her heart. She loved them dearly. This was, without a doubt, twenty-four-hours of firsts.

"Wow! I love my sisters, but this! I'm overwhelmed with emotions. Too much love. It's making me nauseous." She wanted to laugh but knew if she did, they would wake up. "Time to get up. I need to get as many answers as possible before I leave for school."

Maeve sat up slowly. A sharp, stabbing pain pierced through her head like a sword. She paused holding her head in between her hands.

"Oooh, the pain is horrific. I need to get a grip on it. Mam will make me stay home if she thinks I'm in pain. I can't have that."

Maeve moved very gingerly to her bathroom. She did not want to chance the girls waking up. Their talking and fighting would be too much for her brain this morning. She finished brushing her teeth and thought she heard someone talking. There were voices floating up the vents in her bathroom from the kitchen.

"What now?"

It was usually quiet in the early morning. Mam never had the radio on – not even to hear any news. Maeve thought, Pa must be home sick from work. No! He never takes off. He'd have to have a 105 fever to stay home.

Maeve placed her hands on her belly and started rubbing it. She was starting to feel anxious. Maeve instinctively reacted positively. She rebuked the negativity instantly.

Today, Maeve knew how strong and confident she was. There would be no way a feeling in the pit of her stomach would overcome her emotions.

Maeve listened intently through her heating vent to try and decipher the voices in the kitchen. It was impossible from her room.

"Wait." Maeve paused to listen. "Why were there two different female voices? One was Mam's, for sure. I can't figure out the other voice. I guess I'll be surprised."

She rushed to finish getting ready. It was driving her crazy not knowing the other person's identity. She quietly closed her bedroom door while lovingly glancing at her sisters. She tiptoed down the hallway and headed down the wooden stairway, stepping carefully.

"Please, please, please...don't creak. Not this morning. I don't want anyone to hear me."

Maeve could hear Mam and Pa's voices. She listened intently. The mystery voice seemed so familiar. Maeve slowly crept to the kitchen alcove where no one could see her. When she peaked around the corner, she saw Mam pouring coffee for Pa. He was not sick. Maeve knew he stayed home because he was worried about her. She could see the back of a woman. The woman turned toward Mam. It was Auntie Rio!

Maeve did her best to eavesdrop on her parents and Auntie. She was a bit too far away and had a tough time hearing every word. She made out bits and pieces of their conversation. Maeve heard her Auntie say the word "tower". Tower! That grabbed Maeve's attention.

"This can't be a coincidence. I have a vision last night about a tower and now they're talking about a tower."

Maeve knew that her dream was truly a vision. A vision that connected the events at school yesterday and who she really was. Maeve listened pensively. There were creases on her forehead from straining so hard to hear a very cryptic conversation.

Maeve wished she had taken two ibuprofens before heading downstairs. Her head was pounding. It was going to be difficult to convince everyone that she was well enough to go to school. Her symptoms were worsening. The conversation continued in the kitchen as Maeve quietly slipped away. She hoped to find headache relief in the first-floor powder room.

34 The Kitchen

Both Treasa and Rio chimed in at once, "Can't it wait? She needs more time, Niall. She is only sixteen. This is a huge responsibility for a girl her age."

Niall replied, "Listen, there's nothing we can do. The timetable has shifted. Maeve needs to know everything that is ahead of her…and us. She must understand that yesterday was the beginning. Lying about her destiny will not protect her. We must be forthright and honest. Our orders are clear."

Treasa tried to interject, "But, but I don't…"

Niall lifted his eyebrow. Treasa stopped. She knew it was not Niall's fault. Everything that was happening was beyond their control. The orders were from the Hierarchy. She must keep her composure. Every part of her wanted to protect her daughter. She nodded at him and he continued.

"Maeve will learn of her birthright tonight. We believe she may already have figured out who she really is. Specific protocols are in place to guarantee her safety. Liam and Shae have directives to keep answers to her questions limited. Too much, too soon may be counterproductive. It would not be prudent to have her on edge – looking over her shoulder to see if danger is lurking in every corner."

Both tried to interrupt Niall. He quickly hindered their efforts by quickly adding, "Got it?"

This time both Treasa and Rio nodded at Niall.

"Okay. The orders from the Hierarchy are precise. All Sept members must follow each order. When Maeve comes in, I am to answer her questions with restriction. Understood?" Both rolled their eyes but understood the importance of these instructions. "That means that you cannot add any comments to the discussion. I am sorry to be so adamant, but the orders are specific. We will explain everything to her tonight. Without a doubt, she will have a ton of questions. Counsel is available over the weekend if necessary. The Hierarchy notified all Sept members. Tonight, only Hierarchy, Protectors, Guardians, Divine Oracles, O'Flahertys, Kerrigans, Ryans, O'Connors, and Cillin Darroch will be in attendance."

Treasa was fraught with worry. Rio tried to allay her fears by saying, "I think that once she gets over the initial shock, she'll be quite relieved. She has been curious about her 'secrets' for a long time now."

"How's that?" Niall asked with concerned.

"Maeve has asked me many questions over the past few months. Specifically, about Mammy and Pa. She knows how devoted they were to each other and that both have passed on. I asked her not to ask you about them. I recommended that she wait until you told her yourself and that it would be when she was much older. Quite older. Niall, what a lie that is now."

Pa took a deep breath before he let out an exasperated groan. Mam added, "I caught her a few weeks ago looking through old photo albums. When I walked in, she had a strange look on her face when I asked her what she was doing. She told me she was just looking at old pictures. It was a very odd and uncomfortable conversation, so I just said 'Okay, have fun'".

Pa looked concerned.

"Mammy and Pap never came up during the meeting with the Hierarchy. I will ask Kían to get a message to Quinn to present to Tomas, Lorcan, and Aengus. It will be faster than waiting for tonight."

Within seconds, Kían appeared. Niall just shook his head. He was always surprised at the expediency of Kían's arrival.

"Kían! After all this time, you'd think your arrival wouldn't surprise me." Niall chuckled. Kían and his family had served as Divine Oracles for the O'Flahertys for centuries.

Kían chortled and said, "It's my honor, Sir. Niall, just so you know, Maeve is in the powder room. Her attempts at eavesdropping foiled. I placed a protective barrier around the three of you enabling her only to hear cryptic words. She will expect answers this morning. She will not concede. I will leave now. I shall wait for the Hierarchy's answer before I return. I do…hmmm."

Niall interrupted before Kían could finish. "Thank you, Kían. As always, your assistance is very much appreciated."

"Before I leave, Sir, I have but one more question to ask of you." Niall nodded in approval. "I would like to ask permission to attend to Princess Maeve again. My orders fulfilled by my presence undetectable over the last few days. Poor Maeve must believe I have abandoned her. Although

Aaron has been visiting her and appearing in her dreams, so I believe that has helped considerably. His visits have brought her comfort. Sir, your permission, please."

"Kían, I think that would be quite wise. Thank you!" Kían nodded to Niall and was gone in a flash of beautiful, silvery sparkles.

35 More Directives

Niall took a deep breath. He knew his wife and sister were going to go crazy over the next piece information he needed to share. "Let us sit back down at the table. Hopefully, Kían will return shortly with good news. I need to tell you something especially important before Maeve's arrival." Treasa bit her lip with anticipation. Rio was emotionless. "So, Ollie and I met with Sloane and Oisín a few weeks ago. Rio, I am sure you have met them. They are Liam's parents." She had some recollection of meeting Ollie and Oisín. "Yes, yes, yes. I suppose I have. A few months after we moved to Rowan, I believe I had Sloane in one of my classes."

"As we all know, Liam and Maeve were born soul mates. Guardian Aveline presented them to the Hierarchy as such upon their birth. Liam's power and strength are of immeasurable size. He showed a mere fraction of his abilities yesterday and did an outstanding job protecting the girls. There is concern that the danger against them and the rest of our people will only worsen. So, in preparation, Oisín's brother, Cathal O'Connor, has been contacted."

Niall momentarily hesitated before he made his next statement. "Cathal was ordered to bring his son, Roark, to Rowan. He will be staying with Oisín and Sloane permanently." Both women gasped. "Yes, you heard me correctly. I said Roark. High Chief Tomas decided that time was of the essence. We unanimously concurred. Cathal delivered the boy late last night. He will remain in Rowan permanently. As foretold by Guardian Aveline, she has paired Shae and Roark. Unfortunately, they will meet a few years ahead of schedule. As you both know, they were not to meet until after both finished university. Under the circumstances, it will take place at Hawthorn today."

The news Niall delivered left Treasa flustered. No one spoke of Guardian Aveline as she graced the presence of few. It was rumored that she had beauty, nobility, and grace mesmerizing many by her splendor, elegance, and poise. She was ruler of the Realm of Blessings, a realm between Rowan and Hy-Breasail. While sweet with a silvery speech, her persona could be duplicitous to those whose allegiance was against Rowan and Hy-Breasail. Aveline's intercession in the circumstances about Maeve made Treasa even more fraught over her daughter's safety.

Treasa reacted as any other mother trying to protect her child would. Her face turned bright red which was never a good sign. Through gritted teeth seething in fury said: "Niall O'Flaherty!!!! Ooh! I could just smack you aside the head. This is too much." Niall allowed her to continue. He knew it was in his own best interest. "If it were not for you following orders, ugh, there are no words. Our daughter, the family...I am infuriated! And...poor Shae! Shae has not a clue the enormity of her calling. Aveline appointed me as her advisor upon Branagh's death. Then, no one has the courtesy to inform me of the change until now. Tighearna bíodh trua agat, Lord, have mercy!!!"

Rio patted Mam's back and whispered, "It will be fine. I will help you. I'm sure a transfer to Rowan and a position at Hawthorn will happen expeditiously." Rio looked toward Niall for confirmation. "Should this be my assumption?"

He nodded in concurrence and replied. "Yes, Rio, your relocation is immediate. Sept members packed your home; and the contents moved to Auntie's old home next door. Remodeling has taken place. All hidden built-ins replicated to hold the sacred relics from Hy-Breasail. It will be ready for occupancy at the end of the school day."

Rio acknowledged Niall with a firm head nod and a look of relief. Niall continued: "My darlin', Treasa, I'm deeply sorry. I know you are angry. You know, as well as Rio, that orders are orders. We must heed those made by the Hierarchy to protect our whole family. Caitlín, Bridget, and Breana are particularly vulnerable. There is great potentiality for the girls to become targets. They will be safe, I promise. I would have kept you apprised of everything but had no authority to do so. I truly am sorry.

Treasa remained silent. There was nothing they could do. Treasa had been praying for a miracle hoping to spare this generation from the danger unfolding. She had to trust in the plans set forth. She took a deep breath and replied, "Niall, I know how difficult it must have been for you to keep this secret. My reaction was extreme. I apologize. Although inevitable, I did not expect any of this for another ten years. I prayed for the protection of this generation. My prayers were ignored."

Niall responded, "My darling Treasa..." Niall hesitated before continuing. He had difficult news to share. "Soo...There's more. As you know, Liam and Roark have a strong bond, stronger than cousins. It is a bond that few warriors possess."

Treasa and Rio raised their eyebrows. Niall motioned for them to be patient.

"Last night, Liam and Roark were briefed on the Hierarchy's plans for them in the coming years. The Hierarchy will anoint Liam as the new leader of the Patrons of Warriors when Aengus steps down. Roark will be by his side. Aengus will train both until that day." Rio and Treasa looked distraught when Niall mentioned Aengus's name. Aengus was the Hierarchy's oldest and mightiest warrior. No other warrior had been as powerful in over 1,000 years until Liam and Roark. Treasa began pacing the kitchen wiping everything and anything she could get her cloth on. It was impossible for her to sit. Niall walked up to her placing his hands on her waist and pulled her into him.

He whispered in her ear, "Mo gra....it all will be fine. No worries. I promise. We are strong and prepared." He guided her to her seat at the table. "Sit down, Treasa. There is just one last thing you need to know. The Hierarchy believes that the Sept may be at risk. For protection, Guardians are at Veil na Tairsí. Aengus has uncovered several members of the Sept who have turned their allegiances to Fergus. The rumor is that Fergus will attempt a takeover of Hy-Breasail by kidnapping Maeve."

Rio and Niall's baby brother, Fergus, had become infuriated when Guardian Aveline announced Maeve as successor to the throne. He made many attempts to cross Veil na Tairsí. All attempts thwarted by Guardian Aveline. A trial before the Hierarchy commenced wherein Fergus lost all titles and was exiled from Rowan and Hy-Breasail.

"This has been a lot of information in a brief period, so I have to remind you that only I have been authorized to talk to Maeve. She should be walking in any second. I know how hard this is going to be for you, Treasa, but it is necessary." Treasa had no choice but to concede.

36 Breakfast

Maeve's footsteps echoed down the hallway. Niall, Treasa and Rio looked at each other, nodded, took a deep breath then stared intently at the kitchen entryway. Maeve noticed that the talking had abruptly stopped. She knew they heard her coming. The floorboards were creaking all the way. So much for making a quiet entrance.

Maeve thought, "Here goes nothing." With a cheery, light tone in her voice, she greeted her Mam, Pa, and surprise guest.

"Good morning! Oh, Auntie Rio, I didn't know you'd be here."

Strangely, Maeve had only been able to catch snippets of their conversation. Random words like Princess, Sept, Hierarchy, and Hy-Breasail. Suddenly, upon entering the kitchen, words were coming at her like bullets from a machine gun. She gave each of them a quick kiss on the cheek then plopped herself down in her chair. She needed to barrier the barrage of words coming at her. She closed her eyes for just a second and wished them away. She felt relief flood over her as her mind had quieted.

Maeve began to eat her breakfast, but the room was strangely quiet, making her feel uncomfortable. Pa was being so awkward. He was fidgeting in his chair. Maeve wished he would just come out and say whatever was on his mind. She felt three sets of eyes on her. The adults in the room were at a loss for words. Maeve decided to break the silence.

"Well, the girls came in my room last night to talk. They were super nervous about what happened at school. So...um...well...the four of us cuddled up in my bed. We had our first sister sleepover. It was really special." Maeve waited for a reaction. Nothing from any of them. She continued. "So, I better finish. Shae will be coming soon."

This time she received silent head nods and smiles. Then she heard, 'I've dealt with harder things in the last few hundred years.' It was Pa. Maeve was shocked. Her eyes grew wide. What did he mean 'few hundred years'? He's forty. How was that possible?

Pa pulled out the chair next to Maeve and sat down. He reached out and touched her arm affectionately. Maeve thought 'it's about time someone said something'.

"Maeve, I know you must have a thousand questions. Some I will answer now. The rest will wait for tonight. Yesterday had to be terrifying. We are all thankful you were not harmed."

Maeve looked at him questioningly. Niall placed his hand on hers. Maeve took a deep breath and forced herself to concentrate and let Pa finish talking. The stillness in the room was unbearable. Maeve began to break out in a sweat. Tiny little droplets started to form around her hairline and on her upper lip. She did not feel well at all.

"Sweetheart, you know you have beautiful gifts that have been kept secret. You need who you truly are."

Maeve looked up at all three of them. Maeve could hardly get the words out. She became overcome with emotion - anger, relief, happiness. "You ALL knew! I only thought Mam knew. Everyone has been keeping secrets from ME!"

Pa continued. "Let me explain. I promise it will make sense."

Maeve began stammering. "Why couldn't you have told me something? I felt so ALONE! I knew Raegan and Declan were like me only because we've been able to speak without words since before, we could talk."

Pa moved closer to Maeve. He did not want to invade her space, but he needed to embrace her energy. She needed calming. She needed to go to school today, for Shae. Her absence could make things even more complicated. So, he scooched his chair closer to hers. "I know you have felt isolated, scared, confused, plus a multitude of other emotions. I must explain. Long ago, we moved to Rowan for protection. We are from a realm called Hy-Breasail. It is a beautiful place. We wished for you, Liam, and Shae to have normal lives. You are the future of Rowan and Hy-Breasail."

Maeve turned white. She looked faint. Thoughts were swirling in her mind like a tornado. "Liam? Shae? Did they know? Our people. What? Me and the girls or Me, Liam, Shae and who?"

Pa placed his arm around Maeve's shoulders to steady her and gave orders to Treasa and Rio. "Treasa, get her a cool rag for her forehead. Rio get her a glass of water. Quietly, please. We do not want to wake the girls. That is all we would need right now. I think she's going to faint." Pa pulled Maeve closer to him and whispered in her ear. "Shhh, my baby girl. Relax. You need not fret. Take a deep breath and relax. I will explain everything. I promise."

Pa then placed his hand on the nape of Maeve's neck. She felt a cool rush flow over her. It was as if 1,000 butterfly wings had brushed against her body. She instantly felt better. Maeve's eyes grew wide and a huge smile crossed over her face.

"Pa, your gift? It's like Grandpa's. He healed me once. A long time ago." He nodded and spoke to her through his eyes. No words verbalized. "Your grandfather has been watching over you since before you were born. He has been showing you through dreams your Kingdom. He sent you Kían. The same as he did for me when I was your age. Kían is a Divine Oracle. He has been a trusted friend to our family for generations. He will never leave you. Maeve's eyebrows furrowed in question.

"Maeve, he has never left you. The Hierarchy instructed him to keep away. Your experiences last night were imperative. With him nearby, a shield of prevention would stop Grandpa Aaron to share visions with you. As we speak, he is meeting with High Chief Tomas to get permission to attend to you. He has missed you." Maeve felt she was dreaming. Pa continued, "The four of you were born to be united forever. You may not remember the fourth. You will be reintroduced today. When you get to school, it will feel like yesterday was a normal occurrence. It will keep you safe. Do you understand?"

Maeve nodded her head.

"One last thing, my Maeve. You are my world. Your destiny is greater than you have ever imagined. You, my darling Maeve, are the Princess of Hy-Breasail. One day you will be Queen. I know this is overwhelming for you. There are others. Many women and men that form the Hierarchy of the Sept. You, Shae, Liam, and Roark will be meeting everyone tonight. High Chief Tomas, Quinn, Lorcan, and Aengus will come to discuss your future – all your futures. I promise this will make more sense. Your Mam and Auntie are going to burst any second. I love you."

Maeve threw her arms around Pa: "Oh, Pa. I am so relieved. I don't feel alone anymore. But you do know that I have a million questions?" Maeve could still feel the butterflies fluttering up and down her body. She felt so much peace. She was so grounded. Maeve looked at her Mam and Auntie. Surrounding them and floating throughout the room were the most glorious, glittery sparkles.

Treasa and Rio had tears in their eyes. Maeve was not surprised that Mam and Auntie had heard the whole conversation. They looked as if they were going to swallow her up in emotion. Maeve knew that they would both be vying for her attention any second. Talking over each other. Suddenly, as the dam of Mam and Auntie was about to burst, Shae beeped her horn. Maeve was so relieved.

Thank God for Shae and her punctuality. Mam and Auntie did not get in one word. Maeve grabbed her stuff, kissed everyone, and ran out the door.

37 The Drive

Maeve ran to Shae's car. She felt as light as a feather. She sighed with relief as she buckled her seatbelt. Shae looked tired this morning yet still incredibly beautiful. Shae's beauty sprang from a loving, genuine heart. Maeve gave her best friend a quick hug. Shae asked, "What was that for?"

Maeve replied, "You know." Shae smiled back at her, her smile radiating through her eyes. "I do, my friend." Maeve was beaming. "Pa told me about us. At least some of it. Are you okay?"

Shae replied, "I'm doing amazingly well. I thought yesterday was crazy, and then last night my dreams felt real. I didn't feel like I slept at all."

Maeve grabbed Shae's arm. "Oh, my gosh, me too! Mine were incredible. Like I was watching a movie but at the same time I was part of it. Crazy, right?"

"I would say yes if I didn't have the same type of dreams. So, not crazy at all."

"Did Papa K tell you about the meeting tonight? I forgot to ask where it was."

"Yep, your house after dinner. Around seven o'clock. Are you okay?"

"Truly, I'm fine. Better than I have been in an awfully long time." Maeve smiled lovingly at her best friend. Shae was so relieved to finally be able to talk freely with her best friend. "I'm so relieved you know. Now, we can talk without secrets. It wasn't right to keep things from you."

"I know, Shae. I felt the same. If it wasn't for Kían, I would have gone nuts." Maeve realized she had mentioned Kían. She looked like she had divulged the biggest secret. Shae giggled.

"Maeve, I've always known he was real. You know why?" Maeve shook her head. "No?" Shae hesitated for a nanosecond. "Well, I had an imaginary friend, too." She laughed. Maeve looked at her in disbelief. "Kían was my friend too. When you would slip and mention him, I wanted you to know he was real. I had to keep the secret. I think the Hierarchy thought we were too young to share secrets. It was safer for us to have our own."

Maeve stared at Shae for a second. Shae watched her. She was not sure what Maeve was going to say next. "Shae, how long have you known? I'm not mad at you. I just wished I did, too."

"Maeve, I've known for a while. I believe I was informed sooner than you so that I would be prepared to support you like I am right now. Honestly, I truly believe it was not done with malicious intent. The Hierarchy's decisions always put your safety first above everything else." Both expended a sigh of relief at the same time then hugged each other tightly.

Maeve almost screamed. "Oh my gosh, let's make a pact that from now on, no secrets. Okay?" Shae nodded her head in agreement as she replied, "Pinky swear?!" Both girls burst out laughing. Maeve half laughed, and half spoke when she said, "Pinky swear!"

The girls drove a few minutes before speaking again. Both had the biggest grins on their face. Maeve turned to Shae and asked: "Shae, do you think it's going to be okay at school?"

"It should be. Of course, there will be a few people who will be annoying. Some will just stare at us. Then there'll be the ones who will want to be in our personal space, which I totally hate." Maeve rolled her eyes. Shae laughed. "We'll be fine 'because it will be like any other day." Maeve chuckled with a hint of hesitation.

"Maeve, Liam will protect us. So, no worries! I promise."

"You're right. Thanks, Shae! Love ya!" Maeve blew Shae an air kiss. Shae smiled sending an air kiss back. She quickly glanced in her rearview mirror. A white sedan with silver flecks had been following them since Maeve's house. Shae felt her belly flutter. "Maeve, you're so lucky. Seriously? Why the puzzled look." Maeve shrugged her shoulders. "You have Liam! If he wasn't like my brother, I would be totally crushing on him. All the girls are in love with him."

"Shae! Stop!"

Shae laughed. "You stop. He's gorgeous and brave. He was amazing yesterday." Maeve blushed. "Yeah, he is pretty great." Maeve giggled a little. "I don't know what I would do without him...or you for that matter."

Shae looked a little sad when she asked: "What are the chances I meet someone like Liam someday?"

"Oh, I think very well. You're beautiful, smart, popular...why wouldn't you?"

"Well, umm, there's Finn."

"Oops, sorry!" Both girls burst out laughing again.

"Yeah, now I get it."

"So, here's a thought. What if I meet him today when we get to school?"

"And who will that be? We know everyone?"

"Well, he's going to be new... and handsome. And he's going to fall madly in love with me as soon as he sees my face." Shae was cracking herself up. Maeve looked at Shae and raised her eyebrows. "Shae, you're killing me." Shae burst out laughing: "Nah, apparently, someone else wants to do that."

"Stop! Not funny. Not funny at all, Shae! We're protected. Remember that." The girls were silent for a few seconds. Then Shae continued. "Back to my dream man. He must have blue eyes and black hair like mine. And drum roll please...the pièce de résistance...a sparkling aura like Liam."

Maeve practically shouted, "You can see it, too?" Shae nodded. "I thought I was crazy."

"Nah, if you're crazy, then so am I."

Before they knew it, they were pulling into the Hawthorn parking lot. Liam was waiting for them. Shae noticed the white car parking a few spaces behind her. Liam helped Maeve out of the car and hugged her tightly. Shae glanced over their shoulders. The driver of the white car was heading toward them. Shae started stuttering. "Ma...Ma...Maeve."

Maeve burst out laughing and asked, "Shae, what's wrong with you? Are you okay?" Shae nodded for Maeve to look behind her. This had to be a joke. Shae knew he was coming to talk to them. This "person" was taller than Liam but just as handsome. Shae almost died. She could see his piercing blue eyes from fifteen feet away. And his hair, was black like hers.

Maeve turned back to look at Shae. She tilted her head and made a face that said: "Are you kidding…your dream is right in front of you…how is that possible". Then they heard a deep voice call out to Liam. "Hey, Li, wait up!" Both girls were speechless. Maeve looked up at Liam as he called out to Shae's handsome stranger, "Hey, Roark. Sorry, man, I had to leave a little bit early to meet up with Maeve."

Liam gently kissed Maeve and let her go as he walked over to the mystery man. Maeve heard him say "cuz". She and Shae locked looks. Shae's face froze. She had a look of bewilderment, excitement, and fear on her face. The guys were bro hugging. Liam turned to the girls and waved them over.

Maeve took Shae by the arm and gave a little tug. Her feet were cemented to the ground. Maeve whispered, "Don't make me pull you. My Pa told me about him this morning. I didn't know he was ROARK. Your Roark." Shae whispered, "stop."

As they walked over to Liam and Roark, both girls looked dumbstruck. Liam gave them an enquiring look that said, "What's up with you two?" Then he continued with his introduction: "Maeve. Shae. This is my cousin, Roark. He's starting at Hawthorn today. He just moved here and is staying with my family." Maeve looked at him quizzically. "He is the secret I was keeping yesterday. So, his mom and dad work with my parents and both your fathers at the Sept." Liam whispered quickly in Maeve's ear. "Are we okay?" She looked up at him to say, "Absolutely."

Maeve watched the interaction between Shae and Roark. It was obvious to her that Shae had just met her Liam. There was no doubt in her mind. She looked up at Liam. She knew he was thinking the same thing.

38 Shae & Ollie

Earlier Shae sat on her bed reviewing the events leading up to yesterday's attack. She noticed Maeve tracking something in the woods. So, engrossed in her conversation with Liam, she had minimalized it. Now, she realized that Protectors surrounded the perimeter of the school. She wondered if, as a Patron, Liam noticed. If he did, he did not show it. Shae knew that Liam should not have left their side. Liam sitting with Miss Almath in the back of class, left her and Maeve vulnerable.

Shae was a running a few minutes behind schedule. She hated being late, but her hair was a wreck. After tossing and turning all night, she had massive bedhead. She stood in front of her mirror flat ironing her hair. It was taking forever. She had just a bit left when she heard a knock on her bedroom door.

"Shae, can I come in?" Papa K asked.

"Sure, Papa, what's up?"

Ollie walked over to Shae's bed and plopped down at its' edge. He was amazed at how much his daughter looked like her mother. Sometimes he caught his breath when looking at her. Her beauty, mannerisms and smile kept Branagh alive.

Shae's big blue eyes were questioning. He needed to talk about yesterday.

Ollie hesitated for a second and gave Shae a loving smile. "I know you're almost ready to leave so I'll be quick. Yesterday was very eventful. Much more so than originally thought." He hesitated a second before continuing. "The Hierarchy has asked me to deliver a message. You must keep answers to any of Maeve's questions minimal. We will all gather tonight at the O'Flaherty's. All questions will be fully addressed tonight."

"Papa yesterday was awfully hard. Maeve was totally blindsided. It's obvious she has known of her gifts for some time. But she clearly did not know the danger that surrounded her. I will obey my instructions. There is no need to worry. I am good at diverting Maeve's attention when necessary. I love her dearly. I must keep her safe."

"That's my Shaelyn. You have handled yourself way beyond your years. Your outstanding loyalty to Maeve and the people of Rowan and Hy-Breasail has not gone unnoticed by the Hierarchy. Your acts of duty and bravery were exemplary. You will receive commendation at a further date. I am so proud of you. Your Ma would be too."

Tears were brimming in Papa's eyes as he lovingly looked at Shae. Shae could see his reflection in the mirror. Her cheeks flushed from their porcelain white to a rose-colored blush. With her complexion and black hair, she looked like a princess herself. Her eyes began to fill with tears. Papa's love for her was beaming like sunbursts around him.

"Remember, I am here for you, always."

"Papa, what if Maeve hates me? I've been privy to her identity the longest. She may feel betrayed."

"Shae, it is not true. Mr. O'Flaherty informed me that Maeve was angry at first, but genuinely looked relieved knowing the truth. He told me that you should not be nervous about this morning's drive to school. You cannot fake the love and friendship you have for each other. Plus, her gifts would have enabled her to sense your insincerity a long time ago. So, no worries, okay?"

Shae nodded in agreement.

"Also, I forgot, you're in for a major surprise…Rio has moved here." Shae's face beamed with happiness. "She will start at Hawthorn today. She is moving into her aunt's old house this afternoon. Rio and Mrs. O'Flaherty will be available to you and Maeve for support purposes."

"That's great. I love her!"

"Both ladies will be a great resource for both of you. They've been waiting for this moment for an exceedingly long time."

"Pa, can I ask you something?" Ollie nodded. "Before you knocked on my door, I was going over the events leading up to the attack. When Maeve and I were walking from my car to the school, I saw Maeve peering over at the woods. The Protectors were in the wooded area surrounding the school. If I could see them, maybe she could too."

"If she asks try not to give her too many details. Just keep it simple. You can tell her they are here to help and protect. We want her to be able to go about her day like nothing has changed. If she seems agitated or overly nervous, it may prompt another attack. You understand, don't you?"

"Yes, of course. Oh, and Papa, sorry, there's one more thing. It's about Liam. Something happened to him during the attack."

"What was that?"

"You know how I've told you about Liam's aura and how it is always illuminated." Papa nodded his head up and down. "Yesterday, it was on steroids. It was incredible. He looked like a mythological god. What if others saw it, too?"

Papa laughed. "Well, I can't imagine but what you've described sounds amazing. I remember seeing pictures of illuminated Warriors when I was a boy. They were astounding. In my lifetime, the mightiest warrior I have met is Aengus. Until Liam, there has not been any other with his strength and power. Remember your sight abilities are stronger than the rest of ours."

"What about Maeve? Do you think Maeve was able to see it?"

"If she did, she may not have realized what it was. She could have thought it was just her eyes playing tricks on her."

"Papa, thank you for being here for me. I feel so much better."

"Shae, it's been hard for all of us. To hide our truth is unnatural, especially from those we love."

Papa rose from Shae's bed, walked over to the door, turned, and blew her a kiss.

"Love you, Papa! I'm going to follow you downstairs and grab something to eat and go. My hair took a lot longer than expected so I've got to run."

39 Destiny

The drive to school was almost perfect. Shae felt closer to Maeve than ever before. She felt an overwhelming sense of gratitude knowing she had not lost her best friend. For the first time, Shae had admitted to Maeve her hopes of having a relationship like hers. Maeve did not bat an eye. She knew how blessed she was to have Liam in her life. She knew he was her soul mate. Shae realized nothing could come between her and Maeve, not even Liam.

Shae knew that Aveline would assign a mate for her. It was all a matter of time. It sounded so old and prudish; but marriages foretold by the Guardians were commonplace in the Hierarchy of Hy-Breasail. Some people knew from early ages, others later. Shae hoped the Guardians revealed her soulmate sooner rather than later. She was starting to hate being the third wheel. Starting? That is so funny, she has been the third wheel since kindergarten.

There was only one thing that unsettled Shae during their ride to school. The car behind her had started following them soon after leaving the O'Flaherty's. Of course, it could be someone from school. But this car was unfamiliar. As class president, she knew everyone. She was letting paranoia get the best of her after yesterday's attack. Shae always felt calm, but she had a weird feeling. Today, she was excited and edgy at the same time. She knew the driver could be a Sept member assigned to protect them or even a family member she had not met yet. It would not be surprising as the Kerrigan Family was a huge clan.

Shae saw Liam waiting for them. He was standing in her parking space. Shae looked at Maeve and shook her head. The girls laughed. They knew Liam was not going to leave them alone for one second. Without a doubt, he blamed himself for what happened yesterday. There was no way he would have known Maeve was in danger. For his sake, they agreed to let him be overprotective today, but just today. Tomorrow was another story. They both did not want anyone hovering over them no matter the reason.

The day was turning out to be unusually normal except for the unknown car. She knew she would forget all about the strange car once class began. Shae felt relieved. Then, a voice called out to Liam. A voice so familiar, as if it were a part of her heart, mind, and soul. How could that be? Only Aveline could make that happen and she had not come to her. She turned toward Liam and the voice. She felt an invisible burst blast through her body. Suddenly, her body reacted as if hit by an ocean's wave.

Shae could not utter a single word. Maeve had to whisper in her ear and tried to coerce her to speak. Shae felt like a blubbering fool. She was so embarrassed until his gaze held hers. She knew he was equally surprised by their meeting. His gaze emitted a powerful sense of knowingness. It flowed through her blood like a raging river. Everything would be okay, strange but okay.

Shae looked at Maeve, then Liam, and, finally, Roark. It was the most beautiful vision she had ever seen. All four of their auras had become intertwined by a silvery thread. The thread glistened like the beautiful aura surrounding Liam. Their souls irrevocably bonded through love, goodness, truthfulness, courage, and strength. It was inexplicable.

Instantaneously, eleven years of memories flashed through Shae's mind like a movie. Shae felt tears forming in her eyes. She would not get emotional. The "movie" lasted only seconds filled with a lifetime of memories. It was the most recent memory that stood out among the rest. It had only been a few months ago. The day Maeve and Liam were officially a couple.

40 Maeve & Liam

Maeve's father finally gave Liam permission to date Maeve. So, Shae and Maeve decided to celebrate with a sleepover. Shae loved having Maeve over, especially living in a house full of boys. Thankfully, the Chief sent the boys to their friends' houses to spend the night. The girls would have the house testosterone free. He always made their girl nights special. For a tough police officer, he was mushy inside. He tried so hard after Ma died.

The Chief ordered pizza and asked Shae what kind of ice cream they wanted from O'Malley's Ice Cream bar. As soon as Maeve came, the girls ran upstairs and locked themselves in Shae's room. He yelled up that he would be right back. He was going to pick up the pizzas and ice cream.

"Girls, you want the usual sundaes?"

Both yelled, "Yes, please!!!"

They were so happy to be together. They had an important topic to discuss. Liam!

"Okay, tell me...I can't wait to hear. How did Liam ask you?"

"Seriously, Shae. I know you know."

"Ugh! Yeah, Liam told me, but I want to hear it from you."

"First, can I tell you something?"

"Sure. Anything."

"I wish I had what you and Liam have. Is that me being a terrible friend?"

"Oh, Shae, you're not. I knew the first day of kindergarten that we would be boyfriend and girlfriend. Can you imagine the look on Mam's face when I told her at dinner? She just half giggled and said oh."

"You were five. She thought you couldn't know that yet. What five-year-old talks about having a boyfriend?"

"True, you're right. If one of my sisters told me that, I would think she was crazy.

Shae noticed that Maeve got dreamy when she talked about Liam. She wondered if that would ever happen to her. "Okay, now back to Liam. Tell me the whole story."

"Okay, this will sound weird, but I feel like we're connected with, like, an invisible umbilical cord. Sometimes, we don't even need to talk, we know what the other person is thinking. Does that make sense? I'm not sure I can explain the feeling."

"Maeve, it does make sense. We have that but in the sister kind of way. The first day we met, I knew we'd be best friends."

"Shae, you'll know when you meet your 'Liam'. I know you will. Don't ask me how, but I do."

Shae dreamily replied. "I hope you're right."

41 The Four

Shae knew exactly what Maeve was trying to tell her that night a few months ago. As soon as she made eye contact with Roark, Shae understood what Maeve could not explain. The feeling was indescribable. It was so vastly different than anything else she had ever experienced.

The newly formed group walked through the parking lot. Kids gathered in groups whispering. Shae knew they saw it too. Maeve, without intention, had become the leader she was born to be. Her beauty and power were beyond magical. Everyone was staring. From left to right, they walked into the front doors of Hawthorn - Shae, Maeve, Liam, and Roark. Shae was so deep in thought she did not realize that Maeve was talking to her until she felt a pinch in her upper arm. Shae jumped. Maeve giggled and whispered to her.

"Hey Shae, your destiny is walking right beside Liam. Darn, he's handsome. Not as handsome as Liam, but then I'm biased." Maeve made an exaggerated dreamy eyeroll.

Shae elbowed Maeve gently and whispered, "In case you haven't noticed Maeve, everyone is looking at you. You've become our leader overnight."

"I have not. Don't be ridiculous. I'm still me."

Then Maeve laughed. Shae shushed her. She knew what she was going to say. She did not want to talk Princess. Maeve wanted to talk about Roark.

"Hmmm, Liam's cousin. So, what do ya think?"

"Stop." Shae whispered. Shae grabbed Maeve's elbow and tugged her closer. "I want to hit you and hug you at the same time. It's a dream. I just described him, and he walks up to me ten minutes later. Maeve, he's not real."

"Shae, you've been waiting for him forever. And he certainly is real."

"Remember the night you started dating Liam? You told me how you felt about him. When I looked into Roark's eyes, I knew exactly what you were talking about. It's weird, Maeve. So weird."

Shae stopped talking and looked over at Maeve. Maeve was ready to burst into laughter. Shae gave her a 'it's not funny' look. Maeve was enjoying every second of it. Shae could not stop herself from laughing with her.

Shae, Maeve, Liam, and Roark formed a small circle in the center hall. Liam announced that he was going to go with Roark to get his schedule. As he bent down to hug Maeve, he glanced at Shae. The Hierarchy had enabled bonded telepathic communication between Liam and Shae. The two people closest to Maeve would be able to communicate without causing Maeve unwanted worry. "She's okay, right?" Shae replied, "She's perfect." Liam was relieved. He bent down and gave Maeve a quick kiss and turned to walk away with Roark.

Roark had been quiet since meeting in the parking lot. He started to walk away then realized he had been a bit rude.

He looked directly into Shae's eyes and said, "It was so nice to meet you both. I've heard so much about *you*."

Shae thought, "did he just say 'you'? No, I'm hearing things...he was just generalizing! He just met Maeve too." Roark was still talking. "I hope we have some of the same classes. It would be great to have a friend to show me the ropes. If not, we can sit together at lunch. Um, so happy to meet you both."

Shae was dying. She felt that he was a figment of her imagination and not real. She turned to Maeve and whispered, "Maeve pinch me."

Maeve laughed and whispered back. "Really, Shae? I already did. Honestly, I think it would be clever to answer him."

Maeve flicked her on the back taking the lead and said, "Welcome Roark! I hope you like it here. See you later." Maeve gave him her signature smile. The one that made everyone instantly love her.

Finally, Shae stammered a reply. "It was great, um, meeting you, too. See you later." Shae stood immobilized for a second as she watched him walk away. Shae was frustrated. "Maeve, I sounded ridiculous. He's not going to like me. I couldn't even form a sentence."

"Seriously, Roarkie-poo was directing the whole conversation toward you."

"You're a jerk. You're lucky you're my best friend." Shae covered her mouth. "Did I say that aloud to a P-R-I-N-C-E-S-S? Oops!" Shae laughed. "Maeve, I'm acting like I've never talked to a boy."

"You're fine. You sounded better than you thought. We've just had a ton going on in the last twenty-four hours. Geez. The attack and Finn all in one day. Then I'm told I'm a princess. Oh, let's not forget, our real home is Hy-Breasail not Rowan. Seriously! This morning, Auntie Rio shows up and your destiny walks up to you in the school parking lot. That's a lot of destiny in a brief time."

"As usual you're right." Shae rolled her eyes at Maeve. "So, this happened. I looked straight into his eyes and could hear him in my heart. But I couldn't talk to him!"

Maeve looked at Shae perplexed. She had the "are you serious" face on. "Shae, get out of your head. It's going to be fine. You just didn't expect HIM to happen today. That's all it is." Maeve was stifling a laugh while trying to whisper. "Heee's your destiny. I have seen the visions. You will be together forever."

Shae was dying. "STOP! We aren't supposed to talk about this stuff here. We're going to get in trouble. That dark entity from yesterday must have infiltrated your mind. You're not really you. I know it."

Neither of them could stop laughing.

"Just the opposite. I'm finally me. I just feel so free. I can finally talk to you about everything. I am so happy."

"Me, too. Crazy, but it has been an incredible experience. We can finally be 100% honest. No secrets."

The girls stared into one another's eyes knowingly. Shae felt herself transcending to a significant memory that she had suppressed for many years.

42 Shae's Gifts

The night of Ma's 35th birthday celebration was a night of immense joy and pure devastation. On the way home from dinner, Shae and her brothers were singing "Happy Birthday" for the millionth time. Ma was beaming with happiness. She loved her kids. Her husband. They were the joys of her life. Shae stared at her Ma. Shae never realized how beautiful she was. Everyone always told her how pretty her Ma was. Now, she could see it, too.

The celebration had been perfect until the drive home. It then became the most horrific night in the Kerrigan family's lives. Just one block from their house, a truck ran a stop sign hitting their van broadside. Ma had been on the passenger side. She died before the EMTs arrived. Papa tried and tried to revive her giving her CPR to no avail. The whole family suffered few bruises and abrasions. Shae suffered the most devastating injury. The impact of the accident caused a severe concussion and memory loss.

Shae could remember two things from that night. First, the EMT from the accident. His skin was a shimmering translucent light. Shae thought she was seeing things. No one had skin like that. Then, he gave her a message. He whispered it into her ear. "Shae you will be okay. Tonight, you will meet someone, a new friend. He will protect you. Do not be frightened of him. His name is Kían."

For twenty-four hours, Shae was in and out of consciousness. She remembered a whispering, melodic voice. The voice was loving and kind. When she opened her eyes, a little man was standing beside her bed. He told her his name was Kían. "Little Shae, you are a special gift to us all. Do not try to talk. You do not need to be afraid. I will protect you. I promise."

Shae tried to reply but remained speechless. She found it frustrating. All these sentences were forming in her mind, yet she could not verbalize them. Kían sensed her frustration.

"Shae, with me, we don't need to speak words. We can talk with our minds."

Shae was relieved. "I miss my Ma."

"I know, sweetheart. That is why I am here for you. Your Ma loved you very much. Even though you cannot see her with your eyes, she will always live in your heart. I promise."

"Kían, what if something happens to Papa? Me and my brothers will be alone. What would we do?"

"Do not worry. Your father is safe. So are your brothers. I need to tell you a few things before you get too sleepy. Can you listen for a bit and then I will answer your questions?"

Shae nodded "yes".

"Shae, you have extraordinary gifts. You see in two distinct ways. The first is like everyone else with your eyes. The second is through a magical eye. Your magical eye allows you to hear and see with your mind. Just like how we are talking right now."

Shae's eyes grew very wide and large. "Don't be afraid. I am going to teach you how to use and control it. You must remember it is a secret. Okay?"

Shae replied, "Okay."

Kían explained everything to her simply keeping in mind that Shae was only a seven-year-old. He told her it would be hard at first because Ma was not with her. She had to remember that he was always around...even when she could not see him. He told her life will behold many wonderful surprises. Shae liked surprises.

Kían told her how happy she was when she met Maeve and Liam. He reminded her how she had rolled her eyes when she learned Liam was a boy.

"Yes, I didn't want another brother, but I'm happy he's my friend."

"Shae, the three of you are more than best friends. You will see. I promise." Shae nodded and replied, "I'm tired."

"I know, sweetheart, sleep now. Remember I am always with you."

Kían kissed her on the forehead and left in a current of effervescent sparkles.

Shae dreamt of her first day of kindergarten. Ma and Papa walked her and her brothers to school. Shae remembered thinking I'm going to meet new friends today. I already know who they are. There's two of them. A boy and a girl. There's Maeve standing by the playground. She's with her Ma. Out of the corner of her eye, she saw Liam. He would be her best friend, too. He was standing with an older girl, his sister. Shae smiled. My two best friends.

Shae started skipping. Halfway there, she paused then turned to look back at Ma and Papa. They were both smiling. Ma had tears in her eyes. Pa looked so happy. She gave them her hugest smile and blew the biggest kiss. Her class was in Line C. She could see it a few yards in front of her. A very pretty teacher was holding up a sign with a glittery C. Shae got on her line. Suddenly, she could hear someone talking in her mind.

Shae thought, I can hear you, but I can't see you. Where are you?"

"Shae, I'm right beside you. No one can see me. My name is Aveline. I am a Guardian sent to deliver a message to you."

Shae nodded.

"You and Liam are here to support, love, and protect Maeve in every way possible. We know you are just a little girl, but we know that you are strong. You should be proud. A long time from now, Liam and Maeve will also learn of their gifts. You, Shae, are a Keeper of the Gifts. Years from now you will bring Maeve to meet Eamonn. It will be a special day."

"Huh, I'm just a little girl. I like gifts."

Aveline smiled, "Dear, this gift is to be kept close to your heart. Only speak of it to Kían. He is always close to you. Do you understand?"

Shae nodded in understanding.

43 Fagen

Shae was relieved that Maeve did not notice her transcendence. She wondered if Maeve transcended too. Its timing was most inopportune. Kían said that in this world it felt like a nanosecond while in another dimension it could feel like days. Shae knew she could not ask her now. School was not the place to have that conversation.

Shae picked up in the conversation right where they left off. They were so deep in thought neither realized that danger was lurking around the corner. The darkness of the upcoming confrontation would be a shock to them both. They shuddered at the same time. A cold chill ran up their spines. Maeve glanced over at Shae and asked, "Did you feel that?"

"If you mean the creepy goosebumps, then yes."

Maeve looked frightened. She wrapped herself up in her own arms and Shae placed her arm around Maeve's shoulders and snuggled her close to her side. Maeve asked: "Did you see anything?"

"Nope, but I definitely had a bad feeling."

"Me too! What should we do?"

"Don't worry. Remember what you told me in the parking lot. We've got this. The four of us together will be fine."

Maeve nodded her head up and down in agreement. She then added, "Well, looks like we've returned to our proper roles. You always know how to calm me down."

The girls continued walking. As they were heading toward their first period class, the warning bell rang. They looked at each other and knew they were going to be late. Just as they looked up Fagen Darroch turned the corner and slammed right into them. They were stunned and at the same time said, "Hey, Fagen, sorry. Are you okay?"

Fagen just glared at them. He did not say a word. Shae asked him again.

"Fagen!!! Can you hear me? You just walked right into us. Say something! Are...you...okay?"

He did not reply. This annoyed her immensely and heightened her defenses. Shae could see hatred spewing out of his eyes. Then, she heard Maeve gasp.

Maeve did not gasp from the collision; it was much worse. In his eyes, she saw something wickeder than hate. It was a dark vortex within a cyclonic sea of red. With vine-like ropes, it pulled Maeve into the blackness deep within his soul. Faster and faster, deeper, and deeper, ropes submerged her into a deep, nefarious hole. Around her was a volcanic wall with sharp tendrils whipping toward her. When they jabbed her skin, she felt thousands of fiery needles piercing through her flesh. The pain was excruciating. She could hear herself screaming.

The tendrils began whipping around her head forming a halo. When it got to a bizarrely fast speed it entered her mind through her orifices. Its hypnotic voice whispered to her: 'you will follow me. We will reign over Hy-Breasail together. Your reign with me will be greater than you can ever imagine. If you follow me, I will let your family, Shae, Liam, and Roark live. If not, they will die, a terrifyingly horrific death.'

Maeve felt overtaken by this dark, evil entity who she could feel depleting goodness from every cell in her body. It was drawing her into its darkness. It would be so easy to concede. She struggled to fight. Suddenly, she felt a burst of energy enter her body through her feet. As the energy filled her, she felt herself grow stronger and stronger. Every single cell in her body was rebelling against the vile entity.

With composure, grace, and a hint of vehemence, Maeve refuted the attack. "I command you to leave me. I will not partake in your evilness. I will not sacrifice myself, my family, my friends, or my people to your darkness. In the end, we will win. Leave NOW!"

Maeve reacted with grace and dignity without sacrificing her God-given strength and intelligence. She felt overcome with a feeling of completeness. She was a Princess.

In a flash, she was back. Maeve shuddered not in fear but to brush off the evil energy that had touched her. She whispered to Shae, "We must talk." Maeve placed her hand on Shae's forearm, nudging her to keep walking away from Fagen. Shae looked at Maeve then placed her hand on top of Maeve's and gave her a reassuring squeeze.

Shae's cheeks were turning red and blotchy. Her heart suffered a vice-like pressure. It was her turn. Fagen was trying to attack her. She felt a storm raging inside of her. Her physical strength was intensifying deep within her inner core. She felt it coursing through her veins flowing everywhere in her body. It triggered growth in her confidence. Her inner core shook with gratitude for this this gift. Combined with her training, she knew this new gift of strength enabled her to protect herself, but more importantly, Maeve.

As she clenched her hands into fists, she thought, you evil bastard, I'm not afraid of you. My strength is immeasurable. If you are smart, you had better start running for shelter. You, Fagen, and your brother, are no match for me. All it would take is one blow to take you down. You'd go running like a dog with its tail between its legs. Be gone, Fagen, or you will have to see my strength for yourself.

Shae felt powerful. She stood before him tall and proud. Alarmingly, she realized that Fagen could hear her thoughts. He replied.

"Oh, Shae, I'm not afraid of either of you. Maeve has seen the fate of those who do not follow me and my people. The world as you know it will cease to exist. I will see you again soon, and next time, you won't be so lucky."

Fagen sneered at Shae. She never expected an altercation today especially with an enemy disguised as a life-long friend. Shae glared back at Fagen. Telepathically he heard her message. I know who and what you are, Fagen. My strength is impenetrable so don't even try to hurt Maeve. Underneath your villainous façade you are nothing but a sullen puppy. Poor, poor Fagen. I feel sorry for you. You are nothing.

Fagen teemed with fury. Before their eyes, he took a deep breath and transformed. No longer was Fagen dark and dangerous, he became the Fagen they loved. The handsome, sweet, kind, and good-hearted Fagen. Taking only a few steps, he hesitated, turned, and sweetly said, "Watch your back."

44 Princess

Shae turned to look at Maeve. Maeve stood in front of her stoically like the majestic, mythical Irish Queen Medb. Shae's gaze met Maeve's. There she saw a tiny glint of satisfaction over their victory. Fagen had lost. Questions ran through both their minds. Without speaking, Shae and Maeve's thoughts ran concurrently.

Who else was part of the Regime? The Regime could be deceptive and duplicitous, an understatement for sure. If Finn and Fagen were examples of its norm, there was going to be quite the battle ahead. The dangers their infiltration would pose were immeasurable. They winced.

Cillín? If Cillín was in the Regime, he fooled not only Aífe, but the Hierarchy. His threat would be much greater. The intelligence he gathered would be devastating. Hy-Breasail would crumble. Could he fool the Warriors or the Hierarchy? It would be impossible. The change in him would be obvious especially to Aífe. Aveline would not have paired them. It was impossible. Unless Aífe was working for the Regime as well.

Their thoughts so deep, Maeve startled Shae by grabbing her wrist pulling her close. Fagen was out of sight, Maeve kept her voice just above a whisper.

"Shae, I need to tell you something extremely important."

"Huh? Sure!"

"Just a second, I want to make sure that Fagen is far away so he can't hear us.

Maeve and Shae stood listening to Fagen's footsteps descending the main corridor. When barely audible, Maeve said, "First, I agree. There's no way that Cillín is working with the Regime. It perplexes me that he did not see the changes in his brothers. How could he have missed it entirely? There's no way."

Shae interrupted. "This is totally unrelated, but I have to say it. In less than twenty-four hours, you have transformed from an ordinary teenager to the Princess of Hy-Breasail. I am so proud of you. You mesmerized me when you handled Fagen's threats. You didn't show one ounce of fear."

It was obvious that Maeve was choosing her words so that she described her vision precisely.

"Shae, danger is imminent. I do not think that anyone coerced Fagen to follow the Regime. I believe the Regime's leader may have no bodily form. It is stronger and eviler than we are prepared. This entity finds hosts that are weak. It enters their body and controls them until the host has served its purpose. Fagen and Finn are still inside. I honestly believe this. It tried to control me and make me succumb to its spell. It was extremely difficult to fend off. I thought I was going to lose the battle, but I called upon my gifts. I could feel myself grow stronger and stronger the more I fought against it. I will not let anyone control me – seen or unseen."

Shae listened intently.

"It was a terrifying experience. At first it filled me with terror. I couldn't see anything but a swirling, cloudlike figure spinning around me. It grew tentacles that entered my ears, nostrils, and mouth allowing messages to enter my brain. That's how I was able to hear it. Each time a tentacle pierced my skin, it sent an electrical current throughout my body. It was terribly painful. It propositioned me to become the Regime's ruler. If I did, I would receive immeasurable riches and power beyond my imagination. If I didn't, the pain that I was feeling would intensify a hundredfold. Ultimately, I would die as would my family and friends." Shae looked at Maeve in disbelief. Maeve continued, "I felt a cold hollowness in the depth of my soul."

Maeve took Shae's hands in hers. Shae could feel a slight tremble, but also, absolute strength. "Shae, it is of the utmost importance that we tell Liam and Roark. They need to contact the Hierarchy. Tomas, Quinn, Lorcan, and Aengus need updates without hesitation. Until we know exactly what we are dealing with, Cillín's allegiance to the Sept is questionable. Time is of the essence. The Patrons and Protectors will need to formulate a plan. The threat of impending attack against Rowan and Hy-Breasail must be stopped."

Maeve and Shae walked toward Miss Almath's class.

"We better get going or we're going to be late.

For a brief time, they enjoyed a moment of levity. It was great that they could still act like teenagers. The question that entered Shae's mind was "for how long?" Maeve squeezed Shae's hand and whispered, "Shae, I'm so glad that you and Liam were chosen for me. I can't imagine doing this alone."

45 Warriors

Shae was so proud of her friend. She felt her throat tighten from holding back emotion.

"Oh, Maeve. We are all here for you. You'll be a brilliant ruler of Hy-Breasail. Seriously, as your friend and advisor, I believe we should get to class, act like everything is normal, then make an excuse to find Liam and Roark. Acting normal is of the utmost importance. We don't want to alarm anyone. Without a doubt, yesterday flustered Miss Almath so we cannot tell her why we need to leave. Plus, I'm not sure we can trust her. We must err on the side of caution. Please take my lead."

Maeve nodded in agreement. There was great concern in her eyes. This was all so new to her. Shae's response was silent. She slightly tilted her head and squeezed Maeve's hand in reassurance. Shae's touch emitted tiny impulses into Maeve's hand emanating throughout her body spreading a sense of grounded calm.

Shae spoke just above a whisper into Maeve's ear, "Maeve, feel the calm. We are safe. The Protectors are shielding us. The building's signage glistened from its brilliant illumination this morning. Did you see it? After yesterday and this morning's encounter with Fagen, I hope the increase in security is strong enough to shield us."

Maeve clenched her teeth and grimaced while squeaking out a nervous chuckle. "I didn't notice, but maybe something we should mention at the meeting tonight. Honestly, I was so involved in teasing you about Roark I wasn't paying attention. Probably not a good habit for a princess." Maeve raised her eyebrow at the same time she mentioned Roark's name.

"OMG. Stop. Seriously, *Princess*." said Shae with a huge grin on her face.

Maeve rolled her eyes and laughed as she said: "Stop calling me Princess."

"If we are in danger, Liam and Roark's senses will know. Warriors know anytime danger is lurking because their senses intensify. If Fagen was a true threat, they would have been there when Fagen showed up."

Maeve looked puzzled. Shae forgot that Maeve did not know all the gifts beholden by the Warriors.

"Oh, that's right, Maeve, all the Warriors have heightened senses. Their senses escalate when real danger is near. Especially near you. That's why Liam has always been able to come to our rescue so quickly. Remember on the playground in kindergarten. And, umm, I'm not sure about Roark since we don't know him yet."

Maeve raised her eyebrow again. This time as if to say: "but you will". They both laughed.

"Stop teasing me. We need to be serious, *Princess*." Shae emphasized "princess" sarcastically. "Ready? Come on, Maeve, let's get to class."

Seconds later, steps away from the classroom door, Shae noticed that Maeve's steps were hesitant. Maeve was so deep in thought she had slowed to a turtle pace.

"We have to go a little faster than a snail or we're going to be late."

Shae hugged her and whispered, "Remember who you are…"

Before Shae could complete her sentence, Maeve interrupted her. "Oh, Shae, I know who I am. I just can't get Fagen's vision out of my head. Not because I don't think we will conquer the Regime; of that I am sure. But will our friends ever be the same?"

Shae pulled her hands away from Maeve and placed them over her heart.

"Maeve, I want you to look at me."

Maeve slowly raised her glance to meet Shae's. Shae continued, "You weren't transcended. No one would be able to do that to you without your permission. Your powers and gifts are stronger than his. Fagen was playing with your emotions. You defeated him. He will NOT harm you. You have the highest protection surrounding you."

"That's not what I mean, Shae. Fagen isn't compliant with this entity. You know, I thought that at first. I honestly believed that our Fagen was gone. Think about it, Shae. We saw him transition from the possessed Fagen to the normal Fagen right before our eyes. He is still in there. I'm 99% sure. It does not consist of men with earthly form. This wraithlike entity enters the bodies of vulnerable men – Fagen and possibly Finn."

Donna Marie George

"Maeve, if true, it is going to be much harder to take it down because it will be able to disguise its appearance, taking the form of even our friends." Maeve nodded in agreement. "I pray if there is even a semblance of them left inside their bodies that they are protected. There's so much that you will find out later today. But, because of what just happened, I will tell you this. The gifts of our people are beyond the imagination of those in this world. We have abilities that are unimaginable to anyone not affiliated with Hy-Breasail. Most of our people in Rowan are not privy to this for their safety. This entity's strength cannot compare to that of the inhabitants of our home."

Maeve was a bit relieved.

"I would like to show you something. But we must cross Veil na Tairsí. We will only be gone for a few moments. Our travel will not make us late for class. It's very much like transcendence."

"The Veil na Tairsí? I don't understand."

"I'm so sorry. Once again, I forgot. Please forgive me."

"Oh, Shae, are you serious? Why would you need forgiveness? None of my ignorance is your fault."

Relief showered over Shae's face as she replied. "Maeve, Hy-Breasail's time is vastly different than that of this realm. If I take you there, we will not be late for class. I think it's time for you to see what we are fighting for. You need to know why you are so important to the people of Rowan. And, to me, of course."

"I agree. I believe it to be imperative. So, yes, I think I'd like you to show me Hy-Breasail."

"Okay, good. Hold my hand, Princess." Shae blushed as she called her friend by her royal name. "We'll be gone but a second. Ready?" Maeve nodded. The glint in Maeve's eye intensified. Shae saw something she had never seen before. She was not sure what it was, but it was magnificent. "Here we go."

46 Veil na Tairsí

Immediately, the girls felt a shroud of peace and tranquility cover them. Crossing Veil na Tairsí had been easy. Beautiful crystal illuminations encircled them. The same crystals that illuminated around the Protectors surrounded them for travel. Upon arrival, Shae decided it would be best to remain at the crossroads closest to the Veil. The village was a distance too far for now. A flood of emotion rushed over Maeve. She could not even express to Shae how she was feeling. She just knew she was home.

"Maeve, we have just crossed Veil na Tairsí. Before us is the pathway to the village of Hy-Breasail beyond that the O'Flaherty Castle. I believe it is of the utmost importance that you see your kingdom and what we are fighting to protect - this beautiful world. As I did not get permission to cross, I will face the consequences of the Hierarchy tonight if necessary."

Maeve was speechless. She could not believe the imagery in front of her. The path to her real home was beautiful, ethereal, magical. Barely above a whisper, Maeve said, "Shae, it's beautiful. It seems so familiar. I think I've been here with Grandpa Aaron."

"It is possible. I know he has visited you. This place is like nothing you've ever seen before." Maeve nodded. "We are safe here and can talk freely. The Regime cannot hear us. We must be brief so if you have questions, now is the time."

Maeve kept staring at the beauty before her and the beauty beside her. Shae's beauty had been unrivaled in Rowan. Now, Maeve saw her best friend in the world transform into a warrior goddess. Her beauty left Maeve speechless.

Shae's black hair with clear blue highlights billowed like ocean waves. Her hair tied in the back with a ribbon of a silvery, shimmering material weaving in a pattern of strength, nobility, and loyalty. Her eyes were cerulean blue with pupils of opalescent stars. Her black, thick eyelashes curled upward with tips frosted with crystals. Her lips a deep rose color. Her cheeks rosy, dewy, and glowing.

Shae wore thigh high, sleek yet rugged boots in the same color as her eyes. Its laces a thin rope-like material replicating the ribbon in her hair. Her metallic-like jumpsuit the color of the crest of an ocean wave. A braht fastened with a dealg in the shape of the Hy-Breasail crest of ocean blue color emblazoned her chest. Shae's beauty took Maeve's breath away. Unbeknownst to Maeve, she had transformed as well.

Emanating from within her body - as if pierced with thousands of pins - was a glistening shimmer interspersed with golden rays of light. Her hair red as fire flowing like a bridal veil on a billowy cloud with a silver and gold crown interwoven in a torrent of silver and gold majesty. Her skin white as the purest snow, a golden sprinkle of freckles dusting each cheek and the tip of her nose. Blue eyes, sapphire in color, with a burst of star-shaped silver from center to end. Her flowy, angelic, and heavenly dressing gowns were of material interspersed with a gold and silver thread offering protection.

Maeve closed her eyes and took in deep, purifying breaths. When she opened them, she found Shae just staring at her.

"What is it?"

"Maeve, you look awesome."

"Well, you haven't seen yourself. So, do you."

47 Eamonn

Out of the corner of her eye, Maeve saw something moving behind the most beautiful tree she had ever seen. A tree formed from thousands of Celtic knots with twisting branches reaching up toward the heavens. Each branch held tiny silver fruit. The fruit looked like apples, each glistening from the light shining down from the heavens. Maeve walked tentatively toward the tree.

Each step filled with a feeling of knowing. Hiding behind the tree was a boy. He would peek his head out and quickly return to safety. The most beautiful eyes peered back at her. Maeve found herself speaking in a foreign tongue. In her head, it sounded like English, but her words were not. She told the sweet little boy: "Little one, it's okay. I will not hurt you. Come here. Let me see you."

"Buachaill beag, tá sé ceart go leor. Ní dhéanfaidh mé dochar duit. Tar anseo, lig dom tú a fheiceáil."

The little being peered sheepishly at her. He was very tentative. Maeve crouched down so that her eyes were at his level. She held her hands out. Hesitantly, he started to shift away from the tree. Then, he quickly returned to safety behind the trunk. Maeve smiled at him. He blinked back.

His eyes were magnificent. Big, round, emerald green with bursts of golden thread emanating from pupil to the edge of its iris. His eyelashes were a beautiful golden brown, his hair a brilliant red of soft, downy curls surrounding his cherub-like face. He had tiny golden freckles covering his face. He wore a leíne, his braht with a pin on his right shoulder of Hy-Breasail's crest – a duplicate of Shae's. Attached to his crios was a pouch. It, too, embossed with the Hy-Breasail crest. His glorious garb matching his eyes except for his leíne which was the color of saffron yellow.

He stepped a bit closer to Maeve. His eyes aglow with recognition. His smile grew and grew, his eyes twinkling with joy. Suddenly, this magnificent creature ran into her arms. He embraced her with an ease that Maeve did not understand right away. She did not push him away yet desired to look into his eyes. She gently moved his little body away from her while keeping him in her embrace, her hands cupping his elbows. She looked down at him and asked "Your name? It is Eamonn. Yes?"

"Eamonn an t-ainm atá ort nach ea?

He replied: "Yes! You know me! I am blessed."

"D'fhreagair se sea! Táaithne agat ormsa, táim beannaithe."

Shae felt like she was rooted in place, the picture before her of untold importance. She let it unfurl as she remained a spectator. Eamonn's name reverberated over and again in her head. It was familiar. Suddenly, she remembered Papa's bedtime stories about Eamonn. Eamonn was an Ancient One and the Guardian of Riches. Shae noticed Maeve's eyes scan his little body, hesitating on the pouch he carried – the pouch. What sort of riches needed protection by a creature so small?

Maeve's gifts magnified after crossing the Veil into Hy-Breasail intensifying her intuitiveness. She knew exactly who Eamonn was and had gained the ability to speak Hy-Breasail's native language, Irish, and a language used fluently in Rowan by few. The gift of this ancient language appeared right before Shae's eyes. She wished that Liam and Roark were here to experience Maeve's transformation. It was truly beyond description.

Eamonn had a tear in his eyes. Maeve smiled at him and said, "Eamonn, I am blessed to be in your presence. Thank you for allowing me to meet you today."

"Eamonn, tá mé beannaithe a bheith I do láthair. Go raibh maith agat as ligean dom bualadh leat inniu."

Eamonn was beaming. He removed himself from Maeve's embrace slowly. He told her, "Do not be afraid, Princess, I mean no harm."

"Dúirt sé léi, ná bíodh eagla ort a Bhanphrionsa, nil aon dochar ionam."

48 The Gift

Eamonn stepped back from Maeve and transformed. An invisible blanket cocooned his body. Soft feather-like wisps unraveled a beautiful cloak. Astounded by his transformation, Maeve and Shae admired Eamonn. Before them he stood tall, broad, muscular - a man of godly proportions. His handsome face was, as if, perfectly chiseled from stone. He wore a full, beautiful beard of red, tinted with glimmers of gold. His hair, thick, red, and wavy tied back into a ponytail with a leather rope encrusted with emerald stones.

Eamonn explained he was unsure if the Princess' gifts would amplify upon her arrival, so he spoke carefully. "Princess Maeve, you have learned much over the last twenty-four hours. I did not want to scare you. My true form can be intimidating. You needed to look into my eyes and see me."

"Banphrionsa Maeve, tá go leor foghlamtha agat le ceithre huaire an chloig fichead anuas, Ní raibh mé ag iarraidh eagla a chur ort. Is féidir le mo fhoirm dhílis a bheith scanrúil. Bhí sé riachtanach gur fhéach tú isteach i mo shúile agus go bhfaca tú mé."

She had understood. He glanced back at Shae. She did as well.

Maeve asked how he knew of their arrival. So, she asked, "Eamonn, how did you know we were coming? No one knew. It was a quick decision."

"Eamonn, cén chaoi a raibh a fhios agat go raibh muid ag teacht? Ní raibh a fhios ag aon duine. Cinneadh gasta a bhí ann."

Eamonn hesitated. "Princess, you are aware time moves differently here. Therefore, I received alerts about your crossing. Here," he patted the pouch that lay against his hip, "lies a gift for you. Rí Aaron had it made for you. He asks that you keep it with you at all times."

"Banphrionsa, tá a fhios agat go mbogann an t-am sin go difriúil anseo. Dá bhrí sin, tugadh foláireamh dom faoi do thrasnú. Seo is bronntanas duit é. Rinne Rí Aaron duit é Iarrann sé ort é a choinneáil leat i gcónai."

Maeve and Shae watched as Eamonn gently opened his pouch. His hand slowly reached in. He looked as if coaxing something to come to him. He spoke no words but Maeve and Shae both recognized that there was dialogue between Eamonn and the object. After a minute, Eamonn had it cradled in his hand. Eamonn opened his hand to Maeve. Maeve and Shae's eyes opened extremely wide. They could not believe it. There sat the tiniest kitten. It was magnificent.

Maeve replicated Eamonn's hands and placed them next to his. The kitten timidly crawled into hers. Its tiny paw touched her palm. The most remarkable thing happened. It turned into a pendant. Its eyes were black onyx, with a body encrusted in diamonds, its necklace a beautifully woven silver. Saddened, Maeve looked at Shae and Eamonn. She asked what had happened to the kitten: "Eamonn, I do not understand. Did he die by my touch?"

"Eamonn, ní thuigim. An bhfuair sé bás le mo theagmháil?"

He replied that he would explain.

"Míneoidh mé."

Maeve asked for him to speak in English so that Shae could learn the significance of this necklace. "Eamonn, please speak in Rowan's language. Shae has not yet learned the beautifully spoken ancient language of Hy-Breasail. It is important that she also know the significance of your gift."

"Eamonn, labhair I dteanga Rowan le do thoil. Níor fhoghlaim Shae fós teanga ársa álainn Hy-Breasail. Tá sé tábhachtach go mbeadh a fhios aici freisin tábhacht do bhronntanais."

Eamonn nodded in agreement. He began to converse in English.

"Your grandfather, King Aaron, had this made for you. The life of this kitten, Ailm, has not ended. He is very much alive. You will be crossing over Veil na Tairsí very soon, that is why he turned into a pendant. His powers are extraordinary. You must wear him always. No matter what. He will provide you with strength, endurance, resilience, and protection plus much, much more. He represents wholeness, intactness, and purity of the soul, all of which you possess."

Maeve gently picked Ailm up. She gasped. In the center of Ailm's belly was the tiniest keyhole. Liam's key and Ailm were one. Maeve placed him over her head and laid him against her chest. She had an overwhelming feeling of completeness. Ailm was radiating heat, not a temperate heat. It was a radiating warmth under the surface of her skin. He was part of her.

Maeve turned to Eamonn. She reached her hands out for him to grasp hers. As he placed his hands into hers, he kneeled in front of her with his head bowed in reverence. Maeve was grateful for his kindness and gift. "Eamonn, thank you for showing yourself to me. This gift from Grandfather Aaron is a true blessing. I am indebted to you. Godspeed."

Maeve gently touched his cheek. Then turning to Shae, she nodded. It was time to cross Veil na Tairsí. Shae took Maeve's hands into her own. Both bowed their head with their foreheads touching. Without moving or saying another word, they transported. When Eamonn looked up, both Princess Maeve and Shae were gone.

49 The Princess Returns

Maeve and Shae opened their eyes. Their heads bowed with hands entwined. They looked up into each other's eyes. A look of knowing flowed silently between them. Liam and Roark were making their way toward them. Smiles beamed at the sight of them. The boys took greater strides to get to Maeve and Shae. There was an urgency in their step. Liam took Maeve into his arms holding her tightly against him. He whispered, "Mo shíorghra" into Maeve's ear.

Maeve wrapped her arms around Liam's neck. Intensely, he looked into her eyes. His gaze gradually moved to her necklace. He took his arms from around her waist and unhurriedly moved his hands to the talisman hanging around her neck. It was the complement to the necklace he had given her a few short months ago. He tilted his head in a questioning gesture but then said, "Ailm?" Maeve nodded in agreement.

"You crossed?" Maeve nodded once again. "Why? You should not have gone alone. What if something had happened to the both of you. I would not have known where you were. Never again. Promise?"

Maeve replied: "It was a quick decision. It was imperative that we meet with Eamonn. Grandpa Aaron made this talisman for me. You do understand?"

"Of course, I do. But you must promise to never go alone again."

Waiting for Liam and Maeve to finish their conversation, Shae and Roark stood nearby side by side, their hands slightly touching. Shae could feel a tingling in the spot where Roark's hand touched hers. He leaned in and whispered in her ear. "Shae, we need to talk." Shae turned her head toward Roark and tilted it so that he could see her face. Shae nodded.

"Are you okay?" asked Roark.

"Yes, I'm wonderful. I'm just speechless." Shae giggled quietly. "Soon enough you'll find it's not normal for me." Roark smiled. Shae felt as if she had died and gone to heaven.

The final bell interrupted them as did Miss Almath. She smiled and motioned them to enter. Each gave her a "good morning". A great surprise awaited them; their classmates greeted them with a standing ovation. Maeve looked up at Liam then to Shae and Roark, nodding at each. Maeve placed herself in the center of the classroom behind Miss Almath's podium. An uncharacteristic behavior for old Maeve, not for Princess Maeve, as she stood to address her classmates.

"Morning! Wow, what a surprise. Thanks so much! Oh my gosh, everyone please sit down." The class sat down quietly. Maeve continued. "What we all experienced yesterday was very scary, but we are all okay. Aren't we?

Thank you for your texts. Waking up to your thoughtful concerns and wishes was overwhelming. We are so sorry we could not respond to you individually. Our doctor placed restrictions on our use of media devices. In addition, our parents confiscated our phones as soon as we got home. Again, thank you all. Now we better quiet down so Miss Almath can start class.

Liam and Shae were staring at Maeve in amazement. Before yesterday, Maeve would never have taken charge of any public speaking opportunity. Shae, yes. Liam, yes. Maeve, never. It was incredible to watch her transform into her birthright. As they took their seats, Liam looked at her and she knew exactly what he was thinking. "You're amazing. I'm so happy to be on this journey with you." Maeve reached across the aisle and took Liam's hand in hers.

Miss Almath thought she was imagining things. She took her glasses off and with subtle motions rubbed her eyes. Before her sat, Liam, Maeve, Shae, and Roark their bodies intertwined with an ethereal rope. Its threadlike bonding emanating light and star-like filaments in the air. Miss Almath thought 'It's happening'. She knew that Maeve was destined to be the Princess of Hy-Breasail, but not now. Yesterday's attack moved up the timeline.

Miss Almath asked Maeve, Liam, Shae, and Roark to stay after class. Miss Almath had a message for them. The Hierarchy ordered a change to their schedules. Not surprisingly, all subjects and periods were exact. At lunch, Maeve, Shae, Roark, and Liam were discussing this change when their cells began vibrating simultaneously. The message said there was a change in tonight's meeting time.

They would now meet right after school. Instructions were for all to drive with Liam. This was crucial, there was to be no reason or excuse to ignore this order.

The afternoon proved boring, especially after the morning meeting with both Fagen and Eamonn. Minutes felt like hours. By eighth period, Maeve and Shae were counting the seconds for the dismissal bell. Maeve had so many questions. The anticipation of the impending meeting was overwhelming. Finally, it rang.

Maeve and Shae popped up from their seats and started jogging to their lockers. Realizing that they were a bit too eager and could get in trouble, they slowed to an acceptable pace. Liam and Roark followed behind them. The two were chatting non-stop without a breath between them. Liam and Roark just looked at each other and shrugged their shoulders. The car ride would be interesting.

Finally, in the shelter of Liam's car, Maeve and Shae were able to tell them of the encounter with Fagen Darroch. They also told them about their meeting with Eamonn. Liam was irate at what had happened with Fagen. Liam would make sure that the Darroch's would be the first order of business at the meeting.

50 The Hierarchy

As they pulled up to the O'Flaherty's house, cars and motorcycles packed the driveway. Maeve let out a big breath. Shae grabbed Maeve's hand. Each gave the other a reassuring squeeze. They remained holding hands until Liam and Roark opened their doors. The group walked to the front door in silence. Liam snugged Maeve close to his side as Roark gently laid his arm around Shae's shoulders.

At the front door, Maeve turned to them. "No matter what happens today, we will always be together. I will make sure of that." Maeve turned and placed her hand on the doorknob briefly hesitating before she opened the door. Before her, in her living room, was an indescribable scene. All the Hierarchy of the Sept and Protectors were in the same room. The Irish tongue of Hy-Breasail was lilting through the air like dandelion fluff parachuting in a summer breeze. As soon as she entered the room, an ocean of quietness took over.

Tomas, Quinn, Lorcan, and Aengus stood in front of the fireplace. Oísin, Sloane, Niall, and Ollie lingered in the dining room. Aengus' presence was a surprise. Treasa, Rio, Aífe, and Cillín were walking out of the kitchen with drinks and snacks on platters. The goal was not to overwhelm

Maeve with formality. All earthly forms were intact - no one was glittery or sparkly except for the Protectors. Maeve and Shae tried not to stare as they were astoundingly beautiful. The Protectors were breathtaking, ethereal forms in the shapes of human beings emitting a peaceful aura. The peaceful aura radiated throughout the room giving it a sense of purity and peace.

Tomas was the first to greet Maeve, Liam, Shae, and Roark. "You're home. We have all been awaiting your arrival. Sit, have a snack, a drink. We've plenty of time before we start our meeting." The men and women of the Hierarchy nodded their heads in agreement.

For no more than a second, Liam pulled Maeve closer to himself. After withdrawing from her side, he turned and looked at her. Gazing into her eyes, he said, "Maeve, I will be nearby. I must go with Roark and speak to the other Patrons. Go, have a snack, relax."

Maeve replied, "Liam, I'm fine. I promise. Go, do what you must."

Liam and Roark met up with the group standing in the dining room. Maeve watched as they all greeted each other. They were speaking Irish again.

"Beannachtaí, Liam agus Roark. Tá go leor lepté againn. An raibh go leor ceistenna ag an mBanphiorsa agus Shae?"

In her mind she heard: "Greetings, Liam and Roark. We have much to discuss. Did the Princess and Shae have many questions?" She expected the response she heard. Maeve thought excellent job, guys. Their reply was perfect. "No. We believe they thought it better to wait. Plus, there were many interruptions today deflecting any opportunities that arose."

"Ní raibh. Creidimid gurgurbh fhearr fanacht. Chomh maith leís sin, bhí go leor idirghabhálacha ann inniu ag sraonadh aon deiseanna a tháinig chun cinn."

The Patrons all looked relieved. They stood patting the boys on their backs. Nodding and joking with each other continuing their conversations in Irish.

Maeve could tell that Mam was very anxious to talk to her. Even though she knew what Maeve's destiny was, being her Mam and letting her go was heart-wrenching. She tried so hard to get away from Sloane and Rio. They knew her too well. Both kept engaging her in the delivery of the trays of food and drink she had prepared for everyone.

Maeve decided to take matters into her own hands. She cleared her throat a few times before making her speech. She hoped that she did not offend Tomas, but she felt the need to say something to the groups that stood before her. It still baffled Maeve that she could speak Irish. Yet, she began, "Fáilte go dtí mo bhaile. Is mór an onóir dom agus do mo thuismitheoirí go bhfuil sibh anseo. Ordlathas, Cosantóirí agus Pátrúin. Tá go leor ceisteanna agam agus táim cinnte go bhfuil ag Shae chom maith. Báin taithneamh as na sólaistí uile a ullmhaíodh. Táim ag súil go dtosóidh ár gcruinniú ag 3:30 in. Tabharfaidh sé seo am dúinn lé haghaidh diospóireachtaí, mar beidh mo dheirfiúracha, Bridget, Caitlín, agus Breana sa bhaile ag 5:30 tráthnóna inniu. Go raibh maith agaibh."

Maeve stepped graciously into her role as Princess amazed at herself and the speech she had just given. "Welcome to my home. My parents and I are honored to have you here. Hierarchy, Protectors, and Patrons, I have many questions as I am sure Shae does as well. Please all enjoy the refreshments that have been prepared. I expect that our meeting will begin at 3:30. This will give us time for discussion as my sisters, Bridget, Caitlín, and Breana will be home at 5:30 this evening. Thank you."

Silence echoed through the room. Slowly, the groups reconvened, and conversation resumed in low murmurs. A rumble of voices rippled throughout the room upon the arrival of Kían. Maeve started to run to him but remembered her position. She stopped dead in her tracks waiting for him to come to her. Kían stood before her, tilting his head down in reverence to his princess. Upon her approval, Kían took her hand and gently pressed it to his lips.

Maeve's eyes filled with tears. No words needed as they had not lost that ability. Kían's eyes spoke volumes. "My princess, I am so sorry that you felt abandoned this last day. I hope you find it in your heart to forgive me. I had no choice but to follow orders."

"Mo banphrionsa, tá brón orm gur mhothaigh tú tréigthe an lá deireanach. Tá súil agam bhfaighidh tú maithiúnas dom I do chroí. Ní raibh aon rogha agam ach orduithe a leanúint."

Maeve replied to Kían. "My beloved friend, no ill will to you ever passed my thoughts. Worry, yes. That is all."

"A chara mo ghaoil, ní raibh droch-smaointe agam riamh fút, nílim ach buartha fút, sin é."

Kían took her by her arm and escorted her to her Mam. Treasa would not have been able to bear another moment without taking Maeve into her arms. As soon as Maeve reached her Mam, she fell into her embrace. The two of them stood there for minutes just holding onto each other until Auntie Rio embraced them. Shae stood inches away lovingly watching the scene before her. Suddenly, all three of them reached their hands out to her, drawing her into their group hug.

The men paid no attention to the Maeve, Shae, Treasa and Rio hugging. Each group was engrossed in their own conversations. Sloane and Aífe kept note of the interaction trying to decipher if the emotions that were flowing between the group would deter the strength and abilities of Maeve in her future endeavors. Aífe motioned to Sloane when the group disbanded noting that Maeve remained strong and focused. This show of emotion did not in any way hinder the Princess' abilities whatsoever.

The groups began to disband gravitating to the living room. Seats had been set up around the room for all the members of the Hierarchy. Tomas stood in front of the fireplace. Without a word, the crowd quieted down, and each person stood before a seat though none sat. As Maeve entered the room, she noticed a chair beside Tomas, a chair that she had never seen before. Tomas motioned for her to stand beside him. Maeve wafted through the room as if thousands of fairies aided her.

Maeve stood beside Tomas. Her chair directly behind her. Everyone in the room stood in wait. Tomas touched Maeve gently on the shoulder in quiet direction. Maeve at once understood she must now lead. Maeve addressed the Hierarchy. "Please sit. Tomas will address us now. Questions will arise. They must wait until we have listened to Tomas' directives".

"Suigh anois le bhur dtóil mar tá Tomas chun labhairt anois. Tiocfaidh cesteanna chun cinn. Caithfidh siad fanacht go dtí go n-éistfimid le Tomas agus a threoracha."

The chair, an understated throne, was minimalistic yet its beauty was boundless. The throne which perched on a dais or platform carved of a silvery wood from Hy-Breasail. Encrusted in the most delicate carvings were the tiniest of jewels. She was able to see and feel the tiny little Celtic knots in her palms. The warmth of the wood brought calm over Maeve radiating a current of peacefulness throughout the room.

51 The Meeting

The meeting began. Tomas gave an overview of the previous day's school incident. News of the attack angered many in the room. Tomas informed the Hierarchy of evidence uncovering the possibility of the attack's orchestration by a member of the Sept. An active investigation was underway as Patrons gathered more evidence leading to the capture of the betrayed. Tomas introduced Liam as the future Patron leader and partner of the Princess.

Liam addressed the Hierarchy. His speech was inclusive of all incidents over the last twenty-four hours. Liam's strength and future were clear in the efficacy of his presentation. "This morning, Princess Maeve and Shae were approached by Fagen Darroch within the walls of Hawthorn. Threats against the Princess and Hy-Breasail were imminent. The Darroch family are high on the list of untrustworthy apart from Cillín. Unfortunately, as a Patron, he will be suspended due to further investigation into his brothers' involvement with the Regime."

"Ar maidin, chuaigh Fagen Darroch i dteagmháil le Banphrionsa Maeve agus Shae laistigh de bhallaí Hawthorn. Rinneadh bagairtí i gcoinne an Banphrionsa agus Hy-Breasail. Ní féidir linn muinín a bheith again as teaghlach

Darroch, seachas Cillín. Faraoir, mar Phátrún cuirfear ar fionraí é mar gheall ar imscrúdú breise ar an mbaint a bhí ag a dheartháireacha leis an Réimeas."

Cillín looked devastated by the news. Maeve watched him discovering a hint of something undefined. It was not the duplicitous expression she had seen from Fagen. She would alert Tomas and Liam privately. It was imperative that she not accuse Cillín of insubordination based on his family's participation in her attack. Cillín would not attend Hierarchy meetings until proven innocent. Maeve noticed Aífe taking his hand in hers. Maeve hoped that she too was not involved. Aífe was Liam's oldest sister. He would be devastated by her involvement.

Liam continued. "This morning Princess Maeve and Shae crossed Veil na Tairsí where they met Eamonn. Eamonn gifted our Princess with King Aaron's pendant for her protection. The Princess and Shae will not cross the Veil without a Patron for their safety and the future of Hy-Breasail. Again, Tomas will address any questions at the end of our meeting."

"Ar maidin thrasnaigh an Banphrionsa Maeve agus Shae Veil na Tairsí. Bhuail Eamonn leo. Tugadh an siogarla ó Rí Aaron dár mBanphrionsa as a cosaint. Tugadh foláireamh don Bhanphrionsa agus do Shae gan an Veil a thrasnú gan Phátrún as a sábháilteacht agus todhchaí Hy-Breasail. Aris, tabharfaidh Tomas aghaidh ar aon cheisteanna ag deireadh ár gcruinnithe."

Maeve waited until Liam finished then stood with her new-found confidence and continued to discuss the Darroch family.

"I am not convinced the Darrochs are the masterminds behind the attack yesterday. Although I left school in shock and anger, I lacked clarity. I did not doubt Finn's hatred. I do doubt his ability to concoct such an elaborate plan. Today, Fagen acted as if he was another. As if, his spirit or soul remained deep within his body overridden by a deep darkness. I believe it was the darkness that attacked us yesterday and confronted us today. I believe that this dark entity can overtake anyone without consent. I believe it preys on the weak. Fagen experienced a distinct transformation right before me. Therefore, I am not convinced that the Darrochs are taking part on their own volition. Until confirmed, Cillín will have no powers or titles for an indefinite amount of time. I am sorry for him, but I have no other choice. We will find the one who is against us. I know deep within the recesses of my heart we have been deceived. Deceived by one whom we all trust. I will not rest until that person or persons are found."

"Nílim cinnte gurb iad na Darrochs na máistrí taobh thiar den ionsaí inné. Cé gur fhág mé an scoil faoi sioc agus fearg, bhí easpa soiléireachta agam. Ní raibh amhras orm faoi fuath Fhinn. Tá amhras orm faoina chumas plean chomh casta a chur le chéile. Inniu, ghníomhaigh Fagen amhail is gur duine eile é. Amhail is dá bhfanfadh a spiorad nó a anam go domhain laistigh dá chorp sáraithe ag dorchadas domhain. Creidim gurbh é an dorchadas a d'ionsaigh muid inné agus a thug aghaidh orainn inniu. Creidim gur féidir leis an eintiteas dorcha seo duine ar bith a ligean thar ceal gan toiliú. Creidim go dtugann sé aghaidh ar an lag. Tháinig claochlú ar leith ar Fagen os mo chomhair. Dá bhrí sin, nílim cinnte go bhfuil na Darroch's ag glacadh páirte ina ndeoin féin. Go dtí go ndaingneofar é, bainfear Cillín dá chumhachtaí agus dá theideal ar feadh tréimhse éiginnte. Is oth liom é, ach fágadh gan aon rogha eile mé. Gheobhaidh muid an té atá inár gcoinne. Tá a fhios agam go domhain laistigh de chúlaithe mo chroí gur mealladh sinn. Mealladh ag duine a bhfuil muinín againn uile as. Ní bheidh mé I mo scíth go dtí go bhfaighfear an duine nó na daoine sin."

Maeve made eye contact with Liam afraid that he may be angry. It was the first time she ever contradicted him in any circumstance. As Princess of Hy-Breasail, she would have to remain steadfast in her directives no matter the effect it may have on every relationship in her life. Relief flooded through her body. Liam's eyes told her everything she needed to know. He not only was in awe of her beauty; he revered her strength, intelligence, and majesty. Maeve could feel tears brimming as he looked down in reverence to her. Taking a deep breath, she resumed her persona as Princess Maeve of Hy-Breasail. Maeve sat back down on her ríchathaoir or throne.

Suddenly, a burst of heated energy began to radiate from Ailm. The key from Liam began to move. The two connected. Maeve could feel immense waves of vibrations pulse through her body. The chair was enormously powerful acting like a conduit between the key and the talisman. Tomas placed his hand on Maeve to reassure her that all was fine. He inconspicuously squeezed the back of her elbow. He knew what was happening. When the rightful heir to the throne wore the talisman and key, it would unearth a powerful energy that would flow through them into Hy-Breasail's heir.

Shae also knew what was happening. It was important that she allay any of Maeve's fears. She had to make eye contact with the Princess, to help keep her focused on her goals. For the first time, Maeve could hear Shae's thoughts in Irish. A rush of fullness ran through Maeve's heart as she heard Shae say, "My dearest friend do not fret. What you feel right now is the new order of Hy-Breasail flowing through your veins. The key and talisman are reacting and will settle in a moment. Breathe." Maeve just smiled at her beloved friend.

"Ná bíodh imní ort, mo chara is gaire. Is é an rud atá á mhothú agat anois ná an t-ord nua de Hy-Breasail ag sreabhadh thríd na feitheacha. Tá an eochair agus an siogarla ag obair agus socróidh siad i gceann nóiméad. Tóg go bog é."

Shae's words of everlasting support were immeasurable.

Minutes passed and Maeve waited patiently for the energy flowing through her body to settle. The surge should have ebbed by now. Instead, it was intensifying inside of her. The surge was growing and changing. None of it made sense. Maeve was confident that Ailm and the talisman completed their quest. Without question, she was bound to the throne of Hy-Breasail. This change brought new meaning. It was a warning, a warning of impending danger.

Maeve scanned the room. Nothing was amiss. No one else could feel this energy. She was sure of it. Surprisingly, not even Shae. Maeve knew she had to deflect any negativity this force projected onto her. She closed her eyes and conjured the strength that she had felt grow in her over the last twenty-four hours. Maeve's feet began to tingle. The tingle burst through her body with the force of thousands of exploding stars. Maeve focused on Tomas' answers to the many questions asked by other members of the Hierarchy. There was no need to cause alarm.

52 Unwelcome Visitors

Maeve felt renewed as Tomas was ending the meeting. She would meet with him and Liam momentarily. It was imperative that they speak before her sisters arrived. She did not want her sisters involved in Hy-Breasail business. All three were nib noses and would have a barrage of questions. Maeve stood up from her seat intent on talking to Liam. Suddenly, a cold shiver flowed through her body. She grabbed the arm of the throne to steady herself. Liam was making his way over to her. Shae waved at Maeve as she was engaged in a conversation with Roark. It was obvious that Shae was unaware of the impending danger. This worried Maeve.

Liam was no further than five feet away from Maeve when the front door burst open. Seconds later, a tall, dark foreboding man entered the house. A hood swooped down over most of his face covering his identity. Quiet filled the room. Maeve saw Aengus place his hand on the hilt of his sword readying himself for battle. The man raised his hand over his head and snapped his fingers. A radiant energy force exploded through the room making everyone immobile.

The man gestured to the door a wavelike command. Maeve scanned the room realizing she alone was not motionless. Following behind the intruder were Fagen and Finn. Their arrival infuriated Maeve. The visitor continued to hover in the doorway. Liam was so close yet unreachable. Anger masked his face. No one could protect her as each had been rid of their strength and power. Maeve had to keep her composure. She would have to act alone.

Fagen and Finn gazed around the room to make sure that everyone was bound and secure. The visitor continued to hover in the doorway. Maeve was unable to make out who it was. She could see that Liam was worried. He was unable to help her. No one could. She thought, why has Ailm and the key become immobile as well? Their powers are not of Rowan. I must try to sit on the Hy-Breasail throne. It is the only way.

Maeve closed her eyes to see if she could find some clarity or direction from another power. She had no luck. When she opened her eyes, the visitor began to surround himself with a swirling mist. His head lifted to the ceiling with his hands outstretched, he chanted something incomprehensible. He then began to move toward her. The mist was filling the room. The mist was black with an iridescent hue that cast a purple shadow. He nodded as if in agreement with an unseen entity. As he did, the mist dispersed around the room transforming into dozens of chains.

The chains twisted shackling every Hierarchy member. None would be able to break through the magic dispelled. Fagen and Finn walked toward Maeve. Maeve placed her hand over Ailm. He had begun to dance on her chest. The key remained immobile. Maeve knew she needed Ailm's strength to defeat the darkness that had entered her home. Without the key, she was defenseless. Uniting them was her only chance to save her people and herself. She tried to unlock the talisman with the key but received sharp shocks electrifying her hands. She let out a small yelp at the pain. Finn and Fagen laughed.

Maeve looked at Fagen. She became perplexed because she could hear his thoughts. "Oh Maeve, I told you this morning I would be coming for you. If you only listened, no one else would have had to be involved. Now, I will take you away from all of them and all they can do is watch. Don't fight us or harm will come to your sisters."

"Oh Maeve, dúirt mé leat ar maidin go mbeinn ag teacht chun tú a fháil. Dá n-éistfeá liom, ni bheadh aon duine eile bainteach leis. Anois, tógfaidh mé tú ar shiúl ó gach ceann acu agus níl le déanamh acu ach féachaint. Ná troid linn nó tiocfaidh dochar do dheirfiúracha."

Maeve gasped. She could feel tears brimming in her eyes. He continued. "Maeve, there is someone waiting for my call. If they don't hear from me, you'll never see your sisters again. This is not a threat." He sneered at her.

"Maeve, tá duine eígin ag fanacht le glao gutháin uaim, mura gcloiseann siad uaim, ní fheicfidh tú do dheirfiúracha arís, ní bagairt é seo!"

Maeve looked over at Treasa. Mam could hear him, too. Maeve could not hear her mother's pleas, but her heart was aglow, it beamed with unconditional love. A gift for Maeve to see to ready her as ruler of Hy-Breasail. The love Mam had for her daughters was the same love Maeve would need to save her people. Princess Maeve was mother to all Hy-Breasail.

Maeve made a demand. She was not sure how Fagen would respond, but she needed to negotiate her own terms. "Fagen, I will come with you, but you must do these things for me. Once we go, my sisters will be out of danger and you are to free everyone in this room. Understood?"

"Fagen, tiocfaidh mé leat, ach caithfidh tú na rudaí seo a dhéanamh domsa. Nuair a fhágfaimid beidh mo dheirfiúracha as contúirt agus saorfar gach duine sa seomra seo. An dtuigeann tú?"

Fagen began to answer her but the hooded guest promptly interrupted. Fagen's leader spoke authoritatively allowing Maeve to know he and Finn were nothing but small soldiers in a much larger army: "Silence. I will answer. Princess, I will meet your conditions. I promise."

"Tost! Tabharfaidh mé freagra. Banphrionsa, comhlíonfar do choinníollacha. Geallaim!"

Fagen called out in front of everyone in the room sated Maeve. She saw the humiliation in his face.

53 The Reveal

After promising Maeve safety to her sisters and the Hierarchy, the man revealed himself. Gasps filled the room. Before them, stood Conall Darroch. The Darroch brothers' father. Rumors spread throughout Rowan when he abandoned his family so many years ago leaving Cillín, Finian, and Fagen in the care of their mother, Catriona. Most believed his departure better for the family. Others hoped him dead. He was known to have a horrific temper matched against Catriona's beautiful soul. His disappearance a blessing in disguise, until now.

Conall continued with a hint of sarcasm, "Well, well, well...my dear old friends. So, nice to see all of you. I am sure you are happy to see me as well. I apologize for you being all tied up. Please do not worry, I will keep Princess Maeve safe. She will be leaving with me shortly. She will remain Princess Maeve of Hy-Breasail until her eighteenth birthday. Then she will become Queen of the new Regime. Yes, the new, more powerful Regime commanded by Fergus, her beloved Uncle Fergus." Maeve could not believe what she had just heard. It could not be true. Poor Cillín. He looked devastated.

"Bhuel, bhuel, bhuel...mo sheanchairde. Tá sé chomh sibh go léir a fheiceáil. Táim cinnte go bhfuil sib ar fad sásta mise a fheiceáil freisin. Gabhaim mo leithscéal as ucht sibh a bheith srianta. Ná bi buartha coinneoidh mé an Banphrionsa Maeve slán. Beidh sí ag imeacht liom gan mhoill. Fanfaidh sí mar Banphrionsa Maeve Hy-Breasail go dtí go mbeidh sí ocht mbliana déag d'aois. Ansin beidh sí ina Banríon ar an Réimeas nua. Sea, an Réimeas nua níos cumhachtaí faoi cheannas Fergus, a Uncail muirneach Fergus."

Maeve knew she had to address Conall. He needed to know that she was not a frail, schoolgirl that he could bully. Carefully, she chose her words while focusing on an inanimate object across the room. She knew looking at Mam, Pa, Liam, or Shae would make her emotional.

She felt it imperative to keep her composure and stature as Princess. No fear or anger to be evident. Focusing helped her remain calm. She knew the strength within her was greater and more powerful than Conall. She did not fear him. She was not scared, nor would she allow herself to be. She would go with Finn, Fagen and Conall without duress

"Conall, your sarcasm is not appreciated. Under my rule, I expect dignity, grace, and respect to ALL. No excuses. Therefore, in the future, as I am to spend the next few years gracing your presence, I will expect nothing more than proper etiquette when addressing all inhabitants of Hy-Breasail. I am sure you understand."

"Conall, níl meas agam ar do searbhas. Faoi mo riail, beifear ag súil le dínit, grásta agus meas ar gach duine. Dá bhrí sin, amach anseo agus mé chun na blianta beaga amach romhainn a chaitheamh i do láthair ní bheidh súil agam le rud ar bith níos mó ná béasaíocht cheart agus tú ag tabhairt aghaidh ar áitritheoirí Hy-Breasail, gan aon leithscéal, táim cinnte go dtuigeann tú é seo?"

Conall knew he had overstepped his authority. His directives were to not let his past get in the way of Hy-Breasail's future. Therefore, he replied to Maeve in the most dignified fashion. In translation many heard: "I apologize, my dear Princess, I let my emotions get the best of me. I have not seen these people for years. Our past was turbulent. I should have been most respectful of you. You took no part in that. The past is the past. Today, we fight for the future of Hy-Breasail. I hope you can forgive me, your majesty."

"Gabhaim leithscéal a Banphrionsa daor, lig mé do mo chuid mothúchán an ceann is fearr a fháil orm. Ní fhaca mé na daoine seo le blianta. Bhí ár n-am atá caite corraitheach. Ba choir go mbeadh níos mó meas agam ort. Ní raibh aon pháirt agat sa mhéid sin. Tá an t-am áta caite san am atá caite. Inniu táimid ag troid ar son todhchaí Hy-Breasail. Tá súil agam go maithfidh tú dom é, a Mhórgacht."

Maeve chose her words carefully. As she spoke, she glared directly at Fagen and Finn. "Conall, I accept your apology. Henceforth, I expect nothing less than respectful decorum from you and any of your cohorts in my presence. We will not address this situation again. Thank you."

"Conall, glacaim le do leithscéal, ach, as seo amach nílim ag súil le rud ar bith níos lú ná cuibhiúlacht measúil uaitse ná do lucht leanúna i mo láthair. Ní thabharfaimid aghaidh ar an scéal seo arís, go raibh maith agat."

Both boys looked down at the floor. Neither had the nerve to look at her. Conall replied. "Thank you, my Princess for your understanding. It will never happen again. I promise."

"Go raibh maith agat, mo Bhanphrionsa as do thuiscint. Ní tharlóidh sé arís. Geallaim."

Conall offered his arm to Maeve. She placed her hand in the crux of his elbow allowing him to escort her out of her home. She walked out tall, brave, and beautiful leaving messages for Liam and Shae. In Irish, he received her message: "A Liam, feicfidh mé arís thú go luath. Gheobhaidh tú mé. Tá mo chroí ceangailte le do chroí. Ní theipfidh ar ár ngrá."

"To Liam, I will see you again soon. You will find me. My heart is yours. Our love will not fail."

Still immobile, Shae was able to let Liam know through her eyes that for the first time, she had heard Maeve in Irish as well. "Do Shae, mo chara is gaire, mo dheirfiúr. Is é Roark do fiorghrá. Le chéile beidh sibh ag cabhrú le Liam theacht ormsa. Tá neart an triúr agaibh gan teorainn, Smaoinigh ar an gCladach. Grá. Dílseacht. Cairdeas. Cabhróidh siad seo libh theacht orm." Even with the bonds of this evil regime, Shae's powers were evolving.

"To Shae, my dearest friend, my sister. Roark is your true love. Together you will help Liam find me. The strength of the three of you together is immeasurable. Think of the Claddagh. Love, loyalty, and friendship. These three will help you find me."

As soon as Maeve and Conall walked through the doorway exiting her house they crossed the Veil. At the same time, the chains shackling the Hierarchy dissipated into thin air; and the entity encircling the O'Flaherty sisters disappeared.

54 Conall

Crossing the Veil with Conall did not compare with this morning's crossing with Shae. Hy-Breasail was stunningly beautiful, that did not change. It was undeniably breathtaking. Yet, there was something new about it. Maeve felt an underlying sense of urgency and upset. It was a darkness - a foreboding feeling of damnation and doom. She could not be sure if this feeling came from Conall or the Uncle Fergus they spoke of.

Conall had not spoken a single word to her since their departure. Maeve was hesitant to start a conversation with him. She was not sure what she would say to him. She had to keep her mind sharp and her demeanor calm and authoritative. Maeve could not understand how they believed that she would join Fergus' regime and leave her loved ones behind. She knew she had to be smarter than them. To think ahead. To try and predict the Regime's actions.

The terrain they walked over was beautiful, very much like where she and Shae had met Eamonn. The trees were magnificent. The trunks interspersed with gorgeous gems of white and blue. Occasionally, Maeve noticed some tree trunks had emerald-like jewels encrusted. These were significantly different than the other trees. The ground was an emerald green mossy coverage. Incredibly soft and easy on the body as they walked. She felt as though the ground was buoyant as if a layer of water flowed underneath.

Unexpectedly, Conall held her arm gently and guided her along the path they were following. She tried not to look at him. If she did, she knew she would have to speak to him. So, she curtly thanked him for his aid while keeping her gaze on the path. Maeve saw something in her peripheral vision. She turned abruptly to see what it was only to trip on a small root jutting her forward. Conall caught her in his arms before she hit the soft earth below her. She turned her head upward to look at him in curiosity.

Maeve stared at Conall. He had transformed into a magnificent warrior. His hair was wavy, long, and dark gray interspersed with white and light tan. His eyes were almond shaped with dark, long, thick eyelashes. The color was a pure green like the sea glass that she collected at Auntie Rio's summer house. There were fine lines at the corners of his eyes like he had spent a lot of time smiling. Maeve sensed a gentleness in his face. Yet, there was a wolf-like resemblance. His beard was long, braided from his chin down to his clavicle. The braid woven with the finest golden thread. His garb was that of the finest warrior. His breastplate encrusted with the Hy-Breasail crest.

Maeve nodded at him acknowledging his gentlemanly behavior. Though she sensed a gentleness in Conall, she refused to let down her defenses. The duplicity of his sons left her questioning his sincerity. She would need more time to even consider trusting him. Maeve remained observant of all that was around her. In the future, she knew it may help her escape her captivity. She hoped that upon arrival at their destination, she could send a message to her loved ones. Hope of all hopes.

Maeve startled when Conall began talking to her. He had been silent for so long. She could not believe what she heard. "Banphrionsa, ní dhéanfaidh mé aon dochar duit. Geallaim. Tá mo chuid idéalach difriúil ná an Ordlathas, ach tá rún maith acu. Ní mian liom ach an rud is fearr le haghaidh Hy-Breasail. Chuala tú go leor scéalta fúm. Tá cuid acu fíoragus cuid eile nach bhfuil."

"Princess, no harm will come to you. I promise. My ideals are different than that of the Hierarchy but are with good intention. I want only the best for Hy-Breasail. You have heard many stories about me. Some are true. Some not."

She was not sure how to respond. She hesitated and Conall continued. He was apologizing for Finn and Fagen. "Tabhair maithiúnas le do thoil do Fagen agus Finian as a n-éagothroime. Bhrís Shae croí Finn. Tá a chuid gníomhartha fós do mhaithe. Tugadh iomardú do Fagen maidir le ar athbhrí ar an bhfírinne agus an fearg a chuir sé sa teachtaireacht ar maidin. Tá mórán foghlama ag mo bhuachaillí. Tá brón orm, ainneoin a gcuid tuairimí agus mothúchán tá tú inár dtodhchaí. Ár Banríona."

"Please forgive Fagen and Finian for their past indiscretions. Finn's heart broke when rejected by Shae. Still his actions are inexcusable. I reprimanded Fagen for the vehemence and anger he delivered his message with this morning. My boys have much to learn. I apologize. No matter their feelings, you are our future. Our Queen." Maeve thought that it had to be a ploy. It had to be. Conall was trying to gain her trust.

In the distance, Maeve could see a huge body of water. Beyond the water was an island with a tower sitting alone. Ailm had been quiet but now she felt a stirring on her chest. He was trying to warn her. Maeve knew she had to pretend to acquiesce to Conall's niceties. It was going to prove difficult, but she was to be queen. Maeve chose her words carefully as to not anger Conall. She tried her best. "Go raibh maith agat, Conall. Is mór agam leithscéal. Ceistim an dáiríreacht taobh thiar de do chuid focal. Labhraíonn tú ar Fin agus Fagen. Ach, chuir an t-ionsaí ag an scoil glúine atá le teacht i mbaol. D'fhéadfadh go leor doibh a bheith gortaithe nó níos measa, marbh. Conas a mhíníonn tú na gníomhartha seo? Domsa, mar Banphrionsa, níl na gníomhartha sin do mhaithe. Ina theannta sin, na bagairtí a rinneadh ar mo dheirfiúracha - banphrionsaithe Hy-Breasail amach anseo! An dtuigeann tú mo leisce glacadh le do chuid focal mar an fhírinne?"

"Thank you, Conall. I appreciate your apologies. I question the sincerity behind your words. You speak of Finn and Fagen. Yet, the attack at the school put future generations at risk. Many people were at risk for injury or worse, death from the attack. How do you explain those actions? As Princess the action is unforgiveable. Plus, the threats made against my sisters, future princesses of Hy-Breasail! Do you see my hesitation in accepting your words as truth?"

Conall's hold on Maeve's elbow tightened. She could not detect any change in his facial expressions. He stopped, turned, and looked down at Maeve. She, too, had transformed as she had earlier with Shae. Her beauty was breathtaking. She could see Conall's eyes soften as he looked down upon her face. His words sincere, "Banphrionsa, tuigim do chuid imní. Ní aon iontas dom go mbraitheann tú ar an mbealach seo. Geallaim nach dtiocfaidh aon díobháilduit féin ná do dheirfiúracha. Ní raibh sna bagairtí a rinneadh níos luaithe ach bagairti gan aon rún iad a leanúint. Ní raibh aon bhaint ag Fergus leis an t-ionsaí ar scoil. Níl a fhios againn cé a bhí taobh thiar don ionsaí."

"Princess, I understand your concerns. It is no great surprise that you would feel this way. I promise no harm will come to you or your sisters. The threats made earlier were just that, threats, with no intention of follow through. The attack at the school was not set forth by Fergus. We do not know who was behind the attack."

Maeve looked up at him questioning and said "Tugadh draíocht dorcha isteach i mo bhaile tráthnóna inniu. Bhí sé an-cosúil leis an dorchadas a tháinig isteach i rang Miss Almath inné. Conas is féidir leat a rá nach raibh aon bhaint ag Fergus leis an ionsaí?"

"Dark magic was brought into my home this evening. It was very much like the darkness that entered Miss Almath's class yesterday. How can you say that Fergus had nothing to do with the attack?"

His face softened more as he explained: "Tá corraíl i Hy-Breasail. Tá go leor faicsin ag iompú i gcoinne a chéile. Táimid ag iarraidh a dhéanamh amach cé atá ag iarraidh Hy-Breasail a scriosadh." His explanation made things clearer for Maeve.

"There is unrest in Hy-Breasail. Many factions are turning against one another. We are trying to figure out who wants to destroy Hy-Breasail."

Maeve was sounding more like a princess. "Más é sin an cás cén fáth nach dtéann Fergus i gcomhpháirt le Tomas. Nach ndéanfadh sé sin an dá ghrúpa níos láidre? Cad a tharlódh dá n-ordóinn é seo?" She was learning quickly, her words stately.

"If that is the case, why doesn't Fergus join forces with Tomas. Wouldn't that make both factions stronger? What if I commanded this?"

Conall hesitated before he spoke choosing his words carefully. "Banphrionsa, níl cead agam an cheist seo a fhreagairt. Is é an comhrá seo ná ceann a chaithfidh tú a bheith agat le Fergus, ní liomsa." Maeve thought his answer remarkably interesting. "Princess, I am not at liberty to answer this question. This conversation is one that you must have with Fergus, not me." Maeve knew now that Conall was a high-ranking officer but not who she needed to persuade to join forces with Tomas.

Conall continued to guide Maeve. Their pace gained some speed. It was obvious that Conall wanted to arrive at their destination before nightfall. The water was no more than one-half a mile away. Maeve was sure that she could see some sort of boat or watercraft waiting for them. Ailm had calmed. With that, Maeve felt a bit more comforted in her new surroundings. But the thought of a boat trip was making her feel a bit unsettled. She did not like water or boats. Maeve concentrated on the breathing exercises she had learned. Her heart caught as she thought of Shae.

Without Shae, she never would have learned to breathe calmly. The more she practiced it the less she felt the tugging in her belly.

55 Truths

As promised as soon as Maeve left with Conall everyone in the O'Flaherty home was able to move freely. Groups formed. Chatter continued. Moments later, Bridget, Caitlín, and Breana came through the door as boisterous as ever. There was a feeling of relief upon their arrival. No harm done as promised. Treasa drew all three girls into her arms and hugged them tightly. They started to struggle and whine about how hungry they were when Treasa let them go. She tried not to cry. They would not understand the danger they almost encountered being Maeve's sisters. They were excited to see Auntie Rio, so, she diverted their attention from the visitors by escorting them into the kitchen to get something to eat.

Liam, Roark, Niall, and Ollie were together planning Maeve's rescue. Tomas interrupted. He ordered them to stand down. Liam was about to protest when Niall interceded. He placed his arm around Liam's shoulder, pulled him back and quietly ordered him to keep silent. All acquiesced. Tomas addressed the four. Shae stood within earshot. She wanted to hear the plan to save Maeve. She could not believe what she heard: "Ní bheidh sé éasca ag aon duine agaibh é seo a chloisteáil. Mar sin, éist sula bhfreagraíonn tú. Ní bheimid ag dul i ndiaidh Maeve. Tá fir ag Aengus i Hy-Breasail ag faire ar ghluaiseachtaí Conall. Go dtí seo, níl aon rún ann dochar a dhéanamh di. Chinn mé gur féarr féachaint agus breathnú orainn. Freastalóidh Hy-Breasail go maith ar a bheith foighneach anois. Má fheicim go bhfuil Maeve I mbaol ar bith, déanfaidh mé an cinneadh seo a athluacháil."

Shae was sure of what she heard Tomas tell Liam, Roark, Niall, and Ollie: "This will not be easy for any of you to hear. So, listen before you react. We will not be going after Maeve. Aengus has men in Hy-Breasail watching Conall's movements. So far, there is no intention of bringing her harm. I have decided it is best that we remain watchful. Being patient now will serve Hy-Breasail well. If I see that Maeve is in any danger, I will reevaluate this decision."

Shae stood in disbelief. She watched Liam's expression. She knew he was not handling this news very well. She was concerned that he would act against Tomas's orders. She did not know what would be more devastating. Waiting around doing nothing or going against the Hierarchy's orders. Aífe came up behind her. She whispered in Shae's ear: "Shae, come with me. We have to talk."

The girls went upstairs into Maeve's bedroom. Shae felt overcome with emotion. Aífe gave her a moment. Shae took her time formulating what she wanted to say to Aífe: "Aífe, I don't understand what is going on. The orders from Tomas are inexcusable. Not going after Conall and Maeve. What if Conall harms Maeve or, worse, kills her."

"Shae, she's okay. Believe me when I tell you Conall will protect Maeve. He has brought her somewhere safe so that no harm will come to her."

It took a minute before Shae realized what Aífe had just told her. Shae was angry. "You're one of them. Get away from me. How could you do this to Liam? Get out!"

"Shae, listen. Conall is not as bad as you think. His intentions are good."

"Seriously, Aífe. After what we endured yesterday. You put your own brother in harm's way. How could you? Aífe! This is unbelievable. Oh, God is Cillín one of them too? Please tell me no. Aífe, tell me!" Aífe did not respond. By that reaction, Shae knew. "I'm telling Tomas now!"

Aífe finally responded: "He knows, Shae. At first, we knew the Sept's Hierarchy and the Regime would never consider an alliance. If there would be no alliance, we had to make sure the Regime's goal was to protect Maeve. So, you see, Cillín and I acted in good faith. We only wanted to keep Maeve safe and save Hy-Breasail. When we gained knowledge of Fagen and Finn's involvement, we knew we could infiltrate the Regime. Fagen and Finn were easy to fool. Fergus not so much. He questioned our loyalties. Over time, we gained his trust. Soon after, we informed Tomas, Quinn, Lorcan, and Aengus. At first, they were furious."

"As they should be, I'm beginning to understand your actions, but why lie. You could have told the Hierarchy before you infiltrated the Regime acting as a spy. It makes your intentions questionable."

"Shae, please let me finish." With a look of consternation, Shae nodded in agreement. She was willing to listen to the rest of Aífe's explanation. "Apparently, the Hierarchy knew what we had been doing. The anger they showed us upon our confession was a farce. Kían had been watching over our moves and reported us to Tomas months ago. They did not believe we were acting as spies for the Hierarchy. We had to convince them. Reprimands were harsh that we received for acting on the Sept's behalf without permission from the Hierarchy. But, if we had not infiltrated Fergus' Regime, the safety of Maeve would be questionable today."

Shae shakes her head in disbelief before she asks: "How can I believe anything you say?"

"You can. If I were lying, I would not be telling you any of this right now. I needed to allay your fears, Shae. Maeve knows she is safe with Conall. I wanted to tell you personally and he allowed me to do so. Cillín and I have a lot of explaining to do, but for now, we needed to make sure that Maeve's abduction looked real. Someone within the Hierarchy has turned against us and we do not know who. We had to ensure her safety."

Shae could not believe what she was hearing. Aífe and Cillín acted as spies. Shae felt betrayed. They were her friends. They were Maeve's friends. She turned away from Aífe.

"You knew Maeve was in danger. Neither of you said a word to me. I'm her closest friend and protector. I need some time. After I calm down, I may find forgiveness in my heart but right now I can't. Please leave!"

Shae stood and listened for Aífe to leave. Questions began to flood her mind. Did Papa know? Was he part of Fergus's regime? Papa loved Maeve. He could not put her life at risk.

Could he? Oh God, at this point anything is possible. Shae fell to her knees.

She felt nauseous. This had all been too much. She sat on the floor cradling herself in her own arms. She jumped when she felt a hand on her shoulder. Shae slowly and tentatively began to turn around to see who it was. Shae felt a flurry of relief flow over her body. It was Roark. Shae leapt into Roark's arms. He wrapped his arms around her and whispered into her ear. "Shhhh. Shae, beidh gach rud ceart go leor. Tá mé anseo. Geallaim nach bhfágfaidh mé thú." Shae felt comforted by Roark's words. "Shhhh. Shae, everything will be okay. I'm here. I promise I won't leave you."

Shae allowed Roark to hold her for a few seconds before she replied. "Roark, I am so afraid for Maeve. After Conall's entrance today, how can we believe that he has Maeve's best interests at heart. I find it hard to believe. No matter what Aífe says." He pulled her up from the floor and directed her to the edge of Maeve's bed. "Shae, have a seat. I have more to tell you." Shae began to calm down. "There is a bigger picture. Let me clarify some things for you. Fergus did form his own Regime. Cillín and Aífe infiltrated that Regime. They acted stupidly, yet, extremely brave. We must remember they sacrificed their lives for our Princess Maeve and Hy-Breasail."

Shae began to talk. Roark placed his finger on her lips gently. "You'll understand when I explain the rest, okay?" Shae was surprised how comfortable she was with Roark. Her experience with guys recently had not been positive especially with Finn and Fagen. He cared about her well-being and not just himself. "Yesterday, after the attack, they called a meeting with Tomas and informed him that Fergus would be willing to form an alliance. Tomas and Fergus agreed upon an agreement late last night. Tomas will lead with Fergus at his right hand. No one has claimed responsibility for yesterday's attack. Therefore, only a handful of us know that Fergus is on our side. It will remain that way for Maeve's safety and the future of Hy-Breasail."

Shae smiled at him. She took his hand in hers. "Roark, thank you for telling me this. Maeve and I are like sisters. I don't know what I would do without her. Knowing that she is being protected makes this a bit easier."

The next thing Shae had to say was going to be difficult as she did not know Roark for but a day. She did not want to sound too overbearing, so she hesitated briefly before continuing. "But I must tell you for the future, you must never shush me again. Under these circumstances I understand, but no one will keep me quiet. I grew up with three brothers and a father who is Chief of Police. I will always speak my mind. You understand, don't you?" Roark nodded in agreement and replied: "Shae, I'm so sorry. I did not mean any disrespect. I just knew how scared you were and needed to explain things so that I could allay your fears."

Shae looked up at him and firmly said: "Understood, but it can never happen again. I do not do well with anyone trying to make me acquiescent. It will never be okay. I have an important job to do in my role as protector of Princess Maeve. My strength and abilities far exceed most men and women. My momentary weakness came only from my concern for my friend and our princess' well-being."

He squeezed her hand to reassure her all would be fine. "It was not my intention. It will never happen again." Shae replied: "Thanks, I'm glad you understand my position. Let us leave this unfortunate incident in the past and focus on our main concern." At the same time, they both said "Maeve" and laughed. The tension between them dissipating. Roark continued: "There has been word that Conall has brought Princess Maeve to safety. She is being protected by Kían's wife, Eachna, and her brother, Díarmuid."

Shae looked shocked that Kían had a wife then shrugged it off. Nothing would surprise her anymore. She suddenly realized her reaction toward Maeve. She never gave thought to how Liam must be feeling. "How is Liam? I'm a mess, so he must be beside himself."

"He's fine now. Tomas filled him in on everything. Although with the history between the Darrochs and the three of you, he was hard to convince. They had to hold him back from Cillín for a moment or two and he looked like he wanted to kill his sister, but overall, he handled it well. Remember, it is difficult for him to leave Maeve's protection in someone else's hands. It's been him since you all met."

"Oh, I know. He's always been there for Maeve and I. Roark we have to go downstairs. I need to talk to Liam. See for myself that he's okay."

"Shae, you can't say anything to anyone about what I just told you. Few of the Hierarchy, Cillín, Aífe, me, and Liam know that Fergus has joined forces with us. It is imperative no one else knows until we are sure who our traitor is."

"OMG, Roark, is my father part of the faction? I need to know. I'm not sure if I'd be able to forgive him if he were."

"I don't know, Shae, but one thing at a time. Let's go find Liam. Let the other stuff figure itself out. If your father was part of Fergus' faction, there is nothing you or I can do about it. Okay?"

Shae nodded in agreement. Roark bent down and gently kissed Shae on the lips.

56 O'Flaherty Castle

Maeve was impressed that she did so well on the water. She did not feel nauseous or even queasy. She was so thankful. It would not have served her well to get sick right now. Conall was continuing in this new role of gentlemen and guardian. Maeve did not know if she should be impressed or nervous about the whole situation. He continued to hover over her making sure that no harm came to her. She had to admit that she was grateful that Conall was protecting her and not Finn or Fagen. She knew without question she would not be able to trust them.

The currach that she and Conall traveled in was wood framed, with a beautiful type of canvas sheathing covering the stiff wicker work. The canvas made from brilliant granite and Connemara marble mysteriously stretched over the hull. Maeve marveled at the work before her made from the magical forces of Hy-Breasail. In Rowan, a vessel made from marble would not stay afloat. Conall rowed the currach from the shore to the small island consisting of twenty-five acres which was to be their home until further notice.

Conall filled her in on the rules of the island. She would have limited freedoms. These restrictions would be to ensure her safety. He instructed that she remain within 200 yards from the perimeter of the castle. Maeve looked up at the castle. It was magnificent. The gardens were lush and beautiful. It was not going to be hard to keep close to her temporary home. There seemed to be a lot that would occupy her time. There were outbuildings that were as beautiful and grand as the castle itself. Now, she felt like a princess. She could not believe the majesty that was set forth before her.

The O'Flaherty Castle built with a limestone infused with glistening micro-diamonds left Maeve speechless. She stood in awe in front of this masterpiece, her new home. The grand entrance of the castle had an archway of Irish vine growing around the doorway creeping up the walls toward the second floor, supplying protection from darkness entering. The castle dwelling had a small turret. Maeve looked up at it with great interest. Conall noticing her gaze upward, said: "Is seomraí maireachtála áille iad Banphrionsa, ag barr an túir seo a mbíonn tú ag féachaint air. Roghnaíodh iad ar mhaithe le do shábháilteacht mar tá na ballaí tiubh agus do-airithe. Cuimsíonn an radharc áilleacht uile Hy-Breasail."

"Princess, at the top of this turret that you gaze upon, are beautiful living chambers chosen for your safety as the walls are thick and impenetrable. The view encompasses all the beauty of Hy-Breasail."

She turned and smiled at him. Maeve reflected on his words for a moment and felt very receptive to that idea. First, for her safety, and second, she thought of the fantastic view she would have of her surroundings. She nodded to him in agreement of his choice of lodging for her.

Donna Marie George

A man and woman stood at the grand entrance of the castle to greet Maeve and Conall. They both looked very much like Kían. Both gave her a very royal welcome, in reverence to her the man bowed and the woman curtsied. Maeve blushed. She did not know how to respond. This was far beyond the welcome she was prepared to receive. Just yesterday, she was a normal sixteen-year-old high schooler. Today, a princess living in her own castle. A castle named after her family. It felt a bit overwhelming.

The woman escorted Maeve to her room so that she could rest and dress for dinner. Maeve followed her up the winding staircase. The banister carved into tiny, twisted circlets. She ran her hands over the curves in the wood. The work was brilliant. At the top of the stairs was a door leading to Maeve's room. The arch of the doorway framed in honeysuckles their scent calmed Maeve. She noticed placed above the honeysuckles and centered over her door was a St. Brigid cross woven from rushes. The placement in the entryway of her bedroom supplied heavenly protection.

Maeve took a deep breath as she opened the door to her new room. It was grand. Maeve laughed to herself. Grand was not a word she often used. The colors chosen purposely to reflect those in her Rowan bedroom making it welcoming and comfortable. Only the colors were the same. The room was at least three times the size of her bedroom at home. The plush bed was immense with a canopy draped with a silvery blue sheer material that with the slightest breeze billowed. She thought she could easily fit her sisters and Shae in bed with her. There were dozens of big fluffy pillows at the head of the bed. They reminded her of marshmallows.

Near the window, there were two overstuffed comfortable chairs with ottomans. Staged in the middle of the two chairs was a medium sized table with a gorgeous reading lamp. The lamp of tiny star-like clusters in silver and ocean blue. Maeve noticed a stack of books sitting to the left of the lamp. The books included those on her personal reading list, plus a bunch more. Centered between the lamp and books was a vase of furze. Without doubt, she knew they were a gift from Kían.

The windows spanned from floor to ceiling with incredible glasswork. Each window depicted a different story in Maeve's life. Her parents, grandparents, sisters, Liam, Shae, and Roark detailed exquisitely. Directly, in front of Maeve was the most current. It was of her, Liam, Shae, and Roark walking into Hawthorn. The significance of this scene touched Maeve's heart. The picture was so lifelike, she reached out to touch it. She could feel a loving warmth emanating from its detail. As she closely examined it, Maeve noticed the illustration of the bonded strength of their friendship. It was an ethereal bonding intertwining their auras with tiny Celtic knots.

Overcome by emotion, Maeve looked at each of the scenes. Two windows were differently shaped than the others. The glasswork, too. The glass did not depict any life event. The doors had dewdrops infused into the glass. They were beautiful. Upon closer inspection, she realized that they were doors that opened onto the balcony. Maeve unlatched the doors and before her she found a scene of immeasurable beauty. The balcony overlooked the grounds surrounding the castle. This view would make being held in captivity more tolerable. Maeve almost forgot that someone else was in the room with her.

57 Eachna

Maeve realized that Conall had not properly introduced her to the woman who stood behind her. Or the man in the foyer just a few minutes ago. Maeve turned to the woman who had escorted her to her room and asked, "Go raibh maith agat as do chuid fháilteachas. Tá mo sheomra go hálainn. Cén t-ainm atá ort, le do thoil? Is mise Maeve." The woman looked shocked at the informality of Maeve's questioning. "Thank you so much for your hospitality. My room is beautiful. What is your name, please? I am Maeve." She hesitated a few moments before she answered Maeve.

Maeve thought she was beautiful. She had wavy and long, silvery blue hair cascading down her back like a feathery cloud. Baby ringlets framed her face. Her hair fastened at the back of her head with beautiful ribbons. Her eyes were like starbursts of gray microdiamonds. Her face was as white as snow with a frosting of silvery freckles splashed across her cheeks and nose. Her cheeks and lips were the color of ripe strawberries. She was a tiny sprite five feet tall. Maeve was in awe of her beauty. She did not realize she was staring at her until this beautiful lady before her startled her as she spoke.

"Banphrionsa, Eachna is ainm dom. Tá áthas orm bualadh leat. Tá mé anseo le freastail ort." Maeve was not comfortable with her answer. "Princess, my name is Eachna. I am pleased to meet you. I am at your service."

She replied to Eachna, "Eachna, tuigim gur mé Banphrionsa Ua-Breasail. Tá sé seo an-tábhachtach domsa. Ba maith liom é dá bhféadfaimis a bheith beagán níos neamhfhoirmiúil. Caithfidh mé dul i dtaithi air seo agus cabhróidh sé liom go mór. Tuigim na foirmiúlachtaí i aiteanna agus ocaidi éagsúla. Nuair a bhíonn muid ag labhairt lena chéile, smaoinigh ormsa mar cara." Eachna looked uncomfortable with Maeve's reply. "Eachna, I understand that I am the Princess of Hy-Breasail. This is all very new to me. I would really like it if we could be a bit more informal. This is something I must adjust to and it would help me very much. I understand formalities in different settings. When we are speaking to each other, please think of me as someone who is a friend."

Eachna did not know what to do or say. It was obvious that she was extremely uncomfortable with this conversation. She was quiet for a moment when someone knocked on the bedroom door. Maeve asked whoever it was to enter her room. Both she and Eachna turned to see who it was. Conall shocked Maeve. He had walked into her bed chamber like it was happenstance. Maeve looked at Eachna and asked: "Cad é a theastaíonn uait nach mbeadh ort fanacht go dtí go ndeachaigh mé síos an staighre don dinnéar?"

"Conall, what is it that you need that couldn't wait until I went downstairs for dinner?

Maeve's directness shocked Conall. Eachna stood nearby, yet a few steps behind Maeve. He responded in English. "Princess, I apologize. I do not wish to make you uncomfortable. I just wanted to let you know that I have had word from Tomas."

"Conall, I understand the urgency, but I would have preferred speaking of such matters downstairs. I'm sure you understand."

"Yes, Princess. I will see you in a few minutes at dinner."

Conall looked flustered. He was not a young man, but it was obvious that he knew he had overstepped his authority when he entered Maeve's chambers. Maeve waited until her door had shut completely before she let out a huge sigh of relief.

Maeve turned to Eachna and gave her a quick hug. At first Eachna was uncomfortable by Maeve's hug. Seconds later, she returned it most generously. Maeve pulled away from her and said, "Thank you, Eachna. This is all so overwhelming. I hope you understand."

"I do, Princess. I, too, understand the need to have a friend, a confidante. It would be my honor to have you place that role upon me."

"Thank you, Eachna."

Eachna knew that Kían would be pleased with her. Kían spoke of Maeve whenever he was home. He was very protective of her. Eachna would do everything in her power to keep her safe. Eachna's bed chamber was next to Maeve's. It was much smaller, of course, but just as grand.

"Princess Maeve, I wish to tell you something. You don't know who I am." Maeve looked at her quizzically but replied. "Of course, Eachna, please tell me." Eachna coyly continued: "I am Kían's wife."

Maeve's face went through a variety of facial expressions - disbelief, shock, elation, and happiness. "Eachna, I am so happy you told me. Honestly, Kían never told me he was married. That is why I reacted the way I just did. I'm going to have to talk to him." She chuckled. "Oh, Eachna, you are lovely. I am sure we will be exceptionally good friends."

"Princess, the man downstairs that greeted you. He is my twin brother, Díarmuid. We are both honored to serve and protect you. Most importantly, be your friend." Maeve felt a huge rush of calm flow through her body. This captivity was turning out to be much more positive than she expected.

"Dinner is soon, Princess. We must start getting you ready."

"Thank you, Eachna."

58 A Plan

Shae and Roark went downstairs side by side, fingers intertwined. Shae could hear Maeve's sisters chattering in the kitchen. Thank God Conall kept his promise. She scanned the room for Liam. He was in conference with Tomas. He looked better than she expected. Papa was in front of the fireplace talking to Niall. Niall's cheeks were fire engine red. He was angry. Furious most likely. Papa was trying to calm him down. Niall and Treasa had to be frantic. Safe or not, Maeve was their daughter.

Shae jumped when she heard a loud bang outside. It sounded like a herd of buffalo charging the house. Shae momentarily thought the worst. Was it another unwanted visitor? No. The door flung open as her brothers flooded the foyer. They had no clue of what had happened a brief time ago. They were laughing hysterically. She had no doubt that they had gotten themselves into mischief on their way over here. Their fiery auburn hair fit their personalities. Papa always called them "mo dhiabhal beag" or my little devils.

The O'Flaherty girls flew out of the kitchen colliding with her brothers. Shae noticed how awkward the situation was for the six of them. They all went silent. She laughed to herself. She had never seen them quieter and more uncomfortable than right now. Shae had to blink her eyes a few times. She thought she was seeing things. Right before her eyes a magnificent force bound the O'Flaherty and Kerrigan siblings together.

Shae squeezed Roark's hand. She wanted to tell him what had happened. He interrupted her by clearing his throat and nodding his head toward Tomas and Liam. "Shae, sorry. Somethings up with Tomas and Liam. Let's head over there. Whatever they're planning, we need to make sure we're part of it."

"No, don't be sorry. I agree. We need to know what the plans are for keeping Maeve safe."

On the short walk across the room, Shae could hear the girls talking about her brothers. Kevin, Aedan, and Patrick were oblivious. They had one thing on their minds, and it was not the O'Flaherty girls. Food was what they lived for. She heard them tell Rio they were starving. Rio laughed and said: "why am I not surprised."

Whether Tomas agreed or not, Shae was determined to be a part of keeping Maeve safe. There would be no room for debate. Roark guided her through the crowded living room to Tomas and Liam. Shae was surprised at the warm welcome she received from Tomas. She expected a prompt dismissal.

"Shae, Roark, perfect timing. We have much to discuss. I was just telling Liam that Princess Maeve is safe. Conall has taken her to a small, protected island in the middle of Hy-Breasail. Kían's wife, Eachna, and his brother-in-law, Díarmuid, are among those that are protecting her."

Shae could not keep silent. This news was a bit confusing. She was happy to hear about Eachna and Díarmuid, although, she was not convinced that Conall was trustworthy.

"Sir, I know that it has been confirmed that Fergus does not wish Maeve harm. I do not mean to be disrespectful, but I must ask this question. Without a doubt, are you sure that Conall will protect Maeve? His sons' actions over the last twenty-four hours have been nothing but questionable. We must watch Finn and Fagen especially Fagen. Finn's hate for me is real, which makes him dangerous; but the evilness that flows through Fagen is immense. When he confronted Maeve and I this morning, there was something quite different about him. I do not think that he is following Fergus' orders. I believe that he may be working with the other faction. If true and Conall is as trustworthy as you say, I am sure he is not aware of his son's duplicity."

All three of the men in front of her, were thunderstruck. Shae was right. Fagen's allegiance turned away from his father and Fergus as well as the Septs. Patrons were working with other sources to find out whose Fagen's leader was. Shae continued, "Sir, if allowable, I believe that it would be in the best interest of Hy-Breasail if Liam, Roark, and I cross the Veil to serve in the protection of Princess Maeve. Between us, Conall, Eachna, and Díarmuid, we will be able to keep the Princess safe."

Tomas hesitated before answering Shae. He looked at Liam and Roark to see what their reaction was to Shae's proposal. Both looked at him in agreement. Liam looked a bit relieved by Shae's suggestion. When he finally answered, he said, "Shae, as you know Fergus and I have come to an agreement. The Sept and the Regime are now one entity. Fergus has stepped down as head of the Regime. He will now be reporting directly to me. Our unification will enable all of us to protect Princess Maeve and Hy-Breasail's future."

Shae waited intently to hear Tomas' next step in the plan.

"Slowly, we have been uncovering defectors from the Sept who had joined Fergus' Regime. Please realize this is an ongoing investigation. Some subverted by order; others by their own initiative. We needed to infiltrate the Regime to gain intel. Shae, your father was involved in this mission. Do not doubt your father's allegiance. He is loyal to the Sept. Unfortunately, Cillin and Aífe acted upon their own initiative. Actions considered unconscionable as they could have jeopardized everyone's safety. Rogue missions are not acceptable."

Tears formed on the ridges of Shae's eyes. She was so relieved. Even more than she was a few moments ago upon her brothers' arrival. "It is imperative that this information not be shared. The three of you, along with Quinn, Lorcan, Aengus, Cillín, Aífe, Conall, Eachna, Díarmuid, and Ollie are aware of this new allegiance. Many others remain remain uninformed. Therefore, this allegiance must be secret. Understood?" All three nodded in concurrence of this new development.

Tomas continued to relay the plan that he and Liam had set forth: "Liam and I have formulated a plan. The three of you will travel via Veil na Tairsí with one condition. Riognach will travel with you. She is one of Hy-Breasail's best trackers - more accomplished than any other Patron in the Sept." The news shocked Shae. Shae never thought of her as anything more than Auntie Rio. Tomas continued, "Upon arrival at the O'Flaherty castle, Rio will act as advisor to Princess Maeve and, to you, Shae. Rio will act as Hy-Breasail's historian and advisor in your new roles in Hy-Breasail. She will assist both of you during this time of transition."

Suddenly, Shae saw a picture flash in front of her. It was that of Mayor Aisling reading Rowan's tale of <u>The Queen of Hy-Breasail</u>. Shae did not want to be rude, but she knew she needed to confirm the message of the vision she had just received. "Sir, I understand. Please, may I ask you something?" Tomas nodded. In Irish, she continued: "A dhuine uasail, an bhféadfainn ceist a chur faoi Bhanríon Hy-Breasail? Creidim go bhfuil sé seo fíor. Is iad Rio agus Niall na cúplaí. Is é Rowan an talamh anaithnid. Agus... Maeve an Bhanríon a rabhthas ag súil léi ón scéal?

"Sir, I know that Maeve is our Princess, but may I ask about the Queen of Hy-Breasail? I believe this to be true. Rio and Niall are the twins. The unknown land is Rowan. And...Maeve is the awaited Queen from the story?"

Tomas took Shae's hands in his and said: "Sea, Shae. Is í Maeve an Bhanríon a bhfuilimid ag fanacht léi. Níl tú i do aonar. Tá daoine eile ann nach bhfuil a céannacht ar eolas acu.Tá Shae, comharbas an réimeas i Hy-Breasail ainmnithe ag Aveline de réimse na mbeannachtaí. Mar is eol duit, ní ceart breithe an choróin. Tá sé bunaithe ar na bronntanais a rugadh le duine amháin. Tá a fhios ag na caomhnóirí cé hiad na rí nó banríon sula dtagann siad. Níl a fhios againne. Bhronn Aveline bronntanais neamhbheo banríon ar Maeve.

Ba í a seanmháthair, an Bhanríon Brigid, a rugadh le bronntanais den sórt sin. Tá sé neamhghnách go leanfaidh comharbas an choróin laistigh den teaghlach céanna. Tá a fhios againn go bhfuil cúiseanna ag na Caomhnóirí."

"Yes, Shae. Maeve is the Queen we have been waiting for. You are not alone. There are others that do not know her identity. Shae, the succession of reign chosen in Hy-Breasail by Aveline of the Realm of Blessings. As you know, the crown is not a birthright. It is based on the gifts that one is born with. The guardians know who the king or queen are before they are born. We do not. Aveline presented Maeve with the unearthly gifts of a queen. Her grandmother, Queen Brigid, was the last born with such gifts. It is unusual that the crown's lineage will remain within the same family. We know the Guardians have their reasons."

Tomas continued in English. "A faction formed against the Queen. Niall and Riognach were incredibly young at the time. The story we read every year is true to original events. Many years ago, members of a faction infiltrated the O'Flaherty Castle killing the Queen and King. Fortunately, the faction left Niall, Riognach, and Fergus untouched. Members of the Hierarchy found them in the nursery crying. It is not known for how long; their nanny had disappeared. For their safety, the three were brought to Rowan."

Shae face reflected the questions formulating in her mind. "I don't understand. I've heard the stories Auntie Rio told Maeve about Grandma Brigid. How is that possible?"

"It is easy. Niall and Riognach both have clear memories of their mother. The Divine Oracles bestowed beautiful memories upon them. It was imperative that we keep her memory alive for future generations. It was undetermined how long it would be before another princess would be born. It was a welcome surprise when Aveline announced that Maeve was our new princess. Never did we think that they would be from the same bloodline. That was a true gift."

Shae placed her hand over her heart. She looked at all three of them. Without words, they all understood what her heart spoke. The emotion she felt had left her speechless but the love on her face and reverence she felt toward Maeve was without end.

59 Branagh

Maeve stood in front of her mirror. The events of today were a bit overwhelming. She wished Liam and Shae were with her. She had a deep yearning in her heart to see them. Sensing her loneliness, Ailm released a burst of love. It flowed throughout her body. Gently, she cradled him in her hand and whispered, "go raibh maith agat, a stór beag" which translated to "thank you, my little dear". As she took off her necklace, he began to change into his true form. He purred lovingly at her, while rubbing his little face against her cheek. Maeve kissed the tip of his little nose before placing him in the small pocket beneath her cape. She could feel his heartbeat in synchrony with hers.

Maeve gazed at her reflection. For the first time, she saw her trueness gleaming. Her aura was colorful, filled with light and love, shining brightly signifying her purity and kindness. Its light brilliantly lit as bright as a lighthouse's beacon. She sighed with relief upon the realization that she had walked through life in naïveté. Its magnifying strength made her more beautiful as it amplified her limitless leadership abilities. She felt a powerful sense of adequacy and strength in her future role of Princess of Hy-Breasail.

So caught up in her thoughts, Maeve forgot that Eachna was still in her room. Maeve became embarrassed. She did not want Eachna to think her conceited. Eachna's face did not reflect disparaging thoughts, it only revealed a motherly type of love and concern. Maeve blushed, her eyes becoming doe-like as she smiled at Eachna, Eachna smiled back with a look of knowingness. Maeve felt overwhelmed by her reaction. Maeve knew she had deep feelings for her. Maybe not love, but a profound sense of caring. Maeve decided to take her thoughts outside and walked out onto the terrace. As she passed Eachna, she gave her a quick hug. Eachna's cheeks flushed as she continued to organize Maeve's belongings.

Moments later, Eachna interrupted Maeve on the terrace excusing herself to get ready for dinner. Maeve acknowledged her making one request. She asked that Eachna move swiftly as she did not want to go to dinner unescorted. Eachna concurred. After thirty minutes or so, Maeve knocked on Eachna's door. There was no answer. Maeve realized she may still be readying herself for dinner. Maeve shrugged her shoulders. She would wait a few more minutes and try Eachna's door again before descending the steps into the main hall. She sat down at her mirrored vanity deciding to look through its drawers.

Kían had thought of everything. Her favorite lip glosses and hand and body creams filled the drawers. Maeve felt a prickle run across the surface of her skin. It made the hair on her arms stand on end. She looked up at her reflection. She was astonished to find another person standing behind her in her reflection. It was a woman, although not Eachna. She looked familiar. She felt a knowingness about her. The woman had black hair and eyes as green as emeralds. After a few seconds, the shock subsided, she realized the familiarity. Maeve stunned herself into silence.

Ailm was squirming in her pocket. Slowly, Maeve turned towards the woman behind her. Surprised, Maeve found herself alone. The woman only appeared in her reflection. She turned herself back around towards her mirror. The woman was still there. Maeve felt a soft brush against her shoulder. It felt as if someone had gently laid their hand upon her. This soft touch gave her a feeling of protectiveness. This motherly figure meant her no harm. The woman was exceptionally beautiful. Emotions overcame her with the realization of the woman's identity. She had not seen her since she was but a little girl. Maeve blinked her eyes to make sure the woman before her was truly who she thought it was. Maeve exclaimed, "Auntie Branagh!"

Auntie Branagh was Shae's mam. Branagh smiled at Maeve lovingly. Maeve could hear Branagh's thoughts: "A chara Maeve, táim anseo chun a chur in iúl duit go bhfuil gach duine againn ag déanamh gach rud inár gcumhacht chun tú a choinneáil slán. Caithfidh tú éisteacht leis an guth beag sin i do chloigeann i gcónaí. Ní thabharfaidh sé drochchomhairle duit riamh. Tá duine amháin nach féidir leat muinín a chur ann. Tá a croí truaillithe le féiniúlacht agus le fonn cumhachta. Ní gá ach muinín a bheith agat as na daoine a d'fhan dilis duitse. Tá orm imeacht. Bí sábháilte, mo mhuirnín Banphrionsa Maeve. Tá mo ghrá leat."

"My dear Maeve, I am here to let you know that all of us are doing everything in our power to keep you safe. You must always listen to that small voice inside your head. It will never give you ill advice. There is one that you trust that you must not. For her tainted heart must be full of selfishness and a desire for power. Only trust those who have remained true to you. I must go. Be safe, my sweet Princess Maeve. My love is with you." Branagh blew Maeve a kiss as her reflection dissipated into the mirror's glass.

Branagh's visitation was unsettling. Maeve could not believe her message. Someone she loved and trusted was not to be trustworthy. Maeve thought this to be the ultimate betrayal. Without hesitation she called for Eachna. When she received no immediate response, she shouted Eachna's name. Eachna flew through the adjoining door. Maeve flew into her arms. Eachna held her tightly whispering: "Banphrionsa, cad is cúis imní duit. Tá mé anseo. Tá tú faoi chosaint. Shhh, a Bhanphrionsa, tá tú sábháilte. Geallaim."

"Princess, what causes you to fret? I am here. You are safe. Shhh, my Princess, you are safe. I promise."

"Eachna, I know. When you were preparing for dinner, Branagh Kerrigan appeared in my reflection. Shae's mam. Shae's mam who died years ago. Has Kían told you about any of my gifts?"

"Some, yes, Princess Maeve."

"It took me a moment or two to remember who she was. We were little girls when she died. I have no doubt in my mind that Branagh Kerrigan visited me."

"Princess, please relax. I know this has been upsetting. If you did see her, it is possible that Branagh came to give you a message or a reassurance. It does not mean that she meant you harm."

"You are correct. She came to warn me of impending danger! A danger from someone that I know and trust."

Maeve felt her voice rise a few octaves. She plopped down on the edge of her bed.

"I'm sorry, Eachna, I did not mean to raise my voice. I am just a bit flustered. We should go downstairs, and I will see if it is something, I should bring up during dinner with Conall. Let us forget about this for now and go downstairs."

"Yes, Princess," Eachna replied. Eachna knew that the presence of Branagh Kerrigan might be of great concern. She would have to get a message to Kían.

60 Goodbyes

Shae, Roark, Liam, and Rio packed their bags, made proper arrangements at home, if needed, and said goodbye to their respective families as directed by Tomas. They were to meet back at Maeve's by 7:00 p.m. There was no way to know how long they would be in Hy-Breasail. The hope was that they would return to Rowan within a fortnight. Shae was worried about her father. He had been quiet as she packed. Now, they were driving in silence. Soon they would arrive at the O'Flaherty's without speaking a word. Her thoughts were a jumbled mess in her mind.

Finally, Shae just blurted out everything she needed to say. "Papa, I was so disappointed in you when I heard you may have joined Fergus' Regime. I didn't know if I could look at you the same way. You have been my everything. My rock since Ma passed. What would I have done if Tomas hadn't told me the truth? My ignorance could have destroyed our relationship. I understand you could not tell me. Even now you can't say anything. So, before I leave, you need to know what I feel. I can only hope that I will be half the Patron you are. I am honored to call you Papa."

The Chief reached over and grabbed Shae's hand. He held it for a long time. Something he had not done since she was a little girl. Tears brimmed in his eyes. He was so proud of his little girl. His reaction was so uncharacteristic, Shae did not know how to respond.

"Papa, what is it? I will be fine. I will be with Liam. He would never allow anything to happen to me. Plus, Roark will be there." The Chief faked a look of surprise. He had not uttered a word in fear that if he did, he would start crying. "Don't look so surprised. I'm sure Aveline sent message to you about us a long time ago. You know he would sacrifice his life for me. So, please don't worry."

The Chief coughed and cleared his throat before he broke his silence. Shae saw him swallow a few times. She smiled to herself. "I know all of these things. But, Shae, you and your brothers are my world. I made a promise to your Ma on the day you were born to keep you safe. Now, I must break that promise and let you go. It is not easy for me. I know you are in competent hands. Plus, there is no doubt in my mind that YOU are capable of immeasurable greatness."

"I love you, Papa. You'll see. The time will go by so fast especially keeping an eye on Kevin, Aedan, and Patrick. They will keep you terribly busy. Before you know it I will be home." The Chief turned to look at her. His eyes were so full of love. He was so proud of the young woman she had become. One of the most important people responsible for protecting Hy-Breasail's Princess. She squeezed his hand.

The car ride flew by. Before they knew it, they had pulled up at the O'Flaherty's. Liam, Roark, Sloane, and Oisín had already arrived. Papa parked right behind the O'Connor's car. Shae could see Auntie Rio walking across her front lawn. The Chief and Shae exited the car and met at the trunk. The Chief took Shae into his arms, gave her a huge bear hug, and kissed her on the forehead. Shae smiled. Her Papa was not one to show affection.

"Papa, question. Where will we cross? This morning it was easy because of what had happened with Fagen. It was as if someone had dropped sparkly breadcrumbs for me to follow. But now, how will we know where to go?"

"Shae, when two or more of the Sept's Hierarchy are gathered a portal can be conjured. The Hierarchy alerted the Protectors and Oracles. They will aid Rio and the rest of you in crossing. The four of you will need strength and power to assist you in travel." Shae nodded in acknowledgement.

They closed the trunk and walked up to the porch together. The Chief insisted on carrying Shae's bag. He said that it was an honor to take care of his girl. Shae's heart was overflowing with love for her Papa. Shae held his arm up the walkway toward the front door. She felt overwhelmed with emotion. She was going to miss him. This would be the first time she had ever been away from Rowan without him. She held onto him tighter.

Shae was shocked when she walked into the O'Flaherty's foyer. Declan and Raegan were there. Even though they did not attend the earlier meeting, it was obvious that the Hierarchy decided they should join them. Shae did not know why but she was a bit jealous. She had known Raegan since kindergarten, but the O'Flaherty's were a close family. She wondered if Maeve would choose Raegan instead of her to be her confidante. They had never excluded her before, but she suddenly felt uncertain of her place in the Hierarchy. Shae squeezed her Papa's elbow. He looked at her with question. Once he realized her concern, he let her know through facial queues that she need not worry.

Tomas and Niall were sitting in the living room in front of the fireplace. They had not moved since earlier this evening. Shae wished she could hear their conversation. She knew it had to be about Liam. They were afraid he would act with his heart and not his warrior training. Aine, Maeve's aunt, was sitting on the couch with Treasa. The thought of Declan and Raegan's crossing the Veil na Tairsí distressed Aine terribly. Shae hoped that they were prepared for the potential dangers they must face. Were any of them truly ready, though.

Treasa kept talking to Aine trying to bring her some comfort. "Sweetie, I know this is difficult. Our children are a gift to us from Aveline. We have known this day was coming. Rio will be with them. Her skill and training exemplary. She will keep them safe."

Donall, Treasa's brother, stood behind his wife. He gently massaged her shoulders trying to bring her comfort. He looked at his sister with concern. They all knew this could end terribly. Yet, they had to remain strong for Aine. Her family was not from Rowan. She did not descend from the Hy-Breasail lineage. She was "coimthíoch" or "outsider".

"Love, I know this is hard. We must keep positive. The Hierarchy has prepared for our princess' arrival for over 200 years. A multitude of action plans are in place to keep our future Queen safe." Treasa gave her a tight reassuring hug. Inside Treasa's heart felt like it was about to explode. She hid her own angst for Aine's sake. Treasa must be strong for her daughter and those who protect her.

Tomas summoned Kían and the Protectors to join the meeting. Upon their arrival and that of the other members of the Hierarchy, Tomas began. "Fáilte! Tá do thiomantas dár mBanphrionsa le moladh. Ní thabharfar faoi deara an íobairt atá á déanamh agat. Cuireadh in iúl dom go bhfaca an Banphrionsa Maeve taispeánadh Branagh Kerrigan. Deimhníonn cuma Branagh gur mó an bhagairt i gcoinne ár mBanphrionsa ná mar a bhíothas ag súil. D'ordaigh mé do Eachna aon cheann de eagla na Banphrionsa Maeve a mhaolú. Go dtí seo, glacfaidh mé leis gur comhartha maith é nach raibh aon nuacht againn go dtí seo."

"Welcome! Your dedication to our Princess is commendable. The sacrifice you are making will not go unnoticed. I have received information from Hy-Breasail that Princess Maeve has seen the apparition of Branagh Kerrigan. Branagh's appearance confirms that the threat against our Princess is greater than expected. I have instructed Eachna to allay any of Princess Maeve's fears. So far I will assume no news is good news."

Shae felt faint. She glanced over at Papa. All the color had drained from his face. He was white as a ghost. Suddenly, she felt a presence behind her. She turned around to find Roark directly behind her. He placed his hands on her waist to ground her. She could not believe what she had just heard. Her mother's visitation meant only one thing. Maeve was in great danger.

Danger that Shae hoped they would be prepared to defeat. Shae knew that a message of this enormity was infrequent and rare. No visitation had taken place since the death of Queen Brigid and King Aaron. She hated to leave

Papa now. He was extremely distraught over this news. Shae felt conflicted. Niall looked over at her. She could hear his thoughts. "Do not worry about your father. You know that I will take care of him. We all will. He needs to stay to be here for your brothers and keep Rowan safe." His words calmed her fears about her father's well-being.

Tomas continued, "I will continue in English as many of you have not received the gift of Irish. As you all know, Princess Maeve visit from an apparition is of great worry. This is the reason Declan and Raegan will join you in travel. Their gifts will increase ten-fold once crossing Veil na Tairsí. They will be able to sense imminent danger. You must heed all warnings. None considered insignificant. Do you understand?" Liam, Shae, Roark, Rio, Declan, and Raegan nodded in unison. "Aveline shall arrive shortly. She will update you on all developments. Our hope is she brings information regarding the leader of this dangerous faction."

Murmurs flooded the room. Visits from Aveline were unheard of. She delivered her messages via Kían as he was her most trusted messenger. Shae felt Roark's grip on her tighten. Liam remained stoic. He did not quiver at the mention of Aveline. Tomas continued. "Eachna and Díarmuid are on high alert. Without question, there will be an attempt on Princess Maeve's life. Gréagoír will arrive at the castle shortly. He will guard Princess Maeve. You will receive all directives from me through him while you are in Hy-Breasail. No one will act independently. Gréagoír will lead. So, NO ONE will divert from directives, under any circumstances. This protocol must be followed." Tomas looked directly at Liam when he made his last statement.

61 Guardians

Eachna told Díarmuid the news about Branagh Kerrigan's visitation. Díarmuid contacted the Hierarchy. Without hesitation, special forces arrived to protect the castle. Protectors from all provinces of Hy-Breasail received instructions to report to its governing Divine Oracle for assignments. Tomas messaged Aveline with instructions recommending all Foreseers to be on high alert. Notification of developments from all Protectors and Foreseers must be prompt.

Aveline would first travel to the O'Flaherty Castle then onto Rowan where she would speak to the Patrons crossing Veil na Tairsí. Tomas requested the assignment of Gréagóir to act as Head Guardian of the O'Flaherty Castle. It was imperative for Princess Maeve's safety as Gréagóir was Aveline's most trusted advisor. Tales of a romantic relationship between Aveline and the Head Guardian circulated both Realms. A tale of marriage or a partnership was rumored for many centuries.

Aveline and Gréagóir dwelled in the Realm of Blessings. It acted as a conduit between both worlds. It was the reason the visitation from Branagh was of great concern. Visitations from apparitions not of royalty were warnings. Allegedly,

Aveline spoke little but when she did whoever she spoke to should take heed. Aveline's words were messages from a higher power. These were clear, concise, and exact. The devout called her angel, the skeptics demonic.

Dinner was pleasant. Conall kept telling Maeve how impressed he was with her and how enchanting she looked. He seemed very worried. It was making Maeve overthink her relationship with him. She felt that he was being genuinely nice with a tidbit of creepy added in. Halfway through their second course, Conall told her that they would have a surprise guest. Unfortunately, she was running a bit late but would be here shortly.

Maeve felt a bit of relief and asked, "Conall, is that why you have been acting a bit out of the ordinary? You've been making me feel extremely uncomfortable." He replied, "Princess, that was not my intention. Our visitor is Aveline. I am a bit nervous. I apologize as my usual demeanor is quite calm. Very few are privileged to meet her. She must have an important message for you."

Maeve could not believe Aveline would visit her. They had spoken in the past, but an actual visit was extraordinary. From the first time they spoke, Maeve became enamored by Aveline, but meeting her in person left her momentarily speechless. She realized she had never replied to Conall. "I'm so sorry. I was just thinking about Aveline's visit. It is quite extraordinary. I have spoken to her in the past though we have never met. I am interested in the message she will be delivering."

Conall continued, "Princess, I am unsure if you know everything about Aveline. Before she arrives, let me educate you about her. It is rumored that she is breathtakingly beautiful inside and out with one exception. If anyone tries to endanger the future of Rowan or Hy-Breasail, she can turn into a vile, ungodly, venomous warrior. This person or persons will endure a horrific, tortuous death. Many have claimed that it is always best to remain on her good side."

Maeve took in every word of Conall's description of Aveline. She could not believe that the beautiful voice that had spoken to her so many years ago could avenge her enemy with so much rage. She continued to listen to Conall intently.

"Díarmuid called upon Aveline to bring Gréagóir to protect you and the castle. He will be joining Aveline. They should arrive shortly. It is rumored that he and Aveline are married. I have also heard some refer to them as partners. Either way, they are a force to respect and honor. Gréagóir is the greatest and strongest Guardian. Very much like our own Aengus. He has not met defeat. Unfortunately, when your grandparents met their demise, he was just a wee lad."

Maeve looked sadly at Conall at the mention of her grandparents. She wished that sometimes Conall would just stop talking. He was in the habit of saying too much. The timing could not be more perfect. Eachna and Maeve both looked toward the entryway. Someone with great strength had knocked on the door. The knock echoed throughout the bottom floor of the castle. Maeve could hear Díarmuid ask whoever it was to enter. Seconds later, she could hear the muffled voices of a man and woman.

Maeve, Eachna, and Conall waited intently to see if the visitors were in fact Aveline and Gréagóir. Within seconds, both Aveline and Gréagoír entered the dining room. The strength and power emanating from them both were undeniable and immeasurable. Aveline greeted Maeve. "My dear Princess Maeve, we are deeply sorry to arrive so late to dinner. Please forgive our tardiness."

Maeve all but sputtered. Aveline's exquisite beauty was overwhelming. Her hair was red as rubies. It ran down her back in hundreds of loose curls. Her eyes were black onyx with silver bursts glistening from pupil through iris rimmed in long ruby red eyelashes with sprinklings of black interspersed. As dark as her eyes were, there was no question that they spoke a million words as if entranced in her gaze. Her skin was opalescent with an aura of silver shimmering all about her. Her gown was a blood red designed in the Victorian era style. Below the bodice a gold band encrusted with tiny pieces of onyx and opal wrapped around her body.

Aveline's chiseled features were stunningly beautiful like *Michelangelo's* sculpture of Mary in the "Pieta". She looked like a Divine Oracle but was much taller, not less than six feet. Both Aveline and Gréagoír looked like two beautiful actors walking the red carpet at the Oscars. Maeve momentarily fell star-struck, then returned to her royal-like persona: "Aveline. Gréagoír. I am so delighted to finally meet you. Do not worry about your timing. We have not yet started our main meal. I am incredibly happy that you are here."

Aveline captivated Maeve. She could not wait to tell Shae. Never had she imagined that she would be sitting and having dinner with Aveline. It was one thing to hear stories about her and hear her speak, but this was an amazing experience. As soon as she had the courage, she could not help but ask her questions about her gifts. "Before we continue, I must thank you for coming to me so long ago. You dispelled my fears about going to school. My life changed forever that day.

Aveline bowed her head in reverence to Maeve. Maeve felt goosebumps rise from her feet to the top of her head. Aveline's presence meant more to her than she thought. At that moment, she knew that Aveline would be one of her most trusted allies. Of this, Maeve had no doubt. "Aveline, if you don't mind, could I ask you a question?" Aveline, of course, could not say no. "Princess Maeve, of course, I am here for you. You may ask me anything you would like. It is my honor to serve you."

Aveline's smile was magical. Maeve felt as if she had become entrenched in the wings of an angel. She felt warm and protected. Maeve swelled with happiness, contentment, and a new sense of strength. Strength that no one or nothing could penetrate. Aveline looked into Maeve's eyes. Maeve could see into Aveline's inner being. She knew that no harm would come to her with Aveline reigning as leader of the Realm of Blessings.

"Thank you. I am genuinely concerned for the safety of those coming across Veil na Tairsí this evening. They are all very dear to me. Do we have enough protection for them to get here safely?" Aveline hesitated for a moment. She wanted to answer this question to relieve any of the fears that the princess might have. "Princess, if I may, I will direct this question to all in attendance this evening. Nothing that I wish to say is meant to frighten any of you. There are some things that you must know before I leave."

Maeve nodded giving Aveline permission to speak. "Yes, of course. It is imperative that you address us all on this situation." Maeve spoke, "Anyone who may have a question for Aveline, please feel free with one exception. I request that questions relate only to the safety of Rowan and Hy-Breasail." Conall was amazed at how well Princess Maeve had adapted in such a brief time.

"First, I would like to confirm that you have seen the apparition of Branagh." Maeve replied, "Yes, Aveline, I have." It was obvious that Maeve's confirmation distressed Aveline. "As you know the Realm of Blessings cannot be breached. No one can enter or leave without my permission. Within my Realm is a portal. This portal acts as a conduit for the dead to pass into the heavens. Very few can return to warn of impending danger. It was not I who gave Branagh passage. Therefore, someone has infiltrated my Realm."

Maeve noticed that the table became silenced by Aveline's message. She knew not why. She realized there was much she did not know about the world beyond Rowan.

62 Aveline's Message

As Aveline watched Maeve, she knew there had been no time to educate Maeve on the Realms outside of Rowan. Aveline then shared the dual importance of the Realm of Blessings. "My dear princess, Branagh coming to visit you is of major importance. It is an Act of Warning to you and all the inhabitants of Hy-Breasail, not excluding the people of Rowan. For me, it is also significant in my finding the threat against you and Hy-Breasail. As we now know, Fergus is not one to worry about." Relief flooded across Conall's face at Aveline's acknowledgement. "The only way that Branagh could cross from the heavens would be under my direct command. As I said, I did not sanction her crossing. I am worried it is one who is close to me, very dear to my heart. This person or persons has limited powers here yet is extremely powerful in my Realm."

Everyone turned toward Gréagóir. Not accusingly but questioning. The reaction was instinctual. Obviously, he and Aveline were close. Who else would such great power and access to the portal? Maeve looked to Conall. His face had become ashen. Eachna and Díarmuid both had an aura of red emanating around them. Maeve began to feel unnerved. She was in more danger than originally believed. It was obvious they, too, were thinking this as well. Even though he was closest to Aveline, Gréagoír's involvement did not make sense. Was there another? Maeve did not know. She waited for Aveline to explain further.

Aveline continued with great hesitancy, "I believe my brother, Manannán, to be our enemy." Conall, Eachna, and Díarmuid looked extremely worried. Gréagoír became furious. Maeve watched as Gréagoír grew in body and strength. Maeve was astonished by his transformation. No one uttered a word.

"Manannán, my beloved brother, is very cunning and manipulative. He is quite different from the people of my Realm. Many call him 'black sheep' as he is unlike any other. He acts without conscience. I believe he infiltrated the Sept, convincing the most vulnerable and angry to follow him. I have been suspicious of him for many a fortnight. I believe I know his followers. Until confirmed, it is unnecessary to divulge their identities. Princess, you will be informed first."

"Aveline, I am sorry about your brother's involvement. It must be difficult for you. I do agree with your summation. I do not want to know the identities of his followers until confirmed."

"Thank you, Princess. May I answer your earlier question?" Maeve nodded for Aveline to continue. "Unfortunately, I will not be escorting Rio, Liam, Roark, Shae, Declan, and Raegan across the Veil. I have spoken to Eamonn and he will meet them and aide in their travels. Specific directives are in place once one has crossed the Veil. Your aunt, Riognach, is a very accomplished guide. The power of the six supplies the group protection until arriving at the castle. Unfortunately, I must return to the Realm of Blessings to ensure the protection of all of our Realms."

Maeve replied to Aveline, "I understand and ask that you leave promptly after dinner to speak with Rio, Liam, Roark, Shae, Declan, and Raegan. You must be forthright with them. I demand, and I say it with the utmost respect, that you do not leave out the tiniest detail. It is imperative that they arrive here safely to me." Aveline nodded in agreement adding: "I concur, Princess. I shall leave expeditiously."

It seemed incomprehensible to Maeve that Aveline's brother could be capable of such hatred. As often as her sisters had driven her crazy, she would never betray them as Manannán did Aveline. Maeve's curiosity over the situation led her to ask, "Before you leave, I must ask why you believe that our enemy is your own brother?"

"Princess, my mother died giving birth to Manannán. Coincidentally, my father signed a royal decree changing the rules of succession to the crown. Upon the death of the reigning Queen or King, the eldest living child will inherit the crown. My father did not feel a crown should be discriminatory. Thus, his changes allowed the crown to pass to a woman, in this instance, me. Mannanán believes this change occurred because my father blamed him for my mother's death. It is, of course, not true. The Oracles foretold my mother's death. My brother does not believe this to be true. So, he takes his revenge out on me."

"I mean no offense to you, Aveline, but I must ask. Then, what part do I have in his hatred toward you?"

"Princess, my brother is stubborn and impulsive. He always has been. My father once told me that no matter what, with or without the royal decree, the crown would never pass to my brother."

Maeve did her best not to react to Aveline's message. She turned to Conall for confirmation. "Conall, I understand Aveline's message. I need to ask. Do you feel the group coming to Hy-Breasail will arrive safely at Veil na Tairsí without the protection of Aveline?"

"Princess, the chances of the group encountering danger is low. The skills beheld by Rio, Liam, and Roark should be beneficial. They should pass through the Veil unscathed. Yet, there will always remain the chance of ambush. Therefore, I can make no promises."

Maeve responded to Aveline in question, "I must add that from my perception Manannán may act against me directly. Would it not be easier to attack the castle when so many eyes will be at the Veil? This, of course, is speculation on my part since I do not know your brother as well as you."

Aveline was amazed at the Princess' intuitiveness regarding the situation at hand and replied: "My dear Princess, you are correct. I have no doubt that this may be the course of action my brother will take." She turned toward Gréagóir. "My dearest, you will remain here with our Princess to protect her against my brother. It is without doubt that our Princess may be right about my brother's plans. So, we must be prepared on many fronts. I believe with you here and Eamonn at the Veil all possibilities have been accounted for."

Maeve continued, "Aveline, take heed. I need you to leave for Rowan now. I thank you for your bravery and the ability to share your misgivings about Manannán. Go, now. Be safe." Aveline bowed her head down in reverence to Maeve, turned, and walked down the long corridor to the main entrance of the castle. Maeve watched as Aveline dissipated into thin air.

Maeve took a deep breath. She asked everyone to continue with their dinner and desserts. "Enjoy. Let us savor this moment of peace and tranquility. We cannot let uncertainty taint our evening. Please finish the beautiful meal the chef has prepared for us."

63 Aveline's Arrival

Upon receiving word that Aveline was on her way; Tomas made an announcement to everyone in the O'Flaherty home. "I have just received word from Díarmuid that Aveline will be arriving shortly. She will be updating us on a situation that has arisen. It will affect the travel of Rio, Liam, Roark, Shae, Declan, and Raegan. I will allow her to explain."

Shae turned to Roark, "Why did he bother mentioning a change if he won't give us details? All he needed to say was that she would be arriving shortly with news. Now, all the parents in the room look more nervous than they were before. Aine looks like she's going to have a heart attack."

Roark whispered: "Shae, as our High Chief he has to apprise us of every situation. It is his duty. Princess Maeve would expect nothing less." Shae half rolled her eyes and answered: "You're right. I know I'm overreacting. I can't believe you just called Maeve, Princess Maeve. It sounds so odd. But it also sounds so right." Shae moved closer to Roark. She found comfort being near him. Just the slightest touch brought her a sense of completeness. It did not go unnoticed by Ollie. Or Rio and Treasa.

Everyone in the room jumped when they heard the loud pounding on the front door. Treasa and Niall ran to the door with expectation. Both turned to look at Tomas, waiting for him to give the order to open the door. Tomas nodded to Treasa giving her the honor of welcoming Aveline into her home. Shae saw what she thought was excitement on

Treasa's face as she began turning the knob. A collective breath radiated throughout the room.

Treasa opened the door to find Aveline standing majestically with an air of beauty. Treasa welcomed her home in graciousness. In Irish, she spoke: "Aveline, fáilte. Is mór an onóir dom tú a bheith mar mo aoi agam. Tar isteach agus glac sólás anseo agus tú ag tabhairt do theachtaireachta dúinn go léir."

"Aveline, welcome. I am honored to have you as my guest. Please come in and take comfort here while you deliver your message to us all."

Her entrance was humbly understated. Yet, Shae heard herself gasp. She quickly covered her mouth in embarrassment. Aveline's beauty had taken her breath away. All eyes followed Aveline. Her sprightly stride was buoyant as if gliding on an invisible cloud. Aveline acknowledged everyone as she passed them. Most did not speak. All were in awe of her beauty and overcome by her visitation. Tomas greeted her by taking both her hands in his; he then gently kissed her on both cheeks. Aveline responded graciously as she turned toward her audience.

"Hello, everyone! I am Aveline from Réimse na Beannachtaí or the Realm of Blessings. Please sit. I come with news and to allay some of your fears. Moments ago, I left Hy-Breasail. It was there that I spent a few moments with Princess Maeve at the O'Flaherty Castle. She is well. With Tomas' permission I am to communicate updates from Hy-Breasail."

Shae noticed that Tomas was equally enamored by Aveline as everyone else in the room. He replied to Aveline: "Of course Aveline, please proceed with Princess Maeve's message. Aveline placed her hand gently on his arm and said: "thank you, Tomas." She turned gracefully to face those in the room to share Maeve's message.

"After the events of yesterday at the Hawthorn, it is obvious that Princess Maeve is in great danger. I have acquainted her with my suspicions. There has been the most disturbing news received from Réimse na Beannachtaí. The portal from my Realm has destabilized. As a result, the inhabitants can move freely between all Realms, including Hy-Breasail. There are only two with power to open this portal. Myself, and, my brother, Manannán." There was a collective gasp.

Aveline continued: "Upon the death of my father, Manannán was ordered to be placed in protective custody. This order confined him to Réimse na Beannachtaí. My father noted his lack of loyalty to me, my home, and Hy-Breasail. In retaliation of this order, we expected him to make attempts to harm the people of Rowan and Hy-Breasail in the greatest way possible - through the death of Princess Maeve. Losing her would be crippling across many Realms. This personal battle between siblings has extended beyond the imaginable. Réimse na Beannachtaí and Hy-Breasail will battle together against my brother. For that, I am so sorry."

Shae was about to interrupt Aveline with a question when Roark gently nudged her to keep quiet. "There has also been another development. Many have infiltrated the Sept who we believe are followers of Manannán. I believe that someone coerced Finn and Fagen Darroch to join forces with him and innocently brainwashed them into believing Fergus was the culpable threat. Cillín and Aífe's infiltration into Fergus' Regime revealed this to us. Earlier today, the Hierarchy moved both to a safe place for protection. It was imperative to protect them from Cillin's brothers and/or Manannán himself. Princess Maeve is being apprised of this new development by Gréagoír and Díarmuid as we speak."

Aveline continued, "Rio, Liam, Roark, Shae, Declan, and Raegan, will come with me. We need to speak privately. Please, the rest of you excluding Tomas and Aengus, find refuge at Rio's home. Quinn will join you and be available for questions. All shall be respectful to those seeking answers. It is of the utmost importance that we come together as one. I will not tolerate discord among us. Please understand. Thank you."

64 A Private Meeting

Rio, Liam, Roark, Shae, Declan, and Raegan stood and watched as their family members left the O'Flaherty home to go next door. They knew it would be the last time they would see them until their return from Hy-Breasail. Shae started to feel a bit misty. Niall walked out the door his arm around Ollie. It was obvious to Shae that her Pa would be okay with Niall by his side. Treasa held the same posture with Aine. Shae thought how sad Aine looked. It was best she left sooner rather than later. Sitting around was just delaying the inevitable. No matter what, the six of them would be leaving soon for Hy-Breasail.

Mam called Bridget, Caitlín, and Breana a few times before they made their way downstairs. The three barreled down the stairs like a herd of buffalo. Chattering away like no one else was in the house. Shae looked up at them trying to get their attention. They were oblivious to her multiple attempts. All three of them stopped in her tracks as soon as they realized that Aveline was standing at the bottom of the stairs. Shae was astonished at their transformation. In the ten years that Shae knew the O'Flaherty's, never had the girls been quiet as church mice. The transformation was unreal. It was an absolute shame Maeve and Mrs. O did not have the pleasure of this experience.

The girls were the last ones out the front door trailing a few feet behind the Kerrigan boys. Aveline followed behind the group of six shutting and locking the door behind them. Shae heard her say, "Enchanting group, aren't they? Their futures will be very entertaining." Shae was not sure if that was a good thing or not.

Aveline glided through the room. She stood quietly in front of the fireplace. The room became eerily silent. Shae thought of Father Roan during high holy mass. He would stand at the altar and the church would at once be quiet. Aveline had that same power. "I hope that the news I presented earlier was not distressing. I felt it important to educate you on the dangers crossing Veil na Tairsí. I was unable to arrange for another Guardian or Protector to meet you. Aengus and a few of his men will escort you to the Veil but will remain in Rowan. They will aid you in crossing over. We are currently contacting the Guardian of the Riches, Eamonn, to meet you at the Veil. We have great hope that he will be able to greet you there. Then you will travel from Veil na Tairsí to the O'Flaherty Castle. Rio, with your ability and training, you will lead this group. Liam and Roark, I expect that you will not deter from your orders. Do you understand?" Both Liam and Roark responded in the affirmative.

"Shae, you must leave emotion aside. Keep strong and focused whatever challenge you face. Raegan will help you, as you will support her in her new status within the Hierarchy. Roark and Liam, I expect the same of you with

Declan. The twins are, let us say, thrown into the fire. They both received the Gift of Foreseer upon birth. This gift will amplify once they cross over Veil na Tairsí. You must help them if visions occur; some may be terrifying. To Raegan and Declan, they will seem real. Allay their fears by reconnecting them to the present. Many visions will be forewarnings. Heed these warnings. Do you understand?"

All six of them nodded in agreement with Aveline. Rio did not look at all flustered by any of what Aveline had just shared with the group. Raegan grabbed Shae's hand. As soon as she felt Raegan's hand touch hers, she felt settled, grounded. She looked at Raegan and started to thank her, but Raegan stopped her. She did not have to say a word. Shae could hear her voice – her unspoken voice. Raegan told her all would be fine. They would work as a team to keep Maeve safe. Shae squeezed her hand tightly.

Aveline continued, "It is time. Grab your belongings. I hope you packed lightly. The trip will be long and arduous. Are you ready?" Once again, they all nodded in agreement with Aveline. No one felt the need to speak. Her words were all they needed to continue in their quest.

65 The Shores

A few times during dinner, Maeve caught herself staring at Gréagoír. She could not believe how gorgeous he was. He and Aveline were obviously born to be together. They were a beautiful couple.

Gréagoír walked with the same air of majesty as Aveline. His hair was as black as onyx with ruby red highlights running through it. It was wavy and long parted in the middle with two braids on each side cascading down his back. He wore a mustache and beard accented with the same hue as his hair. His beard long and cut square at the bottom. His eyes were green with amber and black speckles. His eyes rimmed with black eyelashes. He had a ruddy complexion which complemented his hair perfectly. His features chiseled like the Divine Oracles. He stood way over six feet tall.

Gréagoír was very engaging during dinner. His stories allowed Maeve to forget her worries. During dinner, he bent over to her and whispered in her ear. He spoke these words of comfort. "Banphrionsa, tá a fhios agam nach bhfuil aithne agat ormsa. Ligeann mo ghrá d'Aveline agus an grá agus an chosaint atá aici duit, Rowan, agus Hy-Breasail, na mothúcháin chéanna a bheith agam. Níl muid murab ionann agus tusa agus Liam, cé gur as Réimse eile muid.

Ceanglaíonn an nascacht atá agam le Aveline iad siúd is breá léi. Deirim é seo ionas go mbeidh a fhios agat go gcosnóidh mé tú le mo shaol. Iarraim ort gan eagla a bheith ort, a Bhanphrionsa. Creid i do chroí an rud a deirim leat a bheith fíor."

"Princess, I know that you do not know me. My love for Aveline and the love and protectiveness she has for you, Rowan, and Hy-Breasail, allows me to have the same feelings. We are not unlike you and Liam, even though we are from another Realm. The connectedness I have with Aveline binds me to those she loves. I say this so you know that I will protect you with my life. I ask you to fear not, my Princess. Believe in your heart what I say to you to be true."

Maeve became overcome with emotion. Yet, she replied: "Gréagoír, go raibh míle maith agat as do chuid focal cineálta. Chiallaigh na focail seo an domhan domsa. A fhios agam go bhfuil duine éigin gar dom ar féidir liom muinín a bheith dílis dom chomh maith le Rowan agus is faoiseamh é Row-agus Hy-Breasail. Ní dhéanfar dearmad ar do chineáltas agus do dhílseacht.

"Gréagoír, thank you so much for your kind words. These words have meant the world to me. Knowing I have someone near that I can trust to be faithful to me as well as Rowan and Hy-Breasail is a relief. Your kindness and loyalty shall not be forgotten."

After dinner, Maeve and Eachna retreated upstairs to their rooms. She appreciated Conall's concern over her well-being, but she had enough of his hovering for one day. Eachna asked Maeve if she needed any help getting ready for bed. Maeve did not want to be rude to Eachna, but she was more than capable of readying herself. She had been for nearly seventeen years. Plus, she just needed to be alone. She washed her face and brushed her teeth and plopped herself down on her bed. It was so strange not to have cell phone service or her computer. Yet, she found it a bit peaceful.

Maeve's thoughts drifted to Liam, Shae, Raegan, and Declan. She missed them so much. She prayed that they arrived unscathed. Together they could face any adversity, even Manannán. Maeve remained hopeful and filled with optimism that her family, her love, and her best friend would arrive soon to help her face the danger that lie ahead.

Maeve laid in her bed with her head propped up so she could look out her window at the vast land that lay outside. She wished that instead of a beautiful landscape of grass, rock, and water her eyes would rest on her loved ones walking toward the castle. It was not but five minutes later she saw what looked like a boat coming ashore. Moments later she could see a group exiting the boat. It looked as if there were six occupants. Was she dreaming or was it an answered prayer? She felt her heart flutter with excitement.

Maeve got out of bed and ran out onto her balcony. She hoped that the group forming on the shores were who she had prayed for. The flutter in her heart quickly dissipated. She felt a tiny twinge of fear in the pit of her belly. She wished she had a pair of binoculars. The quivering in her belly had turned to dread and despair. It was Manannán.

66 Manannán

Maeve began to talk to herself, believing and hoping that by doing so she could change the scene that lay before her. She started to shake. Ailm confirmed the feeling of danger coursing through Maeve's body. He jumped down from her bed and ran to her. Moments before, he had been cuddling up against her. She felt Ailm rubbing his head against her leg. She bent down and picked him up. He crept up her arm and placed his head against her cheek, rubbing his head against her while purring intensely. She cradled him in her hands and asked, "Cad é, beag? Tá mé i mbaol, nach bhfuil?"

"What is it, little one? I am in danger, am I not?

He looked into her eyes knowingly. Maeve was still amazed at the intelligence of her little talisman. He tilted his head to the side as if questioning her. Then, as if he were not unlike her, she could hear his voice: "Banphrionsa, ní cairde iad siúd ar an gcladach. Tá Manannán tagtha. Glaoigh ar Diurmuid agus Gréagóir anois."

"Princess, those on the shore are not friends. Manannán has arrived. Call for Díarmuid and Gréagóir now." Within a second, Ailm turned back into a pendant. Maeve placed him around her neck. She felt his warmth against her heart as she looked out onto the shore.

Maeve called for Eachna with urgency in her voice. Eachna came through the door connecting their rooms without hesitation. "Princess Maeve, what is it? Are you okay?"

"Eachna, I need to speak to Gréagoír and Díarmuid at once. Manannán is here. Look upon the shore. He is not alone. There are many with him." Eachna looked panicked for a moment, then turned to leave.

Maeve grabbed her arm and asked, "Please contact Díarmuid quickly. I do not wish to be alone for long." Eachna understood.

"Yes, Princess. I will do so with great expediency."

Maeve was shocked when there was a knock on her door a moment later. She forgot that as twins Díarmuid and Eachna had the ability to speak to each other telepathically. They were very much like Raegan and Declan. Eachna opened the door to allow Díarmuid to enter. Surprisingly, Conall and Gréagoír also entered the room.

Maeve told them of her sighting. The men slowly walked over to the balcony. Maeve noticed that they remained in the shadows so not to reveal themselves to those on the shore. Maeve walked ahead of them. She wanted Manannán to see her. She wanted to let him know that she did not fear him.

For a moment, her thoughts wandered to the group that she wished had arrived upon the shores of the O'Flaherty Castle. Hoping and praying that they remained safe. Hoping that they did not yet cross over Veil na Tairsí. Praying that their paths did not cross with Manannán's. She did not feel confident that the group would have been able to defeat Manannán and his men. Unfortunately, she knew she could not dwell on their well-being right now. Everyone in the Castle was in imminent danger.

Maeve turned to the men. Her face revealed nothing of the strategic plan she was formulating in her mind. As nervous as she had been moments before, a plan to outsmart her unwanted guests was bringing forth great strength and unfettered focus. She could feel great power stirring within her soul. She addressed Conall, Gréagoír, and Díarmuid.

"Thank you all for coming so quickly. As you can well see, Manannán is here and he has brought an entourage with him. Díarmuid, I would like you to assure the staff that they are safe within the castle walls. I do not wish them to panic about their safety. Also, for continuity, it is of the utmost importance that you continue to be the liaison between the Castle and Tomas. Conall, you will remain in constant contact with Gréagoír and his men ensuring the safety of Hy-Breasail. You will act as my personal advisor. I expect you to keep me abreast of all decisions and actions against our enemy. I also would like you to update me on the whereabouts of Rio, Liam, Shae, Roark, Declan, and Raegan. Díarmuid. Please contact Kían. Please inform me of any new news from Rowan. Thank you."

The three men knew that there would be no more discussion. All three bowed their heads to Maeve, turned, and left the room. Maeve then addressed Eachna: "Eachna, I relinquish you from any responsibilities for the time-being. Your unfailing loyalty has not gone unnoticed. As wife to Kían, I feel closest to you and would like you by my side. As in ancient times, my Lady in Waiting. Will you find this difficult?"

"Princess Maeve, of course not. I am honored that you feel this way about me. It is a blessing. I thank you for this appointment."

Eachna bowed her head to Maeve. Maeve continued, "Thank you very much. I am pleased that you feel as you do. But, when we are alone, please feel free to let go of the formalities. I do not wish for you to feel compelled to keep up with royal protocol during these times. It will please me to just have you as my friend and confidante when we are alone. I understand when others are here to keep up the royal façade as it would be detrimental to my authority over Hy-Breasail."

"Princess, this is true; yet, I understand, and I thank you." Maeve took Eachna's hands in her own and gave them a gentle reassuring squeeze.

Maeve sat and observed Manannán. He was setting up his camp. At one point she caught him peering at her with a telescope. Maeve's concerns about him were minor. Her major was worry was bringing her loved ones to Hy-Breasail safely. Manannán's presence made her feel stronger and braver. He obviously thought his arrival would cause her fear and weaken her resolve. His presence did just the opposite.

67 The Crossing

Shae inhaled deep as if her breath would behold the beloved elements of Rowan. As she knew there was a small possibility that she would never return to her earthly home. She felt filled with a great amount of emotion renewing within her a sense of excitement and strength. Shae knew her journey would ensure the safety and continuity of Rowan and Hy-Breasail. It was her birthright to continue this quest. Roark's grip tightened on her hand as they listened intently to Rio's speech.

"Okay, everyone, it is time. You heard the words of Aveline. As you know, we will be traveling with Eamonn, the Guardian of Riches once we cross Veil na Tairsí. I must reiterate that we must not divert from our mission. It is extremely important that we stay focused no matter what we meet along the way. Do you understand?"

Everyone nodded in agreement. It was imperative that they continue the journey in solidarity. The future of Hy-Breasail, Rowan and the life of their Princess were at stake.

"Let us form the Circle of Travelers. Place all your belongings in the center of our circle. Aengus and his men will aid us as we are all crossing at the same time. It is important that we do not break our connection. No matter what you feel or experience our circle must remain intact."

Rio was the first to place her bags on the crest. The others followed leaving Raegan at the end of the line. Shae watched Raegan as she approached the crest. Suddenly, her body became rigid and her eyes glazed. Raegan was experiencing a vision. Shae watched to make sure Raegan was okay. She noticed Rio's reaction. It made no sense to Shae. Raegan experienced a barely visible momentary pause. It was obvious Raegan's delay irritated Rio. Raegan started to speak, but Shae quickly grabbed her by the arm and pulled her back into her position within the Circle.

Raegan's vision startled her. Frightened her really. Raegan grabbed Shae's hand. She was shaking. As soon as their hands touched, Shae could vividly see Raegan's vision. It was so tangible as if it were happening right before her eyes. Shae whispered in Raegan's ear: "Ná bíodh imní ort, Raegan, cuirfidh mé do fhís in iúl don ghrúpa. Coinnigh mo lámh. Geallaim go mbeidh sé ceart go leor."

"Don't worry, Raegan, I will relay your vision to the group. Just hold my hand. I promise it will be all right." Raegan nodded in agreement. She did not feel comfortable speaking. "Please listen everyone! Raegan just had a vision. I don't know how but when our hands touched, I was able to see it too."

It was obvious that Aengus was concerned about Raegan's vision without even knowing its content. Rio reaction was disconcerting. She was obviously agitated by the news, she glared intently at Raegan. This alarmed Shae. Rio's reaction seemed extreme. She knew she must talk to

Liam and Roark once they were alone. Aengus replied: "Shae, please share Raegan's vision. It is obvious to me that Raegan needs time to recuperate from her vision. Raegan would you agree?"

Raegan nodded at Aengus. He then asked: "Raegan, will you allow Shae to share your vision?" Raegan whispered "yes".

Rio's reaction puzzled Shae. It left her feeling unsettled and questioning Rio's ability to lead their group once in Hy-Breasail. Shae began to share Raegan's vision:

"Okay…Raegan's vision showed me a boat on the shores of the O'Flaherty Castle. Six men were aboard. One of them was Manannán, the rest of the men were unidentifiable. The vision was duplicitous, filled with both urgency and calm. Thus, leading me to believe we need to cross expeditiously. Princess Maeve may need our help more than originally expected."

Rio made a humph noise and turned to Aengus. Shae rolled her eyes in disgust as she watched Rio turn away from her. Rio asked: "Aengus, has our mission changed?" He took a moment for contemplation. Shae saw Liam's posture change, readying for debate against any change in directives. Anxiously, the group waited for Aengus' reply. "No, continue as planned. I am certainly not happy about Manannán's early arrival, yet I believe it imperative you cross sooner rather than later. I will contact Tomas at once to relay Raegan's vision."

For a moment, all seemed relieved by his message until Rio interjected. "Why would we not change our travel plans? I believe we should arrive at the south end of the island instead of the north. The woods will cover us upon entrance. So, our arrival discreet. Manannán will be none the wiser."

Liam was visibly agitated. Shae was right to think that Rio's leadership was lacking. Shae walked over to Liam and gently touched his arm. He quietly said to Shae: "What is she doing? There is no reason for us to change our strategy. She is disrespectful to the Hierarchy's greatest warrior. No one in their right mind would challenge him. I hope we can trust her." Shae hushed him. Liam must heed Tomas' warning earlier. They were not to argue with their superiors.

Aengus was annoyed by Rio's question. He responded to her. "No, Gréagoír and Díarmuid will continue as directed." Then added. "As will you and your entourage. All plans remain unchanged." Rio just nodded her head. Aengus turned to speak with the group. "I concur that his arrival may increase the dangers originally expected. Yet, at this time, our focus must be on the safety of Princess Maeve. Therefore, all travel strategies will remain." Aengus turned to Shae. "Shae, if directives change, I will send a message through Eamonn. He will meet you in the same place as this morning. No one would suspect Eamonn to behold a tactical message as he is the Guardian of the Riches."

Shae stood straight and proud to answer Hy-Breasail's greatest warrior. "Sir, I will meet him upon our arrival. I know exactly where he will be." He replied: "Very good as he will act as escort as well." Turning to Rio, he strongly stated: "I reiterate no changes will be made unless I send a message to Eamonn. Understood?"

With indignation, Rio responded. "Yes! Thank you, Aengus." Rio did not even look at Aengus while responding. She turned away. "Let us proceed. Shae could not believe how Rio disrespected Aengus. He was the oldest, most revered, and strongest Patron of Warriors for a countless number of years. Shae shook her head in disbelief. If Aengus became perturbed by her disloyalty, he did not show it.

Once again, the six stood in the Circle of Transcendence around the Crest of Hy-Breasail. Aengus and his men stood behind Rio, Liam, and Roark placing their hands on their shoulders. Shae could feel the power of these men surging through her body. Rio directed them to close their eyes as she reminded them not to let go no matter what they saw, felt, or heard.

Immediately, Shae felt as if a crushing blast had stricken her. This was so different than when she and Maeve crossed over Veil na Tairsí earlier. She now understood why Aengus and his men had to aid in their crossing. It was much more powerful than she could have ever imagined.

68 Strategy

An hour had passed since Manannán's arrival, surprisingly, he and his men had not moved from their campsite. Maeve asked for two comfortable chairs for her terrace overlooking the shores. Manannán needed to know he would not intimidate her. She was almost positive that two of the men with Manannán were Finn and Fagen. This possibility infuriated her.

Manannán looked up to her, waved, and bowed in exaggerated reverence. Maeve became incensed and began pacing her floors. Anger was growing inside of her. Ailm gently vibrated on her chest. He was calming her. Maeve placed her hand over him and whispered: "Go raibh maith agat."

"Thanks."

Maeve was so thankful for Ailm. She felt peace and clarity flood her body. She needed to keep her composure and not let her age, inexperience, and emotions get the best of her. It was important especially with Manannán taunting her. She must be a leader and not criticized for being an emotional teenager. Strategies coursed through Maeve's mind. Her thoughts interrupted when Díarmuid knocked on her chamber door. Maeve smiled. At least Díarmuid respected her boundaries. She called to him to enter.

Díarmuid was a pleasant fellow. Maeve thanked him for bringing the chairs to her room. She then graciously excused him to continue preparations downstairs. When Manannán descended upon the castle, she did not doubt his intent to harm those she cared about. Of that, Maeve was sure. It was a strategy she would use if she became a deceitful, villainous individual. So deep in her own thoughts, Maeve began to doze off. She could not let her guard down.

Maeve jolted awake from the pounding on her chamber door. Without the opportunity of finding out who was knocking, the door opened. Of course, it was Conall. Conall's interruption angered Maeve. With a face full of disparagement, Maeve stood up and verbally chastised him. She began, "You amaze me, Conall Darroch. You are as thickheaded as your sons. I know now where they have inherited it from. DO NOT enter my bed chamber without permission. I could have been indisposed. Must I say the same thing repeatedly to you like you are but a child."

Conall momentarily became flustered. Then he interrupted her before she could finish her tirade. He knew she was tired, and all of this was becoming stressful. "Princess, once again, I apologize. You must understand that I entered because my message is of the utmost importance.

Maeve was losing patience with him. "What is so important that you enter my private chambers without permission. It must be of EXTREME importance."

"It is, my Princess. I have just received word that our group from Rowan has crossed over Veil na Tairsí safely." A look of relief flooded over the look of consternation from a few moments ago. "Thank you, Conall. That is a great relief. I apologize for my outburst. I could have handled it better. I believe I have been angry with you not for what you have done but what your sons have. Again, I apologize. But please do not enter my private chambers without permission ever again. I beg of you. Now, continue."

Conall looked relieved. Yet, he felt he needed to respond to the Princesses' statement about his sons. "Princess, I cannot excuse my sons' deplorable actions. I was an absentee father leaving them as toddlers with no male role model. For that, I am sorry." Maeve truly felt sorry for the man. He was becoming more tolerable and a bit endearing. This new feeling toward Conall surprised Maeve immensely. "Thank you, Conall. I appreciate your words very much, but your sons were free to make their own choices whether you were there to guide them or not. Please do not blame yourself for the actions of others. They acted upon their own free will. Now, please let us discuss the matter of Manannán further."

"Yes, thank you, Princess." Maeve noticed a glimmer of tears in Conall's eyes. His sons' actions had laid heavy on him. It was of no use, Conall tugged at her heartstrings. Conall's face had softened as if he given a second chance to prove who he truly was. "Eamonn has met with Shae at the Veil. He delivered updates from Aengus. Impressively, he has volunteered his protection during escort to the castle by an alternate route. It will be a great guise to have him as escort. As Guardian of the Riches no one will suspect him as anything but a guide in Hy-Breasail. Fortunately, the danger they may possibly face will be limited as Manannán's powers are restricted in Hy-Breasail."

Maeve could not belief what Conall had just reported. "Wait, you're telling me that Manannán has limited powers here? Why was I not told of this earlier?" He knew this news angered Maeve. He tried to make her understand their intention was not to omit any information. "Princess, we did not think it of importance as we assumed you knew of his limited powers. For all of us, I apologize. We forget how new you are to all of this as you have handled difficult matters with such ease and grace."

Maeve felt nothing but exasperation. "I must be privy to everything from the smallest or greatest significance. I must be aware of even what is assumed I know." Conall tried to explain. "But there was nothing to be done as he has remained on the shores. No attempt of attack on the castle has been detected by the Protectors." Maeve had no intention of allowing anyone to make decisions on her behalf. "Does everyone forget that I am the future Queen of Hy-Breasail. Never omit the smallest of details. Do you understand? Please relay my order to Díarmuid and Gréagoír. Do not leave me in the dark again. Is that understood?"

"Yes, Princess. I will inform them of your wishes." Conall knew he must convey her wishes or there would be consequences. "Thank you, Conall. I wish to address something of greater importance. Our inactiveness shows weakness. We will go to him. He will not have the upper hand especially with his weakened powers. We will not wait."

Conall hesitated to respond. He chose his words carefully as to not anger Maeve. "Princess, you do not understand. There is more." Maeve was becoming agitated. She thought how much more was she not aware of. Calmly, she asked. "There is more?"

Conall knew Maeve would be calling upon the Hierarchy. It was what he would have done if in her position. Conall replied hesitantly. "Yes." Maeve turned toward the shores. With her back turned away from Conall, she replied: "I will meet you downstairs. Please alert Díarmuid and Gréagoír. We will be having a serious chat." Conall bowed. Yes, my Princess, I understand. We will be waiting for you."

Maeve had an agenda formulated for her meeting with Conall, Díarmuid, and Gréagoír. First, she would send a message to the Hierarchy. It was incomprehensible to not keep the Princess apprised of all concerns regarding Hy-Breasail, and Rowan. Secondly, she would address communications with her staff to correct the situation expeditiously. All must keep Maeve apprised of matters concerning the safety of either Realm. Most importantly, she would confront the greatest enemy of Hy-Breasail and Rowan. Manannán.

69 News

Moments later, Conall knocked on her chamber door. Maeve granted him access. She asked: "Tell me. Are they ready for me downstairs? I will be there shortly." His reply is not what she expected. "Yes, Princess, but there is something else. I have an update to share." Maeve anxiously waited for her news. "Tell me Conall of this news you have heard."

"It is from Aveline. She has sent a message to Gréagóir. She believes that Manannán has reconsidered attacking the castle."

Aveline's update perplexed Maeve. It left her curious. "And what does she base this information on? More importantly, since when did she have this so-called epiphany. I saw her but a few hours ago. She warned us of him. Why the change?"

Conall, too, was leery of this new update. "She declares that no one knows him better than she. She told Gréagóir that if he came here to attack, he would have already done so. The question to be answered is 'why then did he come at all."

Maeve turned from Conall suggesting the need to process this new intel. She questioned the legitimacy of Aveline's claim. None of the events over the last few hours made sense. First, Maeve's greatest enemy, Fergus, joined the Hierarchy of the Sept. Now, Manannán arrives seeking peace. So, an unknown planted the intel received earlier; someone who infiltrated the Hierarchy. The miscommunications designed to deter us from uncovering Maeve's true nemesis' identity.

It was time for Maeve to lead by her own instinct and no one else's. She could not even trust Aveline at this point. A coup had formed against her, she was sure of it. She must hide her true feelings under her royal façade. She turned to Conall in question.

"So, he has come here with no ill intention. Is that a correct assumption?"

"Yes, Princess, I assume so."

"I remain determined to meet him on my terms, not his. I gave him ample time to contact me. He has not. Therefore, I will make the first move. I will judge his trustworthiness using the gifts beholden to me upon my birth."

"Princess, I mean no disrespect as I have questioned Aveline's true intention, but then I remember the past. She has been loyal to Hy-Breasail for many centuries. Her word has always been truthful and honorable. I believe we should trust her. She claims there is more that she cannot divulge at this time. But, for now, we must not see him as a threat."

"He is her brother, Conall, she wants no harm to come to him. If one of my sisters were in the same predicament, I would do the same. I will meet him openminded without a rush to judgment given my respect for Aveline. Yet, if I find his presence threatening, I will order him to the Castle and kept in the galley. None of us will feel frightened or threatened in our home. I will not allow it."

"I understand your concern, Princess. But we must wait to hear from Aveline before taking drastic actions against him."

"Again, let me express to you how I feel about the matter you have presented to me. I hold Aveline in great regard, but she is not the future Queen of Hy-Breasail, I am. I will handle this situation as I deem fit." Conall nodded in agreement. "Therefore, please let Gréagóir know that I intend for him to accompany me to meet with Manannán. We will not send word as such. I would like for him to experience the element of surprise. He must have no time to plan."

Conall could not argue with Maeve. Her plan was that of a seasoned warrior and ruler. Once again, Conall was impressed by Maeve's ability to take charge of a situation well above her training. "Yes, Princess Maeve. I will do as directed. May I add that I am impressed by your abilities and honored to serve you."

Maeve slightly blushed as she responded: "Thank you, Conall. I appreciate your kind words." Conall bowed in reverence as Maeve continued. "I will be wearing my warrior armor. Manannán needs to know that I am serious in the options I will set forth before him. I am sure that many questions have arisen about my ability to rule my kingdom. I do not intend to sit and wait for the person who is threatening me, my people, and my land to dictate my next move. I do not intend to be rude but if you will please excuse me now. Eachna will attend to my dress. With profound respect and integrity, I ask that you contact Tomas and the rest of the Hierarchy of my intention."

There was nothing else for Conall to add. He cast his eyes away from Maeve as he left the room closing the door behind him. Maeve let out a huge exhale. She then went ahead to the adjoining room of her bed chamber that held her warrior armor. Eachna followed behind. "Eachna, thank you. Now, please get me ready to confront this threat."

Maeve watched as Eachna braided her hair into two platelets then twisted them into side buns. Maeve thought she looked like a princess in a sci-fi movie. This style ensured anyone the inability to grab her by the hair. She wore fitted riding pants and a long tunic type top over which Eachna wrapped a cape. Eachna called the pieces of clothing the Princess' léine, brat, and triubhas. Lastly, Eachna secured Maeve's brat with a brooch of jewels then helped her into her thigh high magical leather boots. She wore a metal breastplate with the Hy-Breasail crest. Eachna handed her a shield to carry. Suddenly, she felt a strange sensation on her skin. It did not hurt but felt quite odd. Eachna sensed her questioning.

"Princess, your clothing will act as protective covering. It is impenetrable."

Maeve looked at her reflection in the mirror. The fabrics were magnificent shades of red, green, purple, and blue transforming her into a strong, magical, ethereal persona. She could not believe her eyes. Her transformation from Princess to Warrior was astonishing. Eachna came up behind her. Maeve noticed something in her hands. It was a crown. One not worn for royal events but worn in battle. It was magnificent. Eachna placed it upon her head. Her own reflection took her breath away. Staring back at her was the doppelgänger sister of Queen Meadhbh of Connacht. Was she seeing herself or a vision? Eachna placed her hand on Maeve's shoulder.

"Princess, you are beautiful. I am honored to be in your service."

Maeve realized she had been holding her breath. On exhale, she replied to Eachna breathily. "Oh, Eachna, please. Without you, I could not have gathered the strength to achieve what I have today." Eachna did not reply. She looked down, blushing. "Well, it is time. I wonder if Gréagoír has gone to the stable. If not, please tell him to ready the horses. I think that is how I will make my entrance." Eachna gazed upward and replied: "Princess, you will be grand and mighty." Maeve quickly hugged her. "Thank you. Let us find the men."

The men were in the gathering room waiting for Maeve's arrival. Maeve stood in the massive doorway. All three of them stopped talking as soon as they realized she had entered the room. They waited for her to speak. Maeve looked at the three of them. Her focus must remain on the task ahead of her. Manannán. Maeve knew she had to address the men that were gaping at her.

"Good evening. I hope everyone was able to get some rest. As you all know, Manannán has camped directly in front of my chamber windows. On a few occasions, he has tried to use intimidation tactics to unnerve me. Before he feels that he has the upper hand, it is imperative that I confront him and his entourage. It is time for him to meet the ruler of Hy-Breasail."

There was nothing Gréagoír, Conall, or Díarmuid could say. Nothing that Maeve was saying went against any directive or message that a prince or king would give. They just stood in wait to hear what else Princess Maeve may or may not convey to them.

"Gréagoír, has Cearul been readied. I feel compelled to make a grander, more authoritative entrance on horse rather than on foot."

Gréagoír responded, "Yes, Princess, Cearul and my steed is waiting for us as we speak. Cearul is expecting you as he has been the royal steed for many a generation. He is powerful and strong. You will feel his strength as soon as you sit on his saddle. He was your grandfather's favorite."

Maeve smiled thinking of Grandpa Aaron. "Thank you, Gréagoír. My grandfather has introduced us, and I agree with you. He is grand." She gestured toward the door and directed, "let us proceed."

70 Darkness

Shae heard Roark whispering her name through the haze. She slowly opened her eyes and found Rio, Liam, Declan, and Raegan standing over her. She knew Roark was cradling her in his arms. She remembered standing in the Circle when she felt something crushing her chest. Everything went black after that. As her vision cleared, she knew they had crossed Veil na Tairsí. But she could not understand why this crossing affected her so significantly while no one else seemed affected at all. Roark's soothing voice was calming to her.

"Roark. Rio. Liam. We must find Eamonn. He's going to help us. I'm so sorry. I don't know what happened to me. Hurry. We need to get to Maeve." Roark cradled Shae in his arms. "Shhhhh, we are all fine. Eamonn is here. We were just waiting for you to join us. Are you okay?"

Groggily Shae replied: "Umm, yes. I was scared, but I'm okay now. Before we crossed, my chest felt heavy. The heaviness crushed my heart. It was a horrible feeling. Can you hold me for a minute more?" Shae needed to tell Roark something privately. She knew she sounded desperate, but it was a good cover. No one would suspect her reaction as anything but fear. She could not risk anyone thinking she was being secretive. It would make her become suspect in their eyes.

Roark bowed his head to hers. To the spectator, they looked as if they were in a lover's embrace. Shae pulled him close enough so he could hear her slightest whisper. "Roark, we are in danger. It is not Manannán. We must be very observant to those in our group. We have a traitor amongst us. The crushing of my chest was a warning. I have my suspicions. I hope I am wrong."

Roark looked into her eyes. He understood. If anything, her role as class president taught her how to react in times of uncertainty. So, everyone could hear, Shae said, "I'm not sure what happened but I'm okay now. Thank you for taking care of me."

Shae touched Roark's face lovingly. "Okay, then. Let me help you up."

Shae started to release herself from Roark's embrace when he took her hands in his. He pulled her up and drew her closer to him. He whispered in her ear. "I know of whom you speak." He held her for a second before letting her go. Shae felt a chill up her spine. If her suspicions were right, the person or persons who had infiltrated their group would reveal themselves eventually.

Shae watched everyone closely. The only person acting differently was Rio. Rio's newfound power had gone to her head. Eamonn was no different than this morning. Shae was in awe of his demeanor. He brought a sense of calm and serenity to the group. Much like Raegan and Declan had at Hawthorn yesterday. The anxiety level in the group diminished as he spoke.

Rio stood up to introduce Eamonn. "Has everyone met Eamonn?"

All either mumbled "yes" or nodded their head in agreement. Then, she addressed Shae in front of the group. "Shae, I'm very worried about you. My assignment is to protect you and the rest of the group. To do so, I believe you may need to return to Rowan." Shae could not believe her ears. Rio had singled her out in front of the whole group. Shae stood in amazement.

"Rio, I'm truly okay."

"Great! I am happy to hear that. But, Shae, you may slow us down."

"Rio, I am fine. Believe me. We need to get to Maeve."

"Please, Shae, be honest. Your health is most important. There are enough of us here to protect Maeve. You must not impede our mission."

Shae, puzzled by that statement, replied to Rio. "Yes, ma'am. I am fine. I do not mean to be rude or disrespectful, but I have told you I am okay many times. I will not impede our mission. If I felt I would, I would have removed myself forthwith. So, there is no need for you to ask me again."

"Okay. I hope you're right."

Rio's behavior and her need to have her eliminated from the group made Shae suspect Rio's intentions. She did not want to jump to conclusions just yet. It could be that Rio was being overly concerned for Maeve's safety. So, Shae decided that she had to weigh each of Rio's words with great caution and a bit of compassion. She listened intently to Rio as she addressed the whole group.

"Now that we are all ready to commence our mission, I need to inform you of some changes in our directives from the Hierarchy. Eamonn will be leading our group to the O'Flaherty castle. We will abort our original plan. I will be stepping down as your leader instructed by Princess Maeve and Tomas. I am second in command working side-by-side with Eamonn. Therefore, I give to you *your* new leader, Eamonn."

Shae noticed how incredibly uncomfortable Rio looked giving up control. Shae thought this mission was getting more interesting. How she wished Maeve were here.

"Hello, my friends. First, let me share with you that this morning Princess Maeve received a talisman from the Guardians. A few of you are already aware of this. I delivered it to her myself. This talisman, Ailm, will act as her guide. He will alert Princess Maeve to imminent danger. Knowing that, I will proceed with a development that has taken place."

Liam looked over at Shae. She gave him a reassuring look that everything was going to be okay.

"Princess Maeve holds all power over decisions regarding Hy-Breasail. As we speak, our princess, accompanied by Gréagoír, will meet with Manannán. She is riding the royal steed, Cearul. As a few of you know, Cearul has magnificent powers and experience in battle. He will act on her behalf if necessary. This should allay any of your fears regarding her safety."

Shae noticed that Liam did not react to this news. It was obvious that Liam concurred with Maeve's decision. Shae felt an overwhelming sense of relief from the group.

Although, the news delivered by Eamonn was upsetting Rio's behavior. Shae suddenly thought how difficult this must be for her. She, of course, is Maeve's aunt so she must be concerned for Maeve's safety. Shae considered this possibility. She also realized that Rio was jealous of her own niece. Of that, Shae was positive.

With everything that had taken place over the last few minutes, Shae had not noticed everyone's transformation. Each person was stunningly beautiful. Rio was a beautiful, hard-ass warrior. Raegan, who always looked quiet and shy, had power emanating from her that Shae had never seen before. She looked ethereal but the strength that was beaming from her was intoxicating. Shae realized that Hy-Breasail not only amplified someone's beauty on the outside; it heightened who each person was on the inside.

Shae could not keep her eyes off Roark. Her heart swelled. It was puzzling to her since they had just met. But Hy-Breasail heightened her senses, especially smells and feelings. Shae smiled to herself. Liam and Roark looked like romance novel models. This amplification of senses was amazing. She knew it could potentially help uncover who the threat against Maeve was.

Suddenly, Shae felt someone staring at her. The intensity of the stare was strong and distracting sending tiny flutters up and down her arms. It was coming from behind her. Shae turned to the direction of the power source. It was Rio standing right next to Liam. Shae looked at Rio and then Liam when a bolt of electricity surged through her body. Liam, Roark, Raegan, and Declan emanated light, strength, and power. Rio was different. Shae could see her strength and power, but there was something missing. There was no light. Shae felt a catch in her heart.

71 The Ultimatum

The ultimatum Maeve would present to Manannán was quite simple. Leave peacefully or by extreme force. Her wish, of course, was for him to choose peace. Any great leader once threatened could not withdraw or negotiate terms with their enemy. So, she knew if she presented an ultimatum, and he declined, Manannán and his followers would suffer great castigations. She prayed that he would make the right decision as she suspected two of his followers were Finn and Fagen. Punishing her childhood friends was something she wanted to avoid especially knowing the devastation it would bring to Conall.

The walk to the stables was short but magical. Gréagoír was to meet her there. She gasped when she saw the magnificent outbuilding before her. No building could compare. Its style was very much the same as the stables she had visited in Rowan, but the detail work was exquisite. Maeve did not think a building used to home animals could be so majestic. There was an aura of magic surrounding it. Shimmering lights like the aurora borealis or Northern Lights gleamed in all directions from the structure before her.

Tears formed in the corners of Maeve's eyes. She became overcome with emotion. Suddenly, the stable doors began to open. The light emanating on the outside of the stable originated from the majestic animals living inside. It was so bright, Maeve had to shield her eyes. Three figures walked toward Maeve - a man with two horses. It was Gréagóir with Cearul. Cearul's beauty was astonishing. Her connection with him proved to be deep and powerful – instantly an insurmountable love flowed between them.

Maeve became overwhelmed by Cearul's majesty. Gréagóir aided her upon Cearul's back. He was much larger than the average stallion in Rowan. Cearul's strength and power radiated and surged through Maeve's body. Cearul was the last puzzle piece needed to complete her transformation from teenage girl from Rowan to future Queen of Hy-Breasail.

Gréagóir mounted his horse with ease and grace. Quietly, he told Maeve they would reach Manannán shortly. If needed they could slow down their pace. "Princess, we can slow our pace to allow you a few moments to collect your thoughts."

"No, Gréagóir, I am fine. Our meeting will be swift. Manannán and I will meet. I will deliver my ultimatum. I will not allow indecisiveness. His decision must be quick. I am optimistic he will choose peace. If not, you will alert the Patrons at once." The Patrons were waiting for the orders she would pass on to Gréagóir. He nodded his head in agreement and responded to his Princess.

"Yes, Princess Maeve." Maeve noticed Gréagoír momentarily gazed into nothingness. She knew he had received a vision.

"Gréagoír, what is it? Have you a message for me?" Gréagoír hesitated. "Oh, I'm sorry. Yes, I have. I apologize. It takes me a moment to return from my visions. May I proceed with a message from Aveline?"

"Of course, you may."

"Thank you, Princess."

"Proceed, please."

"Aveline asked me to convey to you her thoughts about Manannán. She does not feel the message she conveyed earlier was in its totality. She may have misconceived messages from informants regarding Manannán's actions. No doubt he is jealous of her standing in our Realm. But his actions against you would be uncharacteristic. He does not harm those he has no qualms with. She has heard that it is not Manannán whom we should fear. He has come to help you in revealing your true enemy. An enemy with powers equal to yours. She asks that you meet with him before acting harshly against him and his men."

Maeve nodded as she pondered Aveline's message. She understood the notion of sibling rivalry. Her sisters epitomized the concept. In her heart, she knew that it made perfect sense. Yet, she could not allow her heart to lead her quest. Manannán's history of attack at Hawthorn was still fresh in her mind. He was not an innocent. Before deciding his guilt or innocence, the wise decision would be to befriend him. Better a friend than a greater enemy. As the adage claims "keep your friends close, and your enemies closer".

"Gréagóir, I will weigh your message from Aveline with great care. I hope that she is right. If she is, our meeting will end in peace."

A million scenarios of deception swirled through Maeve's mind. There was someone close to her that wished her harm. It was not her parents. Her sisters were too young to formulate a masterful, complicated plan. They could hardly brush their teeth in the morning. She knew it could not be Shae or Liam. She knew them too well. It may well be Roark which would be devastating for Liam and Shae. Maeve knew she had to let go of any intimations racing through her mind. She took a deep breath and let them go.

With only 100 yards to go, Maeve's suspicions confirmed that flanking Manannán were Finn and Fagen. Maeve felt a tiny tug at her heart. Ailm stirred a bit reassuring her that all would be fine. As soon as she laid eyes on them, Maeve knew Aveline's message was factual.

"Gréagóir, here we go."

Cearul and Gréagóir's steed trotted along steadily. Maeve felt Gréagóir watching her. She knew he was trying to decipher her emotions. She would control the events about to unfold. She would not, could not, allow anyone to overrule her.

On the shores surrounding the O'Flaherty Castle, the men awaited the arrival of Princess Maeve and Gréagóir. Manannán stood in front of his men. His stance was wide legged with one hand on his waist; the other on the pummel of his sword. Maeve turned toward Gréagóir. His stance was identical except for one hand resting on his horse's bridle.

Maeve rolled her eyes a bit thinking how differently men thought than women. Both expect this meeting to become confrontational. Maeve would take control of the meeting expeditiously. She would not allow these men to greet each other in violence. Without Maeve's order, there would be no act of violence against Manannán and his men.

It took but a minute to reach the men. Maeve found Manannán's face free from malice. Upon her arrival, he signaled to his men to bow in reverence to her. Maeve could not believe her eyes as she watched Finn and Fagen follow Manannán's example. Neither of them looked at her with malice or hatred as she had experienced over the last few days. She turned her focus on their leader. Manannán.

Maeve noticed he held himself with the air and majesty of a Prince. His clothing was identical to Gréagoír. He had the same features and coloring as his sister, Aveline, but more chiseled and manly; yet, they could have been twins. He was much taller than his sister and much more muscular; he reminded Maeve of the professional wrestlers Shae's brothers watched. What surprised her the most was the gentleness gleaming through from his gaze. This discovery would not change her plan. She had experienced far too much these past few days to trust him so quickly.

Maeve began, "Welcome! I am Princess Maeve, and you are Manannán. Yes?"

"Yes, Princess.", Manannán replied.

"I see you have traveled far with some of my friends. I will be curt. I wish to know your intentions. I will present you two options. Peace or war. If you choose peace, my home will be open to you. If you choose war, I am sad for you. You will experience a wrath no other has endured in Hy-Breasail."

Manannán was impressed with Hy-Breasail's princess. His smile genuine.

"Thank you, Princess. You see, I understand the plight I have set forth. Your hands are bound, and an ultimatum is your only choice. I am here for many reasons. I am sure my sister originally believed that my goal was to hurt her by attacking you. Let me assure you that I am not."

Maeve looked to Gréagóir. He had not yet let his guard down. Maeve was grateful. She had to remain suspicious of Manannán's intentions. Maeve allowed him to continue.

"There are many out there, Princess, that wish you harm. More than you know. With me are my men, who also felt that way. I am ashamed to admit that I, too, felt the same. We have all changed. News of Fergus' alliance with the Hierarchy as well as Conall's allegiance to you are just part of our change of heart. Aveline has uncovered a truth hidden from us all. Our former leader hid behind Fergus; used him as her pawn. We were all led in hatred. A hatred so deep for you that she filled our heads with lies. Please believe that it was Aveline that set us free from her grasp by enlightening us to the truth."

The word "she" reverberated in Maeve's mind. As well as questions. Why did a woman threaten her? This news shocked her. Was jealousy or hatred fueling this threat? She listened keenly to Manannán hoping to uncover her nemesis' identity.

"Her abilities match yours. Yet, she is crafty with her powers. She has not shown herself to any of us. She can infiltrate our minds through a magic that is beyond any we have yet experienced. That is why we have all come together to help you win the battle against her. Unfortunately, since we do not know her identity it will be through the intuitiveness and gifts of all our people working as one to fight in the battle against her wickedness."

Maeve thought of her experiences over the last few days. She knew the unknown entity had overtaken Finn and Fagen's bodies. She saw bits of goodness left inside of them. She felt relief flood through her body. Ailm stirred every so lightly against her chest. They had not turned against her. Poor Finn. His battle with the entity began long ago. She knew it. The incident between him and Shae was not of his doing. She could not wait to tell Shae.

"So, Manannán, my threat is close to me. Someone I know well. Am I to trust your words? Finn and Fagen, my friends, cannot look at me. Their behavior these last few days are nothing short of shameful and cowardly. Both of you look at me."

Both Finn and Fagen looked up to Maeve, their Princess. Sadness flooded their emotions. Maeve felt sorry for them both. Yet, she remained indifferent in her speech. She spoke directly to them.

"Finn. Fagen. The Hierarchy, the Sept and your family concur. The actions you have taken over the last few days have been reprehensible. I am not sure how to deal with both of you. I do now know that your actions were out of your control. I wish you had turned to someone, anyone, for help. For now, I will believe you had no part in your ill will toward me. We will deal with your actions at a future time, if at all. For now, I must trust my instincts and adhere to the advice of your sister, Manannán, and bring all of you to the safety of my castle."

Manannán began to speak. Maeve would not have it. She raised her hand to quiet him.

"Please, I am not finished. Gréagóir, please alert the Patrons to place our "friends" in protective custody." Maeve turned to the men before her and continued. "We will guard you from this person you speak of. I am sure she will try to harm you as your allegiance has turned to me. You all have much to prove. Trust me, I await your show of loyalty toward me, Rowan, and Hy-Breasail. Your actions must speak louder than your words. At that time, I will allow you more freedoms. Gréagóir, please let the Patrons know of our plans."

Within seconds, a group of Patrons appeared and surrounded the group. Their arrival startled Maeve's visitors. Immediately, their hands were bound with an impenetrable silvery cuff. Maeve saw a flicker of fear in Finn and Fagen's eyes. She did not flinch. Manannán, once again, tried to speak. Maeve motioned to Gréagóir to have him silenced. She had heard enough. She would continue speaking of this matter with Gréagóir, Conall and Díarmuid.

72 Light vs Darkness

Eamonn, with Rio by his side, led the group along the safest route. Rio walked close behind. Shae could not keep her eyes off the two. The darkness emanating from Rio was equal to the bright illuminous light from Eamonn. Their strength was comparable, but what their hearts held not so much. She hoped the reason behind the illumination difference was resultant from living in different realms.

Eamonn slowed his pace before turning toward the group to give a quick update. In Irish, he spoke: "Thaistil muid i bhfad. Níl an cladach i bhfad uainn. Beidh Caomhnóirí ann dúinn. Tabharfaidh siad coimhdeacht dúinn chuig Banphrionsa Maeve. Ní dhéanfaidh siad cumarsáid leat. Ní labhraíonn siad ach Gaeilge ársa, teanga atá ag fail bháis. Dá réir sin, ní labhróidh siad ach liomsa agus le Rio. Tá tuiscint theoranta ag cuid agaibh. Coinnigh i gcuimhne go dtosóidh sibh ceachtanna chun ár bhfíor-theanga a labhairt nuair a shroicheann sibh Caisleán Ó Flaithbheartaigh."

Rio translated for him: "We have traveled far. The shore is not far off. There the Guardians will meet us. They will escort us to Princess Maeve. They will not communicate with you. They speak only ancient Irish – a dying language. Hence, they will only speak to me and Rio. Some of you have limited understanding. Keep in mind that upon your arrival at O'Flaherty Castle, you will begin lessons to speak our language."

Eamonn turned to Shae and smiled. Suddenly, Shae received the gift of the Irish language. She had never learned it before. Of course, as a child she had picked up words here and there from listening to her Ma, Auntie Kat, and Mrs. O. But now, she understood every word. Like a burst of lightning words began to course through Shae's mind including Rio's thoughts. Shae's heart skipped a beat. Rio's thoughts permeated vehemence and loathing.

"The audacity of you, Shae. To think you have any right to speak to Eamonn without my permission. I will not allow it. You must learn who your leader is. One way or another you will follow me. You will have no choice. You will not make any attempt to intercede in my obtaining my goal. If you do, I will end you."

Shae shuddered. She felt sick to her stomach. The Rio that stood before them masked with sincerity and love was not the beloved Rio of her childhood. This Rio's heart overflowed with hatred and loathing. This epiphany terrified Shae. The cloak or façade stopped them from seeing Rio for who she truly was, a venomous traitor.

Shae squeezed Roark's hand. He looked down at her. Without speaking, he knew. The one they searched for stood with them, was one of them. She felt a glitch in the communication that her and Roark shared even in their brief time together. Rio was trying to come between them. How this frightened Shae. Rio had great strength here, more than the Hierarchy realized. They were all in danger. She felt it deep within her soul.

Suddenly, Shae knew the cause of the crushing feeling in her chest a few moments ago. It was Rio. She had tried to incapacitate and deter her from journeying any further. It explained Rio's disappointment when Shae declined rest after crossing. Rio's façade was unraveling right before her eyes. Her dark aura was not resultant from growing up in Rowan. Her darkness originated from the jealousy that filled her heart. Shae almost screamed: "you were born here; your aura should be light and pure. What has happened to you?"

Memories flashed before Shae. Recollections of happiness and joy shared with Rio and the O'Flaherty's. Playing games, shell collecting, eating ice cream, amusement parks, dinners, etc. Every night at the beach they played games and watched movies. Nothing was out of sort. Every visit was fun and filled with the exciting adventures kids loved to enjoy at the beach. Shae was disappointed in herself that she held such a blind eye concerning her beloved friend's aunt. Even more disturbing was how Rio was able to fool her family and worse yet the Hierarchy.

Shae watched as Rio's strength grew exponentially. Her dark aura began swirling. The closer to shore they traveled the darker her aura grew. Shae hoped that Roark and Liam's gifts could uncover Rio's true nature. Tomas' directives echoed in Shae's mind. How was she to sit back when she had uncovered the most villainous deception. He had said that no one must act unless there was an imminent threat. But Rio has been an imminent threat for the last few days. Shae knew she must act. At that time, Rio's status as leader would cease to exist. It was of the utmost importance that Roark and Liam knew of Rio's duplicitous loyalty. If a battle ensued, Rio's strength would be devastating to everyone. More so if other dark forces were involved. If they did not know of Rio's deceit, Rowan and Hy-Breasail's defeat would be inevitable.

Shae felt Rio's discreet glare. It caused chills to run down her spine. She would not react. It would give Rio more power. Shae knew Rio would dispose of her quickly and quietly. She was Rio's greatest threat as was Raegan as they both were Maeve's closest confidants. It was inconceivable that Rio would try to end both her and Raegan. It would bring attention to herself and her identity as the threat against the Princess. But Shae knew it would be most beneficial to Rio's plans. With her and Raegan out of the way, Rio would have a direct line to Maeve undoubtedly allowing her to trick Maeve and take over her crown.

Rio's strength was growing stronger. Dark shadows appeared in Shae's peripheral view. She knew now that they were the shadows of Maeve's youth. Maeve told Shae many stories of them scaring her as a child. These shadows were not imaginative. They had been caste by Rio all along. Rio had fooled everyone. Shae knew she must remain calm and passive. Rio need not know that Shae's gifts had evolved. Shae now knew Rio's true feelings toward Maeve as well as the people of Rowan and Hy-Breasail.

Shae notice that the dark entities had formed a border surrounding the group. It would be difficult to escape. Shae prayed that Roark and Liam saw them too. She could not imagine that Eamonn did not. His powers were greater than all of theirs. Shae felt an impulse to get closer to Eamonn. No matter the consequence, Shae knew she must warn him and the awaiting Guardians. In her heart, she knew Rio would make it an impossibility, but it was a risk Shae had to take.

73 Deception

Manannán and his group settled in a protected part of the Castle. Maeve retreated to her chambers. She left explicit directions with Gréagóir, Conall, and Díarmuid not to disturb her for any reason. With one exception, the arrival of Eamonn, Rio, Liam, Roark, Declan, Shae, and Raegan. This news would be welcoming. Maeve needed to review the events of the day. She walked out onto her balcony with Eachna steps behind. Realizing this, she turned and politely insisted that Eachna retreat to her own room until needed.

"Eachna, please. I appreciate your willingness to serve me, but, right now, I need to be alone. I must have no distractions or interruptions. Please understand. Thank you."

Eachna became despondent upon her dismissal. Maeve would not allow hers or anyone else's despondency rule over her decisions. Eachna would heed her instruction.

Maeve reviewed the multitude of events that arose over the last forty-eight hours. She was sure she had missed pertinent clues uncovering her nemesis. There was someone, other than the obvious, Finn, Fagen and Manannán, who were part of this coup. Whoever he or she was, they had hidden their identity very well. She continued to list people of question. It was clear that her nemesis' followers had a prevalent presence in Rowan and Hy-Breasail. Her list must be extensive. She would not discriminate. She would include all men, women, family, and friends. She crossed off people that she was confident were innocent.

Maeve cut many from her list with conviction. Doubts of collusion could not shroud her judgement as the Sept left her suspect of everyone. She knew she had to see everyone as suspicious no matter their position or familial relationship. Two questions needed answering. First, who left her doubtful of their allegiance to Hy-Breasail? Secondly, who would gain the most by her demise? She easily deduced the list to three people of suspicion. Conall, Aveline, and an unknown. From the three, she needed to figure out the trueness of their loyalty to her.

Conall's sudden appearance left her wary. Although, he did have a genuine concern for her safety. Maeve was 99.9% sure he was trustworthy. Then there was Aveline. It was disturbing to imagine her leading the Regime. Yet, Aveline's contradictory messages left Maeve cautious of her loyalty. Conall and Aveline's actions of late left Maeve no choice, but to question their alliance to Hy-Breasail. Yet, Maeve had a nagging feeling that she was missing someone else. She was sure there was another. This process was becoming emotionally exhausting.

Maeve decided to sit outside and enjoy the beautiful view from her balcony. The shore looked empty with Manannán and his men now her guests. At first Maeve thought she was seeing things. Across the water on the shores far away, it looked as if a storm was brewing. The clouds above Hy-

Breasail were angry. The elements were changing before her eyes. Green lightning bolts shot out of the clouds hitting the ground below. She heard footsteps behind her. It was Eachna. Maeve turned to ask her what she needed.

"Eachna, do you need something?" Eachna looked extremely uncomfortable. "No, ma'am, I was just checking on you. There is a horrible storm brewing across the water." Maeve raised her eyebrows in question. Not an hour ago she made it clear to Eachna that she needed to be alone. "I appreciate your concern. Everything is fine. It is nothing more than a storm. Please leave. I have work to do. I need not be disturbed." Eachna hesitated. "Now, Eachna, or I will call upon Gréagoír to remove you from my chambers. Now, I implore you."

Eachna turned and left. Maeve sat and watched her walk away. "I know she's Kían's wife, but I will not stand for insubordination." She thought she could have been too casual too soon in their relationship. Eachna's actions angered Maeve sparking questions about her allegiance. The possibilities were endless. Eachna could either be here to protect her or she could be a spy for the faction. Kían would be devastated by the latter.

Before meeting with the men downstairs, Maeve decided to take one more look at the developments on the shores. She stepped onto the balcony and saw that the storm had worsened. The lightning bolts were becoming more intense and frequent. Images began to run through Maeve's mind. Some she had to push away. She needed to keep positive. One of the images gave Maeve confirmation that she was missing an especially important clue. This clue would lead her to her enemy. There was a feeling of disdain that she just could not shake. If she could only figure out its origin, it would help her immensely in her quest to uncover her threat.

Maeve thought of Eachna. She had been a devoted confidant and friend to her over the last day or so. She felt a twinge of guilt being so curt. She knew she must apologize to her at some point. But in all honesty, she was the ruler of Hy-Breasail and that must take precedence over someone's feelings or even the most loyal of friendships. Maeve knew now that she should have kept her at arms-length. It would have made today easier. She accepted fault as she should have not treated her as friend so soon considering the danger at hand. Yet she had done so anyway in respect for Kían.

Maeve's senses heightened. She quickly left her room. She knew Eachna was peering at her through her cracked door. Maeve turned in time to watch Eachna gently close her door. She did not have time to apologize or question Eachna's motives. There were bigger worries at hand. She needed to distance herself from Eachna. The issue with her was inconsequential. She knew deep within her heart she need not worry about Eachna's allegiance. Maeve descended the great hallway staircase swiftly.

The room grew eerily quiet when Maeve entered the meeting chamber. Conall, Gréagoír, and Díarmuid hunched over a table large enough to seat twenty. She experienced déjà vu. In an instant she was back in her kitchen the day after the attack. Mam, Pa, and Auntie Rio sat huddled at the kitchen table. Love and concern flooded the room. Yet, there had been something else. Shock ran through her mind and body charged with an undercurrent of anger. An emotion that she dismissed because of the previous day's events. Now, knowing the depth of the deception she was facing, she knew any scenario was a possibility.

Auntie Rio's support and comfort so quickly was an unfamiliar experience. Auntie Rio was not silent over her adverse feelings toward Rowan. She never attended family or community events unless they suited her. She did not go out of her way for anyone but herself. Maeve realized she only saw Auntie Rio at her beach house or at Christmas. The expediency of her visit after the attack at school was perplexing. She must have received directives from the Hierarchy. That could be the only answer.

Suddenly, Maeve was beginning to connect the dots. Flashes of memories flooded her mind. Only Rio mentioned Pa's past. He never spoke of it. His heart obviously broken by the loss of his parents. Rio knew that. Maeve was sure. Yet, Rio always told her stories of their past in secret. Secrets that are difficult for a child to keep. Rio had hoped to cause a rift between father and daughter. Why did Rio hold such contempt for her twin? It made no sense. Maeve knew the twin bond to be boundless. She saw it between Raegan and Declan. And, now between Díarmuid and Eachna.

Maeve knew her father had become the patriarch of the O'Flaherty clan after his parents' deaths. Rio must have been jealous. Niall was only a few minutes older than Rio so there was no question that he would take his mother's place as head of the family until Aveline announced the next heir to the Crown. Rio must have felt betrayed. Possibly feeling that both should have held this position together as twins. Was she the reason Fergus created his faction against all of them? Maeve tried to make sense of the thoughts coursing through her mind. She felt Ailm move. It was if he was dancing. Not for joy but in concurrence with her thoughts. Her suspicions were mere confirmation of her most deceitful betrayal.

Maeve cleared her throat. Gréagoír stood before her and bowed in reverence. He took Maeve's hands in his. She looked up at him. "Gréagoír, it's her. Do you know of whom I speak?" A mixture of sadness and anger crossed over his face. "Yes, Princess, we have had our suspicions. Now you have given us confirmation."

"I am completely saddened by this revelation. My own beloved aunt. It will be devastating for my father, my family, and all of our friends." Both stood in silence for a moment. It was then that Maeve realized that Eachna was not trying to be annoying. Eachna was trying to warn her but could not find the exact words to do so.

"Gréagoír, we must speak to Eachna. I think she has been trying to tell me something and was unable to because of her allegiance to me and her husband. I believe she knows more than thought. She has been hovering over me for the last hour or so. She kept mentioned the storm brewing on the shores of Hy-Breasail. She was trying to warn me of the storm's origination. She must have suspected Rio as well. She has the kindest of hearts. She knew that the possibility of betrayal by my own flesh and blood would leave me heartbroken. I had hoped with all hope that this would not be true."

Maeve had hardly finished her sentence and Conall was running up the stairs. Díarmuid just stood motionless. He looked like a deer standing in a car's headlights. Maeve could read his mind. "My Eachna, how can this be? How did she know Rio was evil and not tell me? I am a fool. My twin has deceived me. Poor Kían, he will be devastated."

"Díarmuid, let us give her a chance to explain. I realize now how duplicitous my aunt is. She may have taken over Eachna's body as she had done to Finn and Fagen. She is of beautiful heart, so I believe whatever happened between her and Rio has left her conflicted. My aunt is evil with duplicitous wraith; so, I honestly believe Eachna did not act upon her own volition. Remember many of us have been deceived by her and we have known her our whole lives."

Maeve felt his sadness. She, too, had been deceived. Her whole family had. Time was of the essence, she turned to Gréagoír.

"Gréagoír, you know what I must do?"

"Yes, Princess, I do."

Today, Hy-Breasail will change forever.

74 Duplicity

A memory from yesterday soared through Shae's brain. The attack in Miss Almath's class was so much more. The banshee's presence was a message not a threat. In her Irish mythology class, her teacher taught that the banshees came to warn of impending danger. In this instance, danger from a someone everyone in Rowan knew and trusted, especially Maeve. It was Rio. She had formed the Regime. It must have taken years to orchestrate such an elaborate plan. She could not fathom the depths of someone's hatred to obliterate her own family. The O'Flaherty's would be devastated.

Shae did not want to alarm Raegan. Her powers were growing alarmingly fast. Emotion could put everyone at risk. Thankfully, Eamonn had instructed everyone to split off into groups. Rio and Eamonn. Liam, Roark, and Declan. Shae and Raegan. Shae needed Raegan to have a vision. Even with its shocking revelation it would give them the upper hand. Raegan would share it with Declan. Ultimately, defeating Rio could become easier as Declan could warn Roark and Liam as well.

A loud shrill echoed from the surrounding woods, stopping the group. They were in danger. Shae was worried Raegan looked terrified. Liam, Roark, and Declan were readying themselves for battle. Eamonn summoned the men for directives. Rio looked smug and confident. Shae pulled Raegan closer to her. The poor girl's face had become as white as snow. Shae knew she should alert the rest of the group, especially Eamonn. She decided against it. Raegan was having a vision. As much as her first instinct was to share it, she knew it was best to keep it a secret.

Raegan was in a trancelike state. Her eyes had glazed over, and her pupils had become dilated. Her vision lasted no more than thirty seconds. Uncommon for her, as her personality was much like Maeve's, Raegan addressed the group. "Listen to me. You must hear my word." The group turned to look at Raegan. Declan astounded by his sister's transformation elbowed Liam and Roark. She was not one to address groups. She continued, "A darkness is walking amongst us. The banshees tell of impending doom. We must heed their warning. Death is close if we do not. They warn of betrayal within our family, our world."

Upon the completion of her last word, Raegan was back. "What just happened?" Shae wrapped her in a hug and whispered to her, "You just confirmed the danger I have been sensing. Stay close to me. I will protect you."

Raegan pushed herself slightly out of Shae's hug and looked into her eyes. Shae could hear her speak without words. Shae was relieved that Rio could not penetrate Raegan's abilities.

"Oh my gosh, Shae. I know who it is."

Shae replied, "I know, sweetheart."

Raegan looked devastated. "God help us all."

Shae replied, "Can you get a message to Declan?"

"I already have," Raegan replied with a huge smile on her face.

The trees surrounding their path swayed fiercely. Dark entities were taking on human-like forms. Dozens walked among the trees. The trees began to bow as the entities became more powerful. The calmness of the water was shifting. There had been a serene calmness about it. Now, the caps were getting bigger and bigger, the water choppy and angry. Shae looked out over the water and wondered how they would cross if the waves' anger intensified.

Rio's feet had black tinged green torrents swirling about them. Torrents began forming around Rio's wrists. They resembled powerful, braided bracelets. Shae looked up toward the sky. Black clouds accompanied by swirling green surges were overhead. Rio gazed back at Shae with vehemence. There was pure evil and darkness emanating from her. Rio was transforming right before their eyes. The once beautiful Rio was now an ugly enchantress. Rio's traitorous deception was heartbreaking. Rio's deceit would devastate Maeve.

Rio turned toward Eamonn and shoved him to the ground. He landed flat on his back. He glowed with an angelic purity on the ground's soft and cushiony moss-like substance. He looked up at Rio stunned and mortified. She cackled malevolently as she walked over him as if a piece of trash. Everyone was immobile stunned into a state of shock. Rio raised her arms as if to catch the green bolts flashing from the clouds. The bolts pierced through her body. As they did, she grew stronger and stronger.

No fear registered on either Liam or Roark's faces. Power coursed through their bodies. No doubt Rio had been on the watch list of Regime leaders. Both were prepared to defeat Rio. The elements were reacting. Danger was lurking all around them. The surrounding elements were in distress, the trees bowing to their breaking point, the water was cresting, the animals howling or crying in the woods. Declan stood alongside Liam and Roark. The three were ready for battle.

Rio laughed maniacally. She planned to kill both girls first. Shae stood holding Reagan close to form a protective barrier. Shae thought that by shielding Raegan with her own body she could protect her. Rio was too strong. Shae knew as she tired, the barrier would become faulty allowing Rio to attack. Raegan yelped. Shae whispered to her that there was an invisible wall impeding their escape.

Rio gave Shae an ultimatum, "Shae, you must choose a life. Yours or Raegan's. If you don't I will." There was no way either would survive unless fighting in a one-on-one combat. Shae knew she could not win against Rio. She would choose death.

Suddenly, a voice began to speak to Shae guiding her. It guided her to pray. To be strong against evil. Shae grabbed Raegan's hands and held them tightly within her own. Shae stood firmly rooted on the ground of Hy-Breasail. She closed her eyes, bowed her head, and called upon the divinities. All of them - her loved ones who had passed, her angels, and her God above. She could feel an invisible sheath spinning around Raegan and herself. It was spinning faster and faster forming a defensive wall. It would protect them from Rio, at least for a brief time.

75 Sacrifice

Princess Maeve would make the ultimate sacrifice for Hy-Breasail, Rowan, and the O'Flaherty clan. Adorned in her warrior armor, she would fight Rio to the death. The defeat of Rio must be swift for the survival of the kingdom as it was now known. She quickly called upon Díarmuid to scribe a writ on her behalf. The writ would name Liam O'Connor as King of Hy-Breasail upon her demise. The O'Connor's would rule as Patrons of Warriors. Maeve did not want her sisters to succeed her. Rio, upon her capture, would receive a sentence of life in imprisonment in Aveline's realm. Once she entered, she would never be able to return. No matter the circumstance.

Gréagoír rejoiced in the power before him. He bowed down before Princess Maeve. "My Princess, you are forever the Queen of Hy-Breasail." Tears formed in Maeve's eyes. She brought her hand to his chin and raised his head up to meet her gaze. "My dear Gréagoír, it has been my honor to know you. If I do not return, I ask you to please watch over my Liam as you have watched over me. And please apologize to Aveline for my doubts of her loyalty. For that, I am sorry. It is without a doubt that you share a love as great as mine for Liam. Thank you, my friend."

Maeve saw the gleam of tears in Gréagóir's eye. He replied: "Princess Maeve, it has been my honor to serve you. I will prepare to dedicate my life in your service." Maeve released her hand from him and nodded.

Maeve then turned to talk to Conall, Díarmuid, and Eachna. Eachna's allegiance remained unfettered. Maeve's suspicions were correct. Rio had sent a message to Eachna trying to vie her faithfulness to Hy-Breasail. Eachna declined. It was then she knew that Rio was the traitor. Confrontation was not in her character, so she had been unsure how to deliver such unwanted news. Maeve quickly addressed the three who stood before her.

"There are not enough words to express my gratitude to the three of you. I thank you sincerely for being my friends, protectors, and confidants. I hope to see you soon." Maeve had nothing else to say. She turned to Gréagóir, nodded for them to continue as her biggest challenge awaited. They walked side by side in silence to the stables wherein Cearul waited for Maeve.

Maeve mounted Cearul and alone she began her journey to the shores of Hy-Breasail. Suddenly, she began to feel wings unfold. She and Cearul were flying over the waters within seconds. Maeve gasped at his beauty. She turned quickly to glance at the O'Flaherty Castle becoming overcome with emotion then turned to face the sights in front of her. The darkness that pervaded the shores of Hy-Breasail was blacker and more threatening than it had been moments ago.

Maeve called upon the divinities of her youth. Her Grandpa Aaron, her Grandma Brigid, the angels, and her

God. All made themselves known to her as she flew to face imminent danger – her favorite aunt and most dangerous adversary. The divinities were filling her with the greatest and strongest of white light. It was beaming out of her. Maeve became the light in the face of darkness. She brought a sense of hope at her arrival.

Rio looked elated. She waited expectantly for the arrival of Princess Maeve. The protective sheath surrounding Shae and Raegan infuriated Rio. Numerous failed attempts to infiltrate the sheathing, had intensified her anger. The elements were mirroring her emotions. The sea, sky, and animals acted agitated and angry. Liam and Roark had not been successful in their attempts to hold her. With Rio preoccupied with Maeve's arrival, they hoped to overpower her before Maeve came ashore.

Maeve gently kicked Cearul's loins. There was no need to delay this confrontation. Unexpectedly, Rio propelled herself into the air. Rio hoped this would unnerve Maeve, weakening her. Ailm's strength and confidence was searing throughout her body. She found herself fearless. Her concern for Shae, Liam, Roark, Raegan, and Declan intensified. Not more than a football field away from Rio, Maeve gasped. Her Auntie Rio was gone. Left in her place was nothing more than an ugly shrew. This heartless, deviant soul decimated any beauty beholden by her beloved Auntie Rio. Thankfully, Niall would not witness such an abomination.

Out of nowhere, a hand came down from the heavens placing a magnificent sword in Maeve's hand. The sword was mighty and strong but light as a feather. Power radiated from it. It was a gift beholden for a Queen – a gift from the divinities. They too, wanted her to defeat the evil before her. Maeve looked up toward the heavens in thankfulness. "Thank you. I will not fail you."

Rio was moving at a tremendous speed. Before Maeve could blink, she was directly in front of her. "YOU! You have taken everything from me. All of this should be mine." Maeve replied, "What are you talking about? I haven't taken anything from you."

"Oh, yes you have." Rio sounded maniacal. "More than you know." Rio was getting louder and louder. Maeve tried hard to not let the ugly darkness spewing out of Rio affect her. She did not want Rio to think her weak. "Oh, you little girl. It was my destiny to be Queen of Hy-Breasail. Queen Riognach. But no, you, you are an ugly, self-centered shrew."

Maeve let out a stifled laugh at Rio calling her a shrew. Rio was unaware of her own transformation. "You laugh? You insolent child. You will be dead soon enough. Your precious father will be devastated. More than when I killed our parents." Maeve's eyes widened. Rio laughed maniacally. "Yes, it was me. I killed them to inherit the crown and rule the Kingdom of Hy-Breasail. Your father and I would rule together until we married, or I killed him, too. But no, my parents knew. They knew I was evil. So, do you know what they did?"

"What are you talking about?" Maeve knew she could not react to Rio's banter. It would just anger her even more. "Aaron and Brigid O'Flaherty, YOUR grandparents. In their Will, they declared that upon their death, the rightful seat of the throne would skip me. Niall would be patriarch of the family. Aveline to decide the next ruler. Not necessarily an O'Flaherty. They did not find me worthy to become queen."

Her aunt was certifiable. Maeve instinctively knew she must keep her composure. The sight before her was almost comical. Calmly she spoke: "That is not my fault. You do not know what you speak. You speak in fabricated falsities. No one, but Aveline from the Realm of Blessings had any power to secure the future of Hy-Breasail and Rowan. None of this is anyone's fault. It is the history of our Realms. You have become delusional!"

"Ha, I am not. I am sane. Saner than you. I tell you; it is YOUR fault. In the hospital, the day you were born, we all knew. You would be our Queen. As the tiniest babe, it was obvious who you were. Later that night, Aveline visited your parents alerting them of your future."

Maeve watched as Rio ranted and raved insanities. She wondered how did she not know how demented her beloved aunt truly was? "I waited painfully for years. Watching you. Gaining your trust. Your love. It was hard for me to hide the vehemence I felt for you. I should have killed you as an infant. No one would place the blame on me. Things like this happened to wee ones from time to time. I still fought with my feelings. Sweet, beautiful baby with the biggest blue eyes, and reddest hair looking up at me with so much purity and love. Disgusting! It was hard to hate a babe. Yet I did hate you. All of you. Your father, mother, and, ugh, your sisters, the little witches."

Rio's tirade silenced Maeve. The trueness of her aunt's hatred left her dumbfounded. "It was bad enough that you would become the Queen of Hy-Breasail, then your parents named you after the greatest Queen, The Queen of Connacht, Meadhbh. You are not worthy of that honor. You are a travesty. Over my dead body will you rule over Hy-Breasail. Never!"

Maeve felt a rush of anger course through her body. "Enough Riognach! You sound like a petulant child. Look at you! You have destroyed your beauty! Our family! Over what? The crown. What is wrong with you? The atrocities you executed make you a loathsome creature."

"Oh, sweet Maeve, I would have killed my brothers, too. But no, Aveline made sure I could not succeed. She cast protection over them so you would be Queen. You!"

"Riognach! Stand down or I will be forced to..."

"Forced to what, Maeve? Kill me? Go ahead! What are you waiting for? You will never win. This day will forever be seared into their memories."

Rio pointed at the witnesses on the shore below. The sword in Maeve's hand started to vibrate. She could feel the energy surging through her body. She heard "it is time". Maeve thought: Time? "Yes, you heard me. Think not of Riognach as your beloved aunt but as your enemy. The enemy of Hy-Breasail." The voice. It was one that she had heard before. It was Grandpa Aaron.

"Grandfather, no! I can't"

"Yes, Maeve, you must. It is your duty as the Queen of Hy-Breasail. You must think of your kingdom and its people. She is the one who threatens its very existence."

"I understand."

Cearul snorted and moved forward instinctually. It was as if he could read Maeve's mind. He charged at Riognach full force with Maeve sitting in grace and dignity with sword in hand ready to battle. Maeve looked like the Warrior Queen she was born to be. The storm that surrounded Riognach intensified. This did not deter Maeve. As soon as she reached Rio, the battle began. Without hesitation, Maeve set out to end Riognach. There was no question, no doubt even as she glanced down at the shore below her and saw Liam looking up at her. She felt his love connecting his heart to hers. They would be together soon. Maeve attacked Riognach with every cell of her being. As her sword plunged into Riognach, there was a devastating blast. All went dark.

76 Death

Maeve's head was pounding and her body aching. It was so difficult to open her eyes. Maeve heard a voice quietly whispering to her. "Shhhh, Maeve. Rest. You need your rest."The voice was familiar. Maeve fell into a state of unconsciousness.

Faces swirled through her dreams. Liam. Shae. Roark. Raegan. Declan. Mam. Pa. Bridget. Caitlín. Breana. To Hy-Breasail. To the O'Flaherty Castle. She needed to make sure everyone was okay. The kingdom needed her. Why couldn't she wake up? Maeve fought with every fiber of her being to fight through the heaviness holding her down. She needed Liam. She needed to know that he forgave her for killing Riognach. She could not live knowing she had lost him forever.

Seconds felt like hours before Maeve was able to open her eyes the slightest bit. Finally, she was able to open them. She looked around to see where she was. Her body felt laden by heavy weight. She was in her chambers. Enough was enough. If she could defeat an evil shrew like Riognach, she could fight whatever injury her aunt inflicted upon her. Maeve fought through the fog, the pain, the heaviness. With her whole being, she lifted herself to a seated position in her bed. Once situated, she glanced around the room. Nothing had changed.

Sorrow flooded her being. Maeve could not understand why Liam was not here with her. She glanced around the room. Shae was nowhere to be found either. It was all so strange. She thought that Raegan and Declan would be here as well. She scanned the room again with hope. There was no one there. No one at all. She knew something had happened. Something that kept her from them. Tears formed in Maeve's eyes. She never felt so alone. Suddenly, she heard a scuffling sound near her balcony.

Hope surged through Maeve's heart. She was not alone. Suddenly, a man appeared in the balcony doorway. He was very tall, but she had a hard time making out who it was. The light from outside was illuminating his silhouette making it impossible for her to identify him. Slowly, he walked into her room. Tears fell from Maeve's eyes. "Grandfather? Is that you?" It was Grandpa Aaron.

With a huge grin on his face, he quickly moved to her side and took her into his arms. "My darling, my Queen. You are awake. We have been so worried about you. You had quite the battle with Riognach." Maeve was confused. Grandpa Aaron was dead. He could not be here in his human form. It was not possible. "How are you here? I know that Riognach killed you. You can't be here."

It took a few moments for Grandpa to answer Maeve. He took a deep breath before he spoke. "My darling," he said with sadness in his inflection, "You were so brave. The strength of the battle that had ensued was more than your body could handle. When your sword pierced Riognach's body, the energy inside of her reverberated through the sword…and into your body. I'm so sorry, Maeve."

At that moment, Maeve knew. "No, no, no… I can't be!" Maeve began to sob. "Liam, Shae, Declan, Raegan, Roark? Are they alive?" Aaron shook his head in the affirmative. "I need to go back. Please! Tell me how. I need to see them one last time. OMG…," her voice faltered. He took her hands in his then placed them over his heart. "My sweet Maeve, there is no way back.

"Grandpa, no. I'm not ready to leave them yet." Aaron cradled her in his arms as she cried. He rocked her back and forth as if she were a baby. He whispered in her ear words of love and encouragement. Maeve felt him caressing her face. Gently, he kissed her forehead. "My sweet granddaughter, you will see. All of this happened for good reason. Liam is safe. Everyone is safe because of you."

Through her tears, Maeve looked up at him. "What are you saying? How is this good?" It did not feel good. She knew that during her battle with Riognach she would face the possibility of death. But she could not understand how her death could serve her well. Aaron replied: "You will see, my darling. You will see." Maeve looked up at her grandfather in questioning. She could not understand how she would see. Would she be able to visit everyone in Rowan and Hy-Breasail the same way her grandfather had been able to visit her so many times over the years?

"How? Will I be able to visit them as you visited me over the years?" Grandpa Aaron nodded. Maeve let out a huge breath of relief. "At least I can find solace in that." Aaron hesitantly replied. "My darling, yes you may visit with limitations. But your loved ones' ability to see you can only happen with Aveline's permission. It must serve a purpose. Otherwise, it will not be allowed."

"I understand, I do. It will take me some time to get over the shock of my death. But I knew of the dangers I was to face. It was my birthright to fight for the future of our Realm." Aaron's face beamed with love. "My darling, I am so proud of you. There has not been a greater queen since Queen Mebh. The people of Rowan and Hy-Breasail will worship you for all of eternity." Maeve was embarrassed by her grandfather's words.

She continued: "Has Liam been made king as I had instructed?" Aaron held Maeve tighter. "Yes, he has been crowned." There was a slight hesitation in Aaron's speech. "This will be hard for you to understand right now but changes had to be made concerning the future and safety of Hy-Breasail and Rowan."

Maeve looked up at him with great concern. She knew the Hierarchy would make changes resultant of her death. Her grandfather was acting strangely. "Grandpa, I am not surprised by this news. What is it that has filled you with concern?" Grandpa looked as if he was going to cry. Maeve knew whatever it was he felt it may devastate her. "Maeve, this will come as a shock to you but...Aveline has paired Liam with your cousin, Raegan. She will become his queen on her twenty-first birthday." Maeve looked shocked at the news but allowed him to continue.

"This news must be upsetting." Maeve squeezed his hand in hers. She felt a lump forming in her throat making it almost impossible to swallow. She could barely squawk her next sentences. "Grandpa, it is truly a shock. But the future of Hy-Breasail and Rowan must come first. There is no other person, other than Shae, that I could accept as my love's future wife." Grandpa gave her a huge hug. "I am so proud of you, my Maeve." Maeve knew her heart ached with love and a tinge of jealousy for Liam and Raegan. A jealousy that she would not allow to grow and fester as her aunt's once did.

Aaron was so honored to call Maeve his granddaughter. His praises were endless. "Believe me when I tell you that you are a very brave girl and have sacrificed much in your short life. But your sacrifice has saved millions. Your rewards will be great."

"Grandpa, I do not want rewards. I never expected that. I set out to save Rowan and Hy-Breasail and I have. Now that our Realms are safe, and my family and people can be at peace I too can share in the feeling of peace and joy with you and Grandma Brigid."

"My sweet, sweet Maeve, I love you with all of my heart."

"I love you, too!"

Maeve found comfort in her grandfather's arms while tears leaked from her eyes and slowly slid down her cheeks. She fell asleep quickly as the emotion from their conversation overcame her. He gently laid her head down onto her pillow, covered her, and returned to the same position he was in when she had awoken.

77 Reality

Maeve had fallen into a deep sleep. She had lost so much over the last few days – her family, her friends, and, most of all, Liam. Her love for him would never die. The only thing keeping her from totally breaking down was the promise that one day she and Liam would be together for all eternity. Well, her, Liam, and Raegan. Maeve chuckled. She loved her cousin and Liam with her whole heart and wished nothing for them but a life of love and blessings.

Suddenly, a burst of joy coursed through her body. She had defeated Riognach and saved Hy-Breasail. Even though she had suffered the greatest loss in the process – her life and love. The feeling of triumph she felt for regaining Hy-Breasail's safety superseded the sadness she felt over her losses. If she had the same choices to make over again, none of her decisions or actions would change. She believed that without a doubt.

A familiar voice was reaching out to her in her sleep. "Maeve, Maeve, can you hear me?" Maeve tossed and turned in her bed. The voice was becoming increasingly insistent. "Maeve, it's me Meadhbh. Can you hear me? I need to talk to you." Maeve tried so hard to open her eyes." She mumbled, "I'm trying to open my eyes…and I can't. I can hear you though." Meadhbh replied: "Good, good. Listen to me. I have little time. I need you to fight…fight hard. Please Maeve. I beg of you. You must come back. We all need you. Maeve…"

Maeve was so confused. How was Meadhbh able to reach out to her. She was dead. The only answer was that Meadhbh must be dead too. Meadhbh, her doppelgänger, must have died with her. "Meadhbh, what are you saying. Return? I've died. And I assume you have too." Meadhbh voice was getting weaker. Maeve could hardly hear her as she pleaded for her return. "You must return, Maeve. We all need you. Please don't give up." Maeve was not sure what Meadhbh meant. Grandpa Aaron told her she would not be able to return to Hy-Breasail or Rowan without Aveline's permission. Maeve called out to Meadhbh again but received no reply.

Maeve knew she had to wake up and ask Grandpa for his advice. Meadhbh needed her. She could not fail her. She would not. Maeve could feel Grandpa holding her hand. He was caressing her forehead and whispering to her. The whispers were getting louder and stranger. "Shhhh, mo shíorghra. I love you. Come back to me." Even through her grogginess she questioned why Grandpa Aaron would call her "his love". But it was not Grandpa. It was the voice she longed to hear most. It was Liam's voice.

Maeve thought she must be transcending to a past memory. It was the only possible answer. Memories would make the time away from Liam go quickly. An indescribable sadness filled her dreams. She could hear Liam, but she could not see him. She needed to make it stop. It was too soon. Maeve felt desperate as she called out to him: "One day, one day we will be together. I promise. For now, I must leave you." She hoped he could hear her. This thought brought her a sea of calm. Ailm was purring and nuzzling her neck.

Suddenly Maeve felt bound by an invisible force encasing her body in a thick goopy liquid. A tightness around her chest squeezed until she became breathless. Then, a swift current of energy pulled her out of the sea of quicksand. Liam's voice was music lilting in the background. A soft feathery caress on her cheek confirmed his presence. The heaviness Maeve felt lifted and the fog began clearing. Even the clarity of the voices around her were sharper and more distinct. There was a familiar voice speaking authoritatively. It was not Liam but someone new; yet familiar.

Maeve tried hard to distinguish the man's voice from the ocean of others flooding the room. Suddenly, she realized who it was. It was Dr. Lynch. He was the doctor they met in the emergency room after the accident. Irritation-tinged Dr. Lynch's voice. "Please step back and let me check the patient. Don't make me call security." Slowly, Maeve opened her eyes. The room was bright and blurry. "Maeve, can you hear me? Blink twice if you can hear me."

Maeve blinked her eyes twice. She must be dreaming. There was a light flashing in her eyes. She motioned to make it stop. The light was too bright like high beams in a deer's face. It was making her head hurt. He bent over Maeve to make sure she could see him. "Maeve, you were in an accident at school. You have suffered a traumatic brain injury. We have all been very worried about you. Especially, your mother and father. Oh, and Liam, of course."

Dr. Lynch turned to Mam and Pa giving them the thumbs up. "Her vitals look great. Her response is remarkable. We must give her some time to heal. So please make your visits short." He took her hand and squeezed it. "Maeve, I'll be back shortly to check up on you. For now, I think your mother and father need to see you." Dr. Lynch turned and left the room.

Mam and Pa practically ran to her bedside - one on either side. Both kissed her cheeks simultaneously and giggled. Tears streamed down both their faces. Pa finally composed himself enough to say: "Oh, sweetheart, we've been so worried about you. We thought we had lost you forever." Maeve replied: "Pa, you'll never lose me. I will always be with you."

Maeve knew they had to hear that from her. She did not know when they would see her again. Aveline must have arranged this so she could say good-bye. She was sure that she had to return to the O'Flaherty Castle shortly. Grandpa Aaron was waiting for her. She would savor this blessing. The ability to give her loves a proper good-bye was more than she could ever ask for.

78 Truth

Mam and Pa hesitantly moved to give Liam a chance to spend time with Maeve. Maeve knew she did not have much time to spend with him. Liam needed to know how much she loved him and that Aveline's pairing did not upset her.

"Liam, I am so sorry. The battle of Hy-Breasail did not turn out as I had planned. I did not want to die. Will you ever be able to forgive me?" Liam shook his head in disbelief. "You also need to know that I understand Aveline's pairing between you and Raegan. You both have my blessing. I wish nothing but love for the two of you."

"Maeve, what are you talking about? Hy-Breasail? What battle? Me and Raegan? You're kidding right? I love your cousin but not as a girlfriend. You are not making any sense. Maybe I should call for the nurse?" Maeve grabbed Liam's hand in desperation. "I had to kill her to save Rowan and Hy-Breasail." Liam's eyebrows furrowed in question. "Kill who? You're worrying me. Maeve, you seriously need to rest."

Maeve knew she sounded delusional. She spouted one thought after another like a machine gun firing at a target. "Listen to me, Liam. I am not crazy. I killed Riognach. Aveline has arranged this. You and Raegan will reign over

Hy-Breasail. Liam, I am only here to say good-bye. Did you not just hear me? I am dead. I died in the battle against Riognach to save Hy-Breasail and Rowan. You were there. You all were. Eamonn, Shae, Roark, Declan, and Raegan, And, of course, Riognach."

Liam raised his eyebrows. Worry washed over his face. "My love...what are you talking about? You have done nothing. The explosion? There is no way the explosion was your fault. And it did not happen in Hy-Breasail. We were in Miss Almath's class. Don't you remember the presentation?"

Maeve was so frustrated with him. She knew all about the explosion. She was there. She was talking about the events after the explosion. Liam seemed more confused than she was. "What? You were there Liam. You know where Hy-Breasail is. You have crossed Veil na Tairsí. You are a Patron of Warriors. The Hierarchy groomed you for greatness, to be my King. To sit beside me as I rule Hy-Breasail."

"No, Maeve. The explosion was an accident. You suffered a serious head injury. Chief Kerrigan is at the school now with the investigators. There may have been a faulty gas line. So, the fire department ordered the school closed for the next week while they ensure its safety."

Maeve was getting irritated with Liam for the first time. He was not understanding her. "Riognach? Where is she then?" Liam motioned toward the hallway. "Riognach? Since when do you refer to Auntie Rio as Riognach? No one does. Maeve she is here. She has been here since yesterday. She came as soon as she found out about the accident. We've all been here." Puzzlement crossed over Maeve's face.

"Shae? Roark? Declan? Raegan? The girls? Everyone is safe?"

Liam knew that Maeve needed reassurance of everyone's safety. "Yes, everyone. Everyone is fine. Some of us have some scrapes and bruises." Liam chortled, "Miss Almath is a mess. She feels that she put us all in danger. She was here, too, but had to go home. You suffered the worst injuries since you were closest to the explosion."

Maeve was becoming increasingly agitated. Liam was not listening to her. He had to know about Hy-Breasail. "You're not listening to me, Liam. Stop talking about what happened at school. Please!" Liam was on the brink of pressing the call button. Maeve was not making any sense. "I do hear you. But you must keep calm. Dr. Lynch will make us leave. Please, I don't want to leave you."

Maeve pulled Liam closer to her. "Liam, come closer, please." Liam gently hugged Maeve so she could whisper into his ear. "No, what happened at Hawthorn was just the start of everything. There's so much more." Liam leaned over Maeve. He gave her a soft wink and replied quietly. Quietly, but not so much so that no one else could hear. It was important that others in the room were privy to his questioning. "Do you need me to get Dr. Lynch? You're worrying me." Maeve realized that he did understand her. She was so relieved. She must act like she conceded to his explanation. "No, Liam, I'm fine, honestly."

Maeve's revelation sent shockwaves down her neck. She could feel every hair standing on end. She had transcended while unconscious. She grabbed Liam's arm. His gaze spoke volumes. He knew exactly what had happened to her. She then asked everyone in the room to give her and Liam some time alone. "Hey, do you all mind if Liam and I have a few minutes alone." Thankfully, no one objected, not even her parents.

Once everyone left, Maeve threw herself into Liam's arms. There was so much she needed to tell him. "Liam, I know I sounded like a crazy loon. I'm so sorry. I didn't realize at first that I had transcended. I honestly believed that I was here to say good-bye. My transcendence was so real this time. I was not just an observer; I was an active participant. I know this for a fact. The explosion was not a gas leak. I promise you that. Riognach made it happen."

Liam knew the Hierarchy directed him and other Hierarchy members to not divulge Maeve's destiny. Very few were privy to this information. For her safety and the Realm of Hy-Breasail, it was imperative to keep it secret. He had heard of the Gift of Transcendence, but he himself had not received its gift. He kept calm as his training had taught him. Upsetting his princess was inappropriate as her future king.

"Then you are aware of your birthright?" Maeve nodded. "Okay, then." Liam felt relieved. He hated keeping secrets from Maeve. But he could not act against the Hierarchy's directives. "Maeve, we will have to contact Tomas for instructions. Auntie Rio? She's a threat? Are you sure?" Maeve nodded in the affirmative again.

The news of Auntie Rio's plan to annihilate Maeve, Hy-Breasail and Rowan outraged Liam. He loved Auntie Rio. It amazed him that someone so endearing could be so duplicitous. After ruminating this horrible development for a moment Liam continued: "Maeve, the Hierarchy will be shocked by this news. As I am sure you were? I can't believe it myself." Liam never imagined having this conversation with Maeve. None of them were prepared, especially Maeve, for the battle that would ensue. A threat had been prophesied by Aveline to occur in the foreseeable future, but not on the timetable that Maeve had provided.

"Yes, Liam, I know I am to be Queen of Hy-Breasail. I have been to Hy-Breasail and the O'Flaherty Castle. I have met with Aveline, Eamonn, Eachna, Díarmuid, and Gréagoír. It is true about Riognach. She has planned my demise since my birth. She is the one responsible for the deaths of my grandparents. All of this is true."

Liam pushed her gently away and looked into her eyes. Maeve's eyes equated not only to love but truth and certainty. Liam became extremely worried. He knew Maeve had the gift of foreseer, but it put her in extreme danger. He needed to protect her now more than ever. He hoped that Riognach did not know that Maeve knew her true intention.

"Maeve, I believe you. But we can't talk about this anymore. No one must know what you have just told me until we speak to Tomas. We must act as if nothing has happened." Maeve totally understood. "Yes, I do. If Rio finds out I know about her intentions she will attack sooner rather than later. We must act like my rambling was just that."

"I agree. Let's tell everyone to come back in here. I think if we spend too much time alone, Rio may become suspicious. Do you agree, my Princess?" Maeve rolled her eyes at him and replied. "Stop, that's enough. Shhhh….no one can hear you call me that. They'll know I know." He laughed. "Yes, my liege." Maeve punched him in the shoulder. "Get over here and give me a kiss, my King." Both laughed hysterically.

Mam popped her head in the room. "I know you too want to spend all this time alone but there are other people out here waiting to visit." Maeve and Liam replied in unison. "Sure, sorry." Mam laughed at the two of them as she directed the group. "Everyone please come back in. Maeve can't wait to see you."

Maeve and Liam sat holding hands as the entourage reentered her hospital room. Minutes later Dr. Lynch swept in. Maeve was sure that Mam called for him again after her senseless repartee a few minutes ago. "I'm so sorry everyone. The pain in my head is excruciating. If you overheard my senseless banter, I am sure you're extremely worried about me. I am fine. I truly am. Dr. Lynch, may I have something for my headache?"

"Yes, of course. I will order it for you. The nurse will bring it in shortly."

He turned to address the rest of the visitors. "I ask that all of you keep your voices down so as not to make Maeve's pain worse. Now, I would appreciate it if you all would say a quick 'hello'. Maeve's parents and Liam may stay, but I am sorry the rest of you must leave. Maeve, I will dim the lights on my way out. Everyone, I appreciate your cooperation."

Maeve was so relieved. "Thank you, Dr. Lynch." Everyone in the room either nodded or mumbled a quick thank you to the doctor on his way out of her room.

79 Family

Liam held her hand, their fingers interlacing. "Everyone say a quick hello to Maeve then I am sorry you must leave so that she can get some rest." One by one each said hello. Raegan had tears in her eyes as she gave Maeve a sweet, soft hug. Declan by his twin's side gave Maeve a wink and a thumbs up.

Shae could not resist hugging her best friend with tears streaming down her face. Maeve noticed the handsome man standing in the back of the room. Raising her eyebrow, she pulled Shae closer to her and whispered: "And who may I ask is that handsome man standing in the far corner of my room. I may have a head injury, but I believe he has a thing for you. Come on spill it."

Shae rolled her eyes and let out a huge "It's Liam's cousin, Roark. And yes, we have a thing. A lot has happened in the two days you have been unconscious. We have a lot to catch up on."

"I'm sure you do." Maeve giggled. "I love you, Shae."

"I love you, too."

Maeve smiled as she watched her friend walk over to Roark. Shae reminded her of Tigger from "Winnie the Pooh". Shae had a bounce in her step.

Roark sauntered over to Maeve's bed. The O'Connor men were certainly handsome. "Maeve, I'm Roark. It is so nice to finally meet you. I feel like I know you already. Shae has told me a thousand stories over the last two days. I look forward to the four of us hanging out." Maeve noticed a twinge of blush on Roark's cheeks when he said Shae's name.

It made her heart happy to know her friend had met her "Liam". "Roark, it's a pleasure even under these circumstances. I feel like I know you already." Maeve looked at Liam. He knew she had met Roark during her transcendence. He smiled back at her. "We will plan to hang out as soon as Dr. Lynch gives me the thumbs up." Roark gave Liam a guy hug and told him he would see him at home. Maeve gave Liam a quizzical look. He told her that he would fill her in later.

Maeve started to talk to Liam about Shae and Roark when a chill ran down her spine. She looked at Liam. In mid-sentence, Maeve stopped. With the lights dimmed, Rio decided to hide in the shadows. She was standing in the darkest corner of the room. Creepily, she walked over to Maeve's bed. "Why Maeve, it is so nice to see you up and about." Then, she slithered closer to Maeve. She tried to take Maeve's hands in hers. Maeve pulled away.

"Riognach, I appreciate your visit. But, honestly, you must have more pressing things on your schedule than visiting me." Maeve could see through her aunt's façade. She was not sure anyone else could.

"Oh, darling, my only concern is for the welfare of my family. Although, right now, I am getting scathing looks from your handsome doctor. I must leave before I get a scolding. Goodbye, darling. I will see you tomorrow."

The chill became even more intense at the mention of her family. Riognach leaned over and kissed Maeve's cheek. After an uncomfortable pause, she whispered in Maeve's ear. "My dearest Queen Maeve, we must commend ourselves for our outstanding performance. You must know I will be coming for you. Next time, you will not escape death."

"My poor, dear Auntie Riognach, it is you that must be worried. You delude yourself into thinking that you will ever rule over Hy-Breasail. I have safeguards against that. I am no different than my dear grandparents before me."

"Dear, we shall see about that. Savor this life of yours. For it won't be long before you meet your eternal demise."

As Riognach was turning away, Maeve, grabbed her wrist. Staring into her eyes, Maeve replied, "On the contrary, Riognach, it is you who must heed my warning. It is you who will meet your demise. As Queen of Hy-Breasail, I will see to it that your days on this earthly plain will cease to exist. You will not reign anywhere. That I can promise you."

Riognach turned away from Maeve with tremendous fervor. Liam wrapped his arm around Maeve and pulled her closer to him as they watched her enter the elevator. Rio turned and glared at them. Her stare emitting violent electrical pulses filling the elevator. As the doors closed, the pulses remained with Riognach.

80 The Future

Maeve and Liam let out a collective breath. Then turned their attention to Mam and Pa. Mam asked Liam to hang around a bit. It was time to pick up the girls from school. "Liam are you okay with staying with Maeve while we pick up the girls? We'll be back within the hour. I know they'll be so excited to see her." Liam nonchalantly replied. "Of course, there's nowhere else I'd rather be. Take your time. I promise I won't be going anywhere for a long while."

Mam came over and gave him a big hug and squeezed him tightly. "Oh Liam, I don't know what we would have done without you these past few days. Thank you so much." Pa shook his hand fervently. Maeve looked at the three of them with love. She felt so lucky to have such great parents and a wonderful, handsome boyfriend. "Okay, guys, that's enough. We don't want all this praise going to the star football player's head. He will be impossible to live with." Maeve laughed.

Mam was embarrassed. A sheer blush covered her cheeks as she replied. "Maeve, you stop. You're so lucky you're in the hospital. I'd give you a talking to." All of them stood for a moment or two with the hugest of grins on their faces. They were all so happy to be together celebrating Maeve's recovery. "Okay, okay we'll be back soon." Mam threw them both an air kiss.

Liam sat next to Maeve on her hospital bed and pulled her close to him cradling her in his arms. Maeve could not wait for Mam and Pa to be out of earshot. She watched as the elevator doors closed. Both her parents were beaming with joy. What a contrast to her aunt just a few moments ago.

Maeve could not believe the audacity of Riognach's confrontation in a room full of people. Luckily, Maeve had silently called upon Aveline to place a protective barrier between any communication she may have with her aunt. She did not want anyone to be privy to her aunt's deceit. Not until she called a meeting with the Hierarchy. She knew time was of the essence.

Maeve mentally listed the topics that she must be address. First and foremost, she needed to talk about Riognach. Maeve would discuss a secret coronation celebrating her new commission as Queen of Hy-Breasail. This must happen prior to her eighteenth birthday. It was imperative to step up the timeline to prevent Riognach from causing death and devastation to Rowan and Hy-Breasail. Without this change, Hy-Breasail would no longer exist as it was now known.

Maeve angled herself toward Liam. Turning her face upward to look into his eyes, she said with an air of royalty and love. "It is time. We must call upon the Hierarchy. Riognach cannot have any more freedom to act upon her hatred and contempt for me. The lives of the people of Hy-Breasail and Rowan are at risk."

Liam turned his gaze downward reminding Maeve of Gréagoír's reverence to her in Hy-Breasail. Goosebumps coursed through her body. She knew that Gréagoír would be Liam's most trusted confident and soldier in their coming quests. Liam replied, his speech smoky with passion, "Yes, my beautiful Princess." He softly kissed her lips.

Maeve quietly, yet authoritatively gave him her directives. "Tell Kían it is imperative we meet expeditiously. He must contact Tomas, Quinn, Lorcan, and Aengus and other members of the Hierarchy."

Liam smiled at her and replied: "Of course, mo shíorghra. I am here for you." He kissed her forehead, closed his eyes, and called upon Kían. Maeve settled back into Liam's arms. She could see their reflection in the mirror across the room. The reflecting image took her breath away.

Maeve looked as she did in Hy-Breasail. She lay in her royal dressing gown. The crown upon her head shimmering like fireflies on a summer night. Liam sat beside her dressed in king-like fashion. A beautiful crown adorned his head. He reminded her of King Ruaidrí Ó Conchobair from her Irish Studies class. A beautiful rope-like vine of Celtic knots intertwined forming a heart-shaped aura around them. The aura emitting tiny silvery effervescent bursts of light filling the room with a protective sheathing.

Maeve closed her eyes for just a moment of rest. Her heart filled with a sense of peace and contentedness. In less than an hour she would meet with the Hierarchy to discuss Riognach's treacherous plans against her and the Realm of Hy-Breasail. She knew undoubtedly, with the greatest of strength and courage, she would defeat Riognach. Queen Maeve of Hy-Breasail would rule her Realm as no other before her with her best friend by her side.

GLOSSARY OF NAMES

The O'Flaherty Clan
Maeve/
Meadhbh *(MAYVE)* — intoxicating; the source of great joy
Treasa *(TRA-sa)* — strength
Niall *(NILE)* — champion; passionate
Ríoghnach *(ree-OH-na)* — queen
Fergus *(fer-guss)* — a strong warrior, virile
Bridget/Brigid — exalted one, power and virtue
Caitlín *(KAT-lyeen)* — pure
Breana *(bree-AHN-ə)* — high noble
Aaron/Árón *(AR-ən)* — exalted, high mountain

The Kerrigan Clan
Shae/Shaelyn *(shey)* — full of majesty
Ólan/Ollie *(O-lan)* — royal forefather
Branagh *(BRAN-na)* — raven haired beauty
Kevan *(kav-an)* — gentle, kind, intuitive
Rían *(re-an)* — little king
Seamus/James *(Shay-mus)* — supplanter
Aedan *(aid-an)* — born of fire
Padraic *(paw-rik)* — nobly born

The O'Connor Clan
Liam *(LEE-am)* — valiant, strong protector
Roark — illustrious, mighty
Aoife/Aífe *(EE-fa)* — beautiful, radiant
Sloane *(slown)* — little raider
Oisín *(USH-een)* — little deer
Cathal (KA-hal) — battle, rule

The Ryan Clan
Aíne *(AWN-ya)* — brightness, splendor, radiance
Donall *(Don-al)* — proud chief
Raegan *(RAY-gin)* — little king, strong
Declan (DECK-lin) — man of prayer, full of goodness

The Darroch Clan
Conall *(KaaN-aa-L)* — high and mighty
Cillín *(KIL-yan)* — one who suffers strife; bright-headed
Finian *(FIHN-iy-ahN)* — fair
Fagen *(FAY-GUHN)* — rustic, little fiery one
Catriona *(kat-tree-na)* — pure

The Hidden Queen of Hy-Breasail

The Hierarchy

Tomas *(toh-moss)*	twin
Quinn *(KWIN)*	advisor
Lorcan *(LAW-KUHN)*	silent, fierce
Aengus *(eng-iss)*	ancient warrior

Oracles, Protectors, and Guardians

Ailm (AE-luhm)	strength, endurance, healing, protection
Cearul (kar-ul)	fierce in battle
Kían (KEEN)	ancient, enduring, wise
Eachna (ahk-na)	steed, horse, Irish Goddess of Beauty
Díarmuid (deer-mid)	without enemy
Aveline (Av-eh-leen)	pleasant, beautiful, radiant
Gréagóir (GRAY-gor)	fierce
Manannán (man-an-on)	son of the sea
Eamonn (aim-on)	guardian of the riches
Conair (KON-er-ee)	guardian of protection

Miscellaneous

Hy-Breasail *(hy-bra-seal)*	a <u>phantom island</u> said to lie in the <u>Atlantic Ocean</u>[3] west of Ireland.
Rowan *(row-uhn)*	red-haired
Laoch Street *(Lay-och)*	warrior hero
Leíne *(lay-nuh)*	shirt/tunic
brat *(braht)*	rectangular woolen cloak
dealg *(delg)*	brooch
crios *(kris)*	a multicoloured woven woollen belt traditionally worn by men in the Aran Islands
currach *(kuhr-uh)*	a small, round, or broad boat made of wickerwork or interwoven laths covered with a waterproof layer of animal skin, canvas, tarred or oiled cloth.
Veil na Tairsí	Veil of Threshold
Réimse na mBeannachtaí	Realm of Blessings
ṁ fhiorghra *(MEER-ggrah)*	my true love
mo shíorghra *(muh-HEER-ggrahh)*	my eternal love

Made in the USA
Columbia, SC
30 June 2021